ELFRID'S HOLE

AN ANGLO-SAXON GHOST STORY

JOHN BROUGHTON

This book is dedicated to Dawn Burgoyne, my calligrapher friend, who, like me, loves the Anglo-Saxon period.

Special thanks go to my dear friend John Bentley for his steadfast and indefatigable support. His content checking and suggestions have made an invaluable contribution to Elfrid's Hole.

Pseudo-inscription on Aldfrith's tomb as in *Elfrid's Hole*.

Translation:

"Merciful Saviour Christ, write the name of Aldfrith in the book of eternal life and never let it be obliterated, but may it be held in remembrance, through you, our Lord."

Illustration by Dawn Burgoyne

Medieval re-enactor/presenter specialising in period scripts. Visit her on Facebook at dawnburgoynepresents.

Old English translation courtesy of Joseph St John.

The intuitive mind is a sacred gift and the rational mind is a faithful servant.

ONE

JAKE CONLEY WAS IRRITATED. TRY AS HE MIGHT, HE COULDN'T rid his fiancée's cutting remarks from spinning like a carousel around his head. As far as self-fulfilling observations were concerned, Livie— Olivia to her parents—was an expert. She had labelled him an *oddball*, always with his head in some distant century, and accused him of not listening to a word she said. Had he not stomped seething out of their flat and been so many streets away, she might have been justified taking him to task now. He had no destination, no awareness of his surroundings; he was simply striding with the aim to walk off his bad mood...and to think about the Dark Ages. He wasn't considering their relationship. He simply wanted to work out a structure for the novel he had in mind. His greatest desire was to achieve international recognition as an author. This was what Livie couldn't understand, his need for reflection, for the peace to create his masterpiece. She was creative, too, but her passion for the theatre was less reflective, more spontaneous.

Masterpiece? For sure, his ambition was to write a bestselling historical novel. Maybe she'd understand his needs more readily if, with his ability and the necessary luck, the feature film of the book appeared in high-street cinemas and the royalties came his way. He wasn't thinking any of this when the accident happened. Rather more typically, Jake was wondering whether his main character should be a Saxon ceorl or a nobleman and running through the pros and cons of each. If Jake Conley's head was not in the twenty-first century, what could be said of that of the Jeep driver? *He* was so lost in thought, he failed not only to see the STOP sign at the junction but also Jake, who was crossing the road without looking in either direction.

When he recovered from a coma seven weeks later, he was no longer an oddball but decidedly weird. The first unfocused face he struggled to see was that of Livie, with her milk-chocolate complexion and black eyes, whose bedside vigils had gained the admiration of the nursing staff.

"Oh, Jake, thank goodness, you're awake! I'd better call the doctor."

"Livie? Is that you? Where am I?"

"You're in hospital, my love. You had a nasty accident."

"Did you assault me, Livie?"

She gave a nervous laugh. Had she heard him right? Was he simply being provocative? Joking?

"Don't be silly; you were run over by a Jeep on the corner of Percy's Lane and Walmgate. The driver claims he didn't see you, but how's that possible? I expect the police will want to speak to you; they've been three or four times, but you've been unconscious for almost two months."

"Two months! How am I?"

As he spoke, he groaned at a sharp pain in his ribs.

Concerned, Livie left her seat and hurried to fetch a nurse. She returned two paces behind a staff nurse in a dark blue, white-trimmed uniform.

"How are you feeling, Mr Conley?" She beamed at him.

"*Lousy,* and you can call me Jake."

"Well, Jake, the doctors rule out brain damage. We did a CT

scan, and everything's fine given the entity of the blow. You were badly concussed, but all in all, you're a lucky man."

"*Lucky*, am I? You have a strange definition of the term."

Livie tut-tutted, "Jake, don't be unpleasant. The nurse is looking after you very well."

"I'll be as damned unpleasant as I want, thank you, miss. It's *your* bloody fault if I'm in here." He groaned and closed his eyes. "My side's killing me!"

"What do you mean, it's my fault?" Livie's tone was searing.

"Best to humour him, miss, the gentleman's still confused," the nurse whispered.

"Do me a favour, clear off out of here, the pair of you!" Jake attempted to shout, but the effort hurt his two cracked ribs. "Or at least give me something to kill the pain."

The experienced nurse took Jake's sullen-looking fiancée by the arm and led her out into the corridor.

"It's just the impact the poor man got to his head," she said by way of explanation, hoping to soothe the devoted girl's nerves. "Come with me, and we'll fetch the painkiller he needs. I'll get the doctor to check him over. You should be happy he's regained consciousness."

"Oh, I am."

Or so she thought, until she returned to his private room and found Jake gaping towards the window.

"Who's that?" he said, pointing a finger at thin air.

"Who? Where? There's nobody except us."

"Don't be stupid, Liv. Look, he's waving at you."

"Who, Jake? The room's empty, I told you."

"The old geezer. Look, he's got three fingers missing from his right hand."

Livie paled and put her hand to her neck. Her granddad had died four years before, aged 94, and Jake knew nothing of him. She'd only been going out with her fiancé for two years. How then could he know her grandfather, who had lost three fingers in the Second World War?

3

"He's smiling at you, Livie. Why are you ignoring him?"

Mercifully, a doctor came in at that moment and saved her from more of Jake's ravings.

"Good afternoon, Mr Conley, how are you feeling?" The doctor raised a chart from the end of the bed and lifted a couple of sheets attached to a clipboard. He scrutinised the charts and recorded readings. "Mmm, all seems well. We'll soon have you fighting fit."

"Bloody hell, I'm a pacifist, doctor."

"Since when? Ignore his bad manners, doctor, he's been acting strange since he came around."

"I bloody haven't! Why don't you just piss off home, Liv. I don't need you here."

"See what I mean, doctor? He never used to talk to me like that."

The tall, thin doctor, distinguished-looking with the aged skin of a heavy smoker, turned to her.

"Forgive me, miss, I need to examine my patient; would you be so kind as to wait outside?"

Alone, he began to shine a pencil light into Jake's eyes and use his stethoscope before asking Jake to cough.

"It hurts, damn it!"

"Of course, it does. You have two cracked ribs, but to be honest, you got off lightly. There was considerable bruising, ah yes, it's steadily being absorbed. You'll be fine. What about your shoulder? Does that hurt? No? Good. Tomorrow, we'll have a neurologist visit you. The scan suggests you got away with head-butting a Jeep, but we need to be cautious. Concussion can be dangerous. If I were a betting man, I'd say you'll be as right as rain in no time, Mr Conley."

"Jake, please. Tell me, doctor, and forgive me asking, but have you lost someone dear to you recently?"

The medical man's face became as white as his lab coat.

"W-what? Have you been talking to the nurse?"

Jake looked at the doctor with concern. "No, not at all. It's just – I can *feel* your pain."

"Good Lord! I lost my daughter a month ago, she was six."

4

He looked as if he wanted to say more but fought back the urge – who was this fellow to him? He was a private person and had no wish to share his grief. He cut short his visit, and with words of circumstance, he left Jake Conley to take his painkiller. As he walked out of the room with what felt like an icy grip on his heart, he wondered at the exchange he'd just had. If the patient hadn't spoken with Nurse Ashdown, then how could he possibly know about Alice? Doctor Wormald had no time to muse because the patient's girlfriend intercepted and bombarded him with questions.

All he could give her were reassurances about Jake's physical condition. What they were both concerned about, for different reasons and without mooting it, was the patient's mental state.

TWO

YORK, UK, MAY 2019

In the professional opinion of Dr Gillian Emerson, the aggression of her patient, Jake Conley, was simply a defensive shield to protect him in his extremely vulnerable state. He was recovering from a serious accident, and separation from his fiancée if she understood correctly, and coming to terms with a marked personality change. As a respected psychologist, she had no trouble dealing with the aggression, but the personality shift intrigued and, if she were honest, excited her. She had his medical records in front of her as she awaited his arrival for this, their fourth session. Dr Emerson had read and re-read them. All assessments indicated no physical complications but were unanimous about his heightened aggression and mood swings. His long-suffering girlfriend had left him, although the psychologist understood the strain she must have been under.

Here was an indisputably good-looking, intelligent and sensitive – ah yes, there was the problem: he was now hyper-sensitive – person aged twenty-nine, who had turned down an academic career in the University of York's renowned history department in favour of chasing a chimera. *Anyone who puts her mind to it can write a novel,* Dr Emerson mused. She'd thought about it herself, but writing a good one, a bestseller, was a different matter. Whether living his dream was the best condition for Jake's fragile state was another matter and one she hoped to pursue with him when he entered her consulting room.

In he came, sat down, and unexpectedly giving her a charming smile, confessed, "When my GP referred me to you, Dr Emerson, I'll admit I was peeved and reluctant. Just the thought of my being considered a case for a psychologist made me rage. I suppose Livie's breaking off with me gave me the push I needed. But after what's been happening recently, I'm glad to be here."

He'd grabbed her attention; he could see it in her body language. She leaned forward in her easy chair, raised an eyebrow and asked, "What's been happening recently, Jake?"

So much had occurred that he'd describe as strange, so why not start with the most recent, the freshest in his mind? His swarthy, tanned countenance, offsetting his light grey eyes, took on a perplexed expression, which enhanced Dr Emerson's already piqued curiosity.

"Well, a lot, to be honest, like this morning, walking here...this complete stranger, not a tramp or anything, maybe a businessman in a suit...walks up to me and starts pouring out all his problems. I mean, like I was a priest, or, with respect, a shrink ...or his best mate. I'd never seen him before in my life. I mean, it's not normal, a total stranger. Why me? Come on, doc, look at me, I haven't got agony aunt written on my forehead, I'm just an ordinary guy."

Gilian Emerson smiled at her handsome patient. She wouldn't describe him as ordinary, but then, she wasn't insensible to masculine appeal.

"Is that how you'd describe yourself? 'Just an ordinary guy'?"

He frowned and stared out of the window at the scudding, wind-driven clouds.

"I might have done until the accident, but after that...I'm confused. I don't know if it's me that's changed or how the world sees me...or both."

His voice trailed away weakly, and he stared at the psychologist with a look she interpreted as a desperate appeal for help.

"You're probably right. In what ways have you changed?"

"To begin with, I pick up on other people's emotions so quickly. Sometimes, I feel quite drained when I'm around negative people, and I come near to snapping with dramatic ones; I can't stand being near them."

Dr Emerson jotted down a note and, smiling in encouragement, waited for him to continue.

"I've been having disturbing dreams too. The other night... Wednesday...well, I wouldn't call it a dream, more a...a...vision. I saw myself leap out of bed, draw back the curtains, and what do you think? There was this red sports car crumpled against the wall across the road, people gathering, then a police car with its flashing blue light and an ambulance came. Then, Thursday night at exactly the same time, there was a terrible crash like a bomb had exploded. I jumped out of bed, drew back the curtains, and, doctor, even as I tell you, my hair stands on end, I *knew* what I was going to see...it was all there, exactly the same scene, like a film replaying. Do you know, two young lads had taken the bend too fast, lost control, veered across the road into the wall – both killed: dead at twenty! Bloody hell! And I knew it was going to happen twenty-four hours before. But what could I do to prevent it? What *am I,* some kind of freak?"

"Of course not." She smiled, although she found it disturbing. "Premonitions are common phenomena, especially those of tragedies and with extremely sensitive subjects."

"Is that what it is, me being sensitive? I could do without it, I'll tell you. I keep knowing when something's going to happen before it does. It freaks me out, doctor."

She laughed. "Well it could be useful on occasion."

"Then there's the strange feeling I keep getting between my eyebrows."

He touched his brow with his forefinger at the crown of his head. "It's like a dull ache, and it happens whenever I have spiritual thoughts. It got me started on checking out religions and things, I mean, Buddhism and Hinduism – things I know nothing about, at least I didn't. But this strange feeling, it's what they call 'the third eye;' apparently, it's my *chakras* opening up!"

He pursed his lips, looked thoughtful, and fixed her with a disconcerting stare. She glanced at her wristwatch, made a note, and waited, but when he continued to stare and didn't speak, she said,

"You do know there's a physical explanation for all this, Jake?"

Ideally, he would make an effort to explain it himself, but he remained in staring, silent mode. She broke the silence.

"It's not unknown for a *psychic awakening* to occur after a trauma. You received a severe blow to the head, and luckily you came away physically unscathed, but you know, the brain is a very complex organ – scientists still don't have complete knowledge of it. Who's to say what such a nasty bump has triggered off?"

"So I *am* a freak, then?"

The psychologist grinned. "Not a freak but someone with access to parts of the brain that are denied to the mass of humanity. You know, it's probable that so-called primitive man could use some of the brain we can't. Think of water divining; think of seeing auras and so on."

"Are you saying I'm primitive?"

He was teasing her now, she reflected; a pity professionalism made it impossible to flirt – she liked him.

"No, but I'm saying you're not crazy, Jake. In fact, there's an eminent cognitive neuroscientist, Abraham Spark, at London University with a practice on Harley Street, who has written several papers on it. He calls it *synaesthesia*, which is essentially a cross-wiring of the brain in which the senses get mixed up. It affects only about four percent of the population who are known as synesthetes. Jake, *you* are a synesthete! Some might see certain colours when they hear music or smell something that isn't there when they feel a certain emotion. This condition is caused by connections between parts of the brain that are not there in other people, and it can be caused by trauma to the head. I'd hazard that happened with your accident. So you see, Jake, there's a convincing explanation for your present mental state. I'm going to call it *acquired psychic syndrome*, a new sub-category of synaesthesia. Practically speaking, we should seek solutions to help you be more comfortable with it."

"Do you mean medicines, doctor? I'm dead against taking pills."

"Good, because *I'm* dead against prescribing them. No, I mean we should find a solution within yourself that might help."

"Such as?"

"Let's see, you told me you'd like to write a novel. Tell me about it."

"I specialised in medieval history at university; my professor even wanted me to stay on and research the Anglo-Saxon era. It's a love of mine. I want to set a novel in that period."

"Do you have a plan for the book?"

"More or less."

"Isn't there more research you need to do?"

"There is, of course, but I've been distracted of late by what's been happening. I've even changed my eating habits."

"Really?"

"Yeah, it's like I can't stand my favourite junk food anymore. I just want salads and healthy stuff. Burger and chips and – *ugh!* – ketchup is right out of the window."

"Interesting. Before your accident, did you have any hobbies, apart from history?"

"I love hiking, rambling around in search of old country churches."

"Nice. I think I'd like to do that, too, if I had more time. Listen, Jake, can't you combine your interests? I think it would do you a world of good."

"What do you mean?"

"Get your boots and head into the countryside. Do some field work to research your novel. The fresh air will help the creative juices to flow."

His pale grey eyes lit up. "Great idea, doctor! A wonder I didn't think of it myself!"

In spite of his 'intuitive hits,' Jake did not foresee the momentous consequences of this decision, and Dr Emerson would have to re-evaluate her assessment of it *doing him a world of good*. She wondered whether she should have packed him off to Helsinki, where the renowned Brain Research Unit of Aalto University could have given him an MRI scan to study which part of the brain could light up under certain stimuli, but she had felt it unnecessary. It would pander to her medical curiosity rather than help Jake, and it would simply confirm her diagnosis, of which she was as certain as could be.

THREE

YORKSHIRE, UK, MAY 2019

Jake retrieved an ordnance survey map of East Yorkshire from its place on a dusty shelf. He ran his finger through the dust, grunted in disgust at his poor housekeeping, and vowed to clean it as soon as he'd finished with the chart. Gingerly, he spread it out on his desk. He was wary of worsening the creases worn by constant folding and unfolding.

Where to visit to research his novel? Maybe he'd misled Dr Emerson into thinking he had clear ideas about a novel, but that could not be farther from the truth. All he knew was that in theory he'd like to write one about the Kingdom of Northumbria. It gave him so much scope in terms of kings and events, but, as usual, he had whittled away mentally at the choice. There were novels already published about almost every Northumbrian king. As a result, he simply didn't know what to select to make a good story, hence the agonising when the accident occurred.

Faced with the bold array of contours and symbols, his struggle to decide resumed. If he chose a commoner as his protagonist, the story might achieve the originality he craved. But the ordinariness of a ceorl hardly inspired a gripping storyline. How would rambling around the Yorkshire countryside help? Where should he go to get the creative juices flowing? He had a reasonable knowledge of Anglo-Saxon sites in the county. His eyes passed over the modern place names, and he converted them into their Old English titles: York – *Eoforwic*, Leeds – *Loidis,* and so on. During this futile exercise, one name leapt off the paper in bold letters, as if the printed word wished to grab his attention: Driffield – *Driffelda.*

Jake blinked and shook his head. Had that really happened? Was this another of the weird circumstances that had been plaguing him of late? He ignored it and continued his perusal of places until it happened again. There was no doubting it this time; Driffield had caught his attention. It was some thirty miles due east of York and had no Anglo-Saxon association as far as he knew, apart from the name, but the Internet should help.

He spent an hour seeking information and discovered that St Mary's Church in Little Driffield was an Anglo-Saxon foundation. There was also a legend stating that a Northumbrian king, Aldfrith, had a royal palace in the settlement. This monarch had suffered severe wounds in a battle nearby, which subsequently proved fatal. Supposedly, he was buried in St Mary's. This convinced Jake that he should investigate this monarch by visiting Driffield, also because the surrounding area of the Yorkshire Wolds was good terrain for a pleasant ramble.

He set about the logistics of the journey. He considered hiking all the way to Driffield but ruled it out on the basis of conserving energy for country walking. He did not enjoy road walking, deeming it unhealthy and hard on the leg joints. He had not bothered to buy a car. There seemed so little point, with him living in York and it being more convenient to move around the city on foot or by bike. So, public transport it had to be, but he would have to overcome the usual problem, the difficulty of travelling from west to east.

It was only thirty miles from York, but he found that to arrive in Driffield, he would have to catch a coach from the Stonebow, which in an hour and a half would reach Scarborough. From the West

Square of the seaside resort, another short coach trip would end in Bridlington. Jake sighed and shook his head. *I'll bet the Saxons could have done it quicker in the eighth century!* But he knew that wasn't true. With relief, he noted that in Bridlington he would have a ten-minute walk from the bus to the train station. At least he'd be able to stretch his legs. From there, a fourteen-minute train journey would take him to Driffield.

He switched off his computer and set about the dusting, knowing full well that when he got back from his jaunt around the countryside, it would need doing again. That was the numbing, unremitting nature of housework.

Jake was lucky with the weather; a very seasonable sunny day raised his spirits as he emerged from Driffield station. He cast a backwards glance to appraise the mid-Victorian architecture underlying the adjustments to the practical demands of a semi-automated twenty-first-century out-of-the-way station. The northern-line service had served its purpose; now he was free to stride out through the town that separated him from Little Driffield. A glance at his map showed him the best route was via York Road and Church Lane.

After a good half-hour's energetic striding, he approached the object of his journey. The graveyard lay between him and the church. A line of withered daffodils stretched between two trees as if to mark the boundary of the burial site. The tree on the right was a bare skeleton, its trunk infested with shiny green leaves of ivy climbing up to the first of the forlorn boughs. In contrast, the tree on the left presented the lush foliage of late spring. His eyes swept over the sorry daffodils to the contrasting well-tended lawn that hosted a series of slab-topped tombs amid the isolated gravestones. Beyond stood the Grade II listed building, its squat tower with crenellations seeming to him to be out of proportion to the long, buttressed body of the church. But he had to admit to being no expert in church architecture. He loved visiting them but needed to deepen his knowledge. If asked for an honest assessment in that moment, he would have considered himself disappointed by the uninspiring exterior. Inside, his attitude shifted. This, as he had read at home, was a church restored by the great Sir Tatton Sykes at the end of the nineteenth century.

He admired the lavish 'Decorative Style' of the interior with lovely tiled floor, carved pews, pulpit, ornate reredos and rood loft. But what really excited him was the printed leaflet he took in exchange for a small offering. It informed him of the supposed burial in the church of King Aldfrith in 705 AD. It claimed that over the tomb was written *Statutum est omnibus semel mori* (It is appointed for all once to die), but in 1807 the nave and chancel had been excavated and disappointingly, no evidence of the royal remains was found. Yet, Jake could sense the weight of history inside the building, and he knew almost as a revelation that he must write a novel about King Aldfrith. Had he known the rest of what this decision implied, he would never have taken it.

Jake folded the leaflet, pocketed it, then left the house of worship behind. He had found and booked a high-quality bed and breakfast in the countryside near the neighbouring village of Bainton. With this in mind, he found a public footpath that took him in a loop around Southburn and all the way to Bainton. After just another five minutes on foot appeared the Wolds Village, containing much more than his accommodation. After checking in, he went to the tearooms, also housed in a listed building, where tea and cake were welcome after his walking.

As he refreshed himself, he took out the leaflet and read about King Aldfrith, whose wounds were inflicted at the Battle of Ebberston. It informed him that the king was carried and sheltered in a cave near the battlefield before being taken to Little Driffield, where his palace stood on North Hill. This site, too, had been excavated and revealed a motte and bailey castle of a post-Conquest date. As he read, Jake experienced the by now familiar sensation of a 'third eye.' Instead of irritating or discouraging him, it reassured him that he should continue along the lines of this research. With this in mind, he reached into a side pocket of his backpack and took out the map to locate Ebberston. He needed to see this cave and check on the site of the battle.

He cursed under his breath. His finger rested on Ebberston. He'd come south, whereas the battle had taken place north of Driffield. It was a stiff twenty-mile hike to get there. He ruled out coming back to this bed and breakfast the next day. A pity; he liked the look of this accommodation. Reaching out, he picked up a glossy leaflet promoting the facilities. *'In the mornings, Wolds Village serves full Yorkshire breakfast in the farmhouse's original Georgian dining room. The air-conditioned coaching inn serves a traditional English menu, and the tearoom offers homemade cakes. All dishes are freshly prepared using locally sourced produce.'*

A full Yorkshire breakfast appealed. It would set him up for the trek tomorrow. Despite his substantial breakfast, when he arrived in Ebberston, the fresh air and exercise had restored his appetite. He found a gastro pub near the village, and feeling in high spirits after having enjoyed the countryside in full bloom, he strode into the bar, noted the cleanliness, and asked a friendly barman for the menu. In one corner a couple were eating what looked like pork with mashed potatoes, and they seemed to be enjoying it.

Jake had noticed the CAMRA plaque outside the door and looked with appreciation at the line of pumps before selecting a pint of craft beer. After ordering from the menu, he smiled at the elderly barman and said, "I heard there's a cave near the village where a Saxon king was sheltered. Do you know about it?"

The reply came with a strong local accent.

"Oh, ay, lad. Everyone knows abou' *Elfrid's Hole*. It's abou' a mile north o' this 'ere road."

Jake stared at the barman. "So, it's more than just a legend?"

"Oh, ay, 'course. Tha can visit yon if tha's so minded. 'Twere dug up when ah were a nipper, not that ah know owt abou' yon. I reckon they'll have summat abou' yon in t' library ower at Eastfield if tha's interested, like."

Jake remembered from his map work the previous day that Eastfield was some miles off to the east, so for the moment, he filed away the idea of checking out the excavation in the library in his memory, adding only, "The cave's not on private land, then? Can I walk up and visit it?"

"Ay, course tha can. Mind, tha'll find it all blocked off. Tha canna go in yon."

Jake took a long draught of ale and smacked his lips in satisfaction. He hoped the food would be as good as the ale.

"Is there a road up to the cave?"

"Nay, lad," the barman laughed, "tha'd better go up yonder 'ill, past the big 'ouse an' cross t' farmland into t'woods, an' tha' ll find t'track, reet enough. 'Appen there's a signboard across t' opening. Nah then, wha' table's tha' goin' to be sittin' at?"

After a most satisfactory lunch, Jake turned left along the road, leaving the pub behind, and struck out along a lane he hoped would lead him to the mansion the barman had referred to. After a few hundred yards, assailed by doubt, he took out his ordnance survey map, blessing the absence of wind as he opened it out. Quickly, he located the PH on the main road, and not far to the north, farther along this same lane, stood a small country mansion. He pressed on, and coming to the elegant building, skirting it, headed into the woodland behind, on the basis of its being uphill. To the north-east of the house, he came to an outcrop, where he discerned the vestiges of a cave within an artificial stone grotto. Could this be it? He approached and found a weathered board in front of the entrance to a land-filled cavern. Obstructing the entrance was a huge boulder. He had no idea of how much it weighed – a lot! There was writing carved into the board, worn, but still legible:

'Alfrid, King of Northumberland, was wounded in a bloody battle nigh this place, and was hid in a cave; and from thence he was removed to Little Driffield, where he died.'

Jake took out his smartphone and photographed the board for reference. That done, he turned to leave, and as he did, the hairs on his arm stood on end. A curious sensation of being observed and an oppressive feeling of being an unwelcome intruder made him want to flee.

Chastising himself for being an impressionable fool, he nonetheless set off back to Ebberston with the intention of finding lodgings for the night. He also needed to devise a plan of action to get more information about this King Aldfrith or Alfrid or Elfrid, as they seemed to call him hereabouts. So far, he had not entered the village itself.

Through the trees near the country mansion, Jake spied the tower of a church, which when he changed direction turned out to be the Church of St Mary the Virgin of Ebberston. Half a mile outside the village, it stood in leafy surroundings, and Jake, unable to resist adding to his collection of country churches, took several photos of the exterior before attempting to enter the ancient building. It was locked. However, there was a mobile phone number of the churchwarden, Mr Hibbitt, and a notice announcing evensong at 6.30 pm. Loath to disturb the churchwarden, he decided to seek accommodation in the village and come back later to attend the service. There were some questions he needed answered, and the church seemed to be the ideal place to satisfy this need. However, he did not know then that *some* questions are better left unanswered.

FOUR

THORNTON-LE-DALE, NORTH YORKSHIRE, MAY 2019

JAKE WALKED AWAY FROM HIS NEW LODGINGS, SITUATED IN THE picturesque village of Ebberston, back to the main road, where he proceeded to the hamlet of Thornton-le-Dale. His idea was to indulge his hobby and explore the Church of St Mary the Virgin before Evensong. He turned into Hagg Side Lane and surveyed the pleasing form of the twelfth-century Norman church. Towering over the building was a large conifer, and when he approached, he was amazed to find a gravestone half-consumed by the tree trunk. How many decades before it disappeared inside the tree completely?

He walked around the exterior, noting grotesque carved heads with their unsettling features and appreciated the well-tended grave-yard until he came to the back of the building. There, on the north wall, he found something that reminded him of the main reason for his presence in this area. Set in the stonework was a stone depicting what he imagined to be a Viking sword. His flesh prickled as his imagination began to churn. This was clearly a re-utilised stone, most likely from a grave-slab. But whose sword did it represent? Where was he buried? What was this man's story? Jake tried to calm his fervid imagination. King Aldfrith died in 705 AD, so this sword post-dated him by more than a century since Viking raids in the area didn't begin until the ninth century. Nonetheless, the long, narrow slab had set his nerves on edge, and he began to wonder about the soundness of his psychologist's advice to visit the area, given his present mental state.

The south door of the edifice had a wonderful calming effect on him. The scrolled ironwork of the door dated from the late Saxon period and contained a dove carrying an olive branch in its beak. Jake photographed the ornate work and racked his memory. He had seen similar Saxon ironwork on another Saxon door in Yorkshire. Ay, that was it! Nearer York, closer to home, at St Helen's church in Stillingfleet. He pulled out a notebook and jotted down his thoughts on this church's exterior.

It was time to make his way into the building now as people were arriving for the service. An elderly woman with blue-rinsed hair gave him a friendly smile, and emboldened, he asked, "Excuse me, I'm looking for the churchwarden, do you know who it is?"

She gave him a thorough once-over gaze, smiled again, and pointed to a rotund, bespectacled man, who appeared quite approachable. Now was a bad time to disturb him, as the congregation was settling to pleasant organ music. This came to a sudden halt, and the vicar began with the usual Glory Be. Jake was not a regular churchgoer, but on the few occasions he attended, he enjoyed joining in the hymns he knew, and this evening he lent his rich, untutored voice to a hearty rendition of 'Immortal, Invisible God Only Wise...': one of his favourites.

After the evensong concluded and the small congregation dispersed, Jake remained seated, bowed his head as if in prayer, and kept his eye on the churchwarden from under lowered brow. The vicar was outside the door, socialising with his parishioners, but Mr Hibbitt was gathering prayer books and placing them in a neat pile on a front pew.

"Are you alright, my friend?"

The cheerful smile illuminated the chubby countenance of the middle-aged churchwarden.

"Perfectly." Jake outdid the smile. "To be honest, I wanted to have a quick word with you – if you can spare a moment," he added hastily.

"Of course." The man slid onto the pew in front of Jake's and twisted round to give him an encouraging nod. "How can I help?"

Jake introduced himself, rather fraudulently, as a novelist and briefly outlined his idea for a story based on King Aldfrith.

For the first time, the friendly countenance clouded.

"You want to tread carefully there, young man. I take it you've been up to the cave?"

Jake agreed that he had.

"There's been all sorts of odd goings-on up there over the centuries. Mind you, I don't pay much heed to rumours and gossip."

"What's the story of the cave?"

"Do you know about the battle of Ebberston?"

Jake nodded slowly and added, "But there's a lot of doubt surrounding it. Like who fought whom and even whether a battle ever really occurred."

The voice of the churchwarden took on an authoritative tone.

"Oh, a battle was fought, right enough. You've only to look on a decent map and you'll see from the place names; the *Bloody Beck* flows past the *Bloody Field,* and those names go right back to before the Domesday Book. They say the slaughter was so bad that the beck flowed crimson with blood. As to who fought the battle, there are those who say it was Aldfrith rebelling against his father, Oswy, but that's impossible because of the date of the battle. His father was long dead. No, I prefer to think it was a Saxon battle against raiding Picts; now *that* is possible."

"I'm glad I decided to speak with you," Jake offered. "You see, I want to get my tale right. There must be many local historians who would be eager to shoot me down in flames if I get the facts wrong."

The churchwarden grinned. "I'd say most would be pleased to

have us on the map, so to speak. You say you've been up to the grotto?"

"Yes, it looks like one of those follies that rich men used to build."

"Very perceptive." The churchwarden looked around uneasily as if he were in a hurry. "That's exactly what it is. Put up in the late eighteenth century by Sir Charles Hotham-Thompson, the eighth baronet, who owned Ebberston Hall at the time." Jake felt the strange sensation at his forehead again and frowned before jotting the name down in his notebook.

"You should look into him, is my advice. That was a funny business, that of the grotto. You can read his correspondence in the archives at Hull University. He left more than three thousand letters, they say. Now, I really must lock up here. Are you staying in the area?"

Jake agreed he was and named the bed and breakfast establishment.

"Get on over to Hull and see what you can find out. Then we can have another talk and I'll tell you all I know."

He proffered a hand, and Jake smiled into the friendly face but went away feeling more than ever unsettled about this story of King Aldfrith. There was something strange surrounding the whole episode. But what? The churchwarden was defensive. Jake also harboured a curious conviction that it was in his fate to write the tale of what happened on the Bloody Field and to get to the truth of the matter.

As he walked away on Hagg Side Lane, he turned to glance back at the lovely church and saw the churchwarden standing next to the vicar and, without a shadow of doubt, pointing at him. The hand dropped immediately as he turned to look their way. Jake shrugged. Was it his overheated imagination again? It was only natural that a stranger to the sleepy hamlet, asking questions, should create a topic of conversation. Still, he decided, he'd ask his landlady about the grotto when he got back to his digs.

She was the archetype of a bed and breakfast proprietor in Jake's opinion, motherly and cheerful. As soon as he entered her house, there she was, offering him a cup of tea and cake. Relaxing in a chintz-upholstered armchair, sipping his tea, he told her how much he'd appreciated the local church and enjoyed the service.

"Are you interested in churches, love?"

Jake admitted as much but told her he was here for another reason.

"Oh, yes, and what's that?"

"I'm researching a novel about King Aldfrith, the king who sheltered in a cave near here. I went there this morning."

Her face was a picture of concern.

"Nay, love. You don't want to be going up there! I'd steer clear if I was you!"

"Why? Why not?"

"There's them as says that place is haunted. There's been rum goings-on there. Stay away, laddie – that's my advice."

Jake frowned and thought about what the churchwarden had said. Hadn't he used the same expression? *'All sorts of odd goings-on up there over the centuries.'*

He smirked at Mrs McCracken, the landlady. "Surely you don't believe in ghosts? You said it was haunted."

"There's been plenty of witnesses over the years. It's fair to say that none of the local folk'll go near. I know I won't. You don't want to be going up there alone, especially not at night. There's been two deaths at least that I know of."

"Good lord, as bad as that? Who died and when?"

"The last one was just after I moved here. One of them backpackers, he was. A 57-year-old teacher from Wigan, I think. He was found with a gash to his head, stone dead. The coroner said it was an unfortunate accident, but I'm not having that. The poor fellow had all the right equipment, sturdy hiking boots – I don't think for one minute he slipped and banged his head."

"Do you suspect foul play?"

"Well, I'm just a foolish old woman, don't go by what I think.

23

Foul play? Worse, I'd say. *The York Press* reported he was found dead with a look of horror on his face."

"I know that newspaper, and it's generally serious enough. So when was that exactly? And by the way, Mrs McCracken, you're neither old nor foolish!" Jake took out his notebook and hovered a pen over the open page.

She gave him a delightful smile for his compliment, but it was soon replaced by a serious expression.

"Let's see, I came here in September 2004, and it happened about a month later. So, October. I remember thinking, 'What a start!' but luckily, he wasn't staying with me. That would have been simply awful, the police and all! Poor man! That's why I want you to stay away from the cave – it's *cursed!*"

Jake didn't believe that for one moment, but to calm her, he said, "Don't worry, Mrs McCracken–"

"Call me Gwen."

"Don't worry, Gwen, I'm not planning on going there. I have to leave for Hull tomorrow. Can you book me in for another three nights?"

"We're quiet at the moment, so no problem."

"Great. What about public transport to Hull?"

"Your best bet is to take the coach; the 128 stops on the main road at Brook House Farm, and it'll take you as far as Hull. That's the best you'll manage. I should have a timetable somewhere. Ah, here it is! Let's see, there's one leaves at 11.15. It'll get you to Hull in three hours, will that do? You can get to the university from the bus station."

"It might mean I'm late back tomorrow."

"You have a key. You can come in whatever time you like, love."

Jake was tired and went to his room, where he found some leaflets. One in particular caught his eye, about Ebberston Hall. It turned out to be a listed building, a small stately hall with splendid gardens. He picked it up and, lying on the bed, began to read about the house. Disappointed to discover that it was now no longer open to the public, nonetheless, he found the Sir Charles, who had the grotto built, included among the previous owners. It seemed the baronet enjoyed significant prominence in George III's reign. He tossed the leaflet aside and decided to shower and find out more about the man the next day in the university.

FIVE

THE UNIVERSITY OF HULL, MAY 2019

Skilful cajolery, deception and manipulation enabled Jake to penetrate the librarian's stubborn defences and gain access to the Hotham-Thompson archives. The eighth baronet proved an enthralling study as Jake discounted letters that covered the young Charles's scholarly career at various public schools, notably Westminster, and subsequent study of law at the Middle Temple. Unwillingly drawn into the life of this eighteenth-century nobleman, despite his desire to discover anything that might shed light on Aldfrith's Cave, Jake's setting aside of irrelevant material slowed as interest in the personage gripped him. A distinguished military career beginning as an ensign in the 1st Foot Guards saw Charles rise to the rank of colonel in 1762 during the Seven Years' War. From 1761 to 1768 he was also the Member of Parliament for St Ives and in 1763 was made a Groom of the Bedchamber.

'Blimey, this Sir Charles was a bigwig – someone to be taken seriously!'

Piecing together the man's career through his letters was a tedious but rewarding experience, and Jake filled the pages of his notebook beginning from 1768 when Sir Charles transferred as colonel to the

15th Regiment of Foot and retired to Yorkshire, where he succeeded his father in 1771 to the baronetcy and his estate near Beverley. He took the additional name of Thompson on inheriting the Thompson estates in Yorkshire from his wife's family in 1772. He was knighted KB in 1772.

This material gave Jake context for his search, and he began to sift through the post-1771 letters with more enthusiasm, but, frustratingly, he could find little other than mundane matters of family love affairs, the escapades of drunken friends, matters of estate management – such as cottage rental, and condolences; in short, all the major and minor events constituting the life of an eminent nobleman of the period.

It was not until he found a letter dated 1773 and addressed to Sir Robert Wanley of the Royal Antiquarian Society that, with shaking hand, he thrust aside the hollow sensation of a day wasted. He read:

Sir,

In your bounteous good nature, you will surely forgive the impertinence of an approach to your esteemed self through this epistle for which I would ask pardon, if I did not think you would be better pleased if I did not.
To the point, Sir, my solicitation is founded upon the deserved reputation that precedes you as a scholar of all matters Anglo-Saxon within and without the Royal Soc.^y . As most worthy heir to a noble, erudite forebear, viz. your grandsire Sir Humfrey, I beg leave to trouble you, aware naturally of disturbing your employment otherwise in useful and essential study, with a matter of mutual interest, which I believe you will be desirous of appraising. May I draw your attention, Sir, to mysterious and awesome occurrences on my property in the Chafer Wood, at a place known locally as Elfrid's Hole, a cavern upon which undoubtedly your peerless learning will be able to shed light. It is therefore with considerable disquiet that

*I await your reply to my invitation to sojourn at my humble
residence of Ebberston Hall to conduct an inquiry. If it so
pleases you, you may make agreeable progress into Yorkshire to
see all the Fine Seats and Places in this country and I feel sure
you will not be disappointed.*

Your Most Humble and Most Obedient Servant,
Chas. Hotham-Thompson, KG.

Jake re-read the letter and, with growing excitement, copied it
word for word into his notebook. In vain, he sought a follow-up letter.
Coming to the end of the archive contents, he replaced the letters
carefully and carried the box file back to the stern, pinch-faced
librarian who made a show of checking the contents and their condition whilst Jake was effusive in his thanks. Having made a point of
remarking how useful his experience had been, he asked her about
Sir Robert Wanley. She disappointed him by insisting that their
archive did not house the correspondence of this particular knight of
the realm. Instead, she told him that his best chance of finding
anything written by the antiquarian might be found at the Society of
Antiquaries in London. She hunted in a card index and produced an
address – Burlington House, Piccadilly. Jake thanked her and jotted
it down, thinking ruefully that there was much more to writing a
novel than he'd ever imagined.

The next morning, after breakfast, he flipped opened his notebook, found the churchwarden's mobile number and called it. A brief
exchange and they arranged to meet in half an hour at the church.
The man seemed relaxed about the appointment, calming Jake's
doubts about his sincerity.

When he approached the church along the path, a cheery wave
from the stout figure of the warden encouraged him forward.

"I went to Hull yesterday and read through the Hotham-
Thompson letters," Jake plunged straight in.

"Did you? And what did you dig up?"

"A letter to an antiquarian that referred to *'mysterious and awesome occurrences'* at the cave."

"That would be just before Sir Charles had the grotto built and blocked off the entrance to the cavern."

"Unfortunately, there were no other letters to this Sir Robert, so I don't know any more than that vague reference to *occurrences*. Can you tell me anything more?"

"I can, but you'd best be warned not to meddle in matters that don't concern you." The menacing tone of the churchwarden seemed so out of character with his benign presence until Jake looked into the pale blue eyes, which had taken on an aggressive hardness behind the glasses. "Writing a novel's one thing, my lad. From a distance, you can use as much imagination as you like, but stirring up certain forces, that's another matter. I'll tell you all I know and let you judge for yourself."

The wind whistled through the churchyard, the trees creaking and groaning under the buffeting, causing Jake to shiver and pull up the collar of his jacket. So he readily agreed to the suggestion of sheltering in the vestry where they sat opposite each other at a small table. The surplices and other ecclesiastical accoutrements hanging limply from their pegs served to make the small room more oppressive. Jake fought to quell a sense of claustrophobia and listened intently to what his host had to say.

"Whatever happened in the eighteenth century has come down to us as what many would dismiss as old wives' tales. They say that the smallholders at the time began to lose animals, and of course, theft of livestock in those days was a capital offence. Several ne'er-do-wells were suspected, but it wasn't until reports of fires up at the cave became frequent that a band of men went to investigate. They found signs of slaughtered animals such as hides and bones, as well as the charred remains of a fire. They determined to keep a watch on the area and to return to the cavern to apprehend the guilty parties when alerted by a fire.

"Sadly, a local man, too impetuous by far, spotted the glow of the flames one evening and instead of summoning help set off to investigate, telling his wife beforehand what he was about. He never came back. Nobody knows what became of him. That was when Sir Charles decided to look into the matter. There was a rumour that he'd fired off several shots in the woods that evening. Of course, he might have bagged himself a pheasant or two. You know what people are like at exaggerating everything. Certainly, it didn't help that when Sir Charles returned to the Hall, he gave instructions to his tenants to stay well clear of Elfrid's Hole. Soon after these events, as you know, Sir Robert Wanley, a famous antiquarian, came to investigate the cave. And here's the most curious fact: the vicar of St Mary's at the time kept a diary where he affirms that Sir Robert arrived as a sociable, jocund personality and left as a haggard, haunted, and irritable individual. It was he who encouraged Sir Charles to fill the cave with rocks and to block off the entrance. Then, of course, after the fashion of the time, Sir Charles built the grotto around the entrance. It stands there, as you've seen, as a folly to this day."

Jake looked at the earnest countenance of the churchwarden and could see that the man was disturbed by his tale.

"There's more, isn't there?"

"There is. People have lost count of the tragedies associated with that place. More than two hundred years have passed, but the curse of Elfrid's Hole continues. We're talking about travellers disappearing without trace, headless bodies, and even raving madmen. Don't look at me like that! I'm not making this up. You can check it out easily enough, Mr Conley."

"It's not that I don't believe you. Just that...if it's as bad as you say, how come the cave isn't more notorious throughout the land?"

"People here want a quiet life. We can do without that kind of notoriety. You see, in 1951 the cave was cleared out and excavated. Do you know what the archaeologists found? No? Nothing to do with the Anglo-Saxons. Far older. They found the remains of seven humans, five adults and two children, along with flints, pottery, antlers and animal bones. The finds were assumed to be early

Neolithic, but no dating was done, and strangely they have gone missing. That's caused gossip and wild speculation. The cave was sealed after the excavation with a large boulder. As I say, we can do without notoriety. The last bad happening was the death of a visiting schoolteacher–"

"In 2004, Mrs McCracken told me. The poor fellow slipped and cracked his head."

"That's what we'd like people to think, but there may be another far more sinister explanation."

"What do you mean?"

"Never mind. Just stay away from Elfrid's Hole. We wouldn't want an *accident* to befall you, would we? I believe it's our concerted effort to keep visitors away from the Hole that's reduced the frequency of sinister events. Let's keep it that way, shall we, Mr Conley?" He made no effort to keep the aggression from his voice.

"Are you threatening me?" Jake stared hard at the plump churchwarden of the innocuous appearance and contrasting voice.

He gifted Jake a warm smile and made an apologetic open-handed gesture. "Just the opposite. I'm trying to protect you from your own curiosity. I'd hate anything to happen to you, young man. Look, why don't you find another king to write about?"

Jake thanked him, shook hands, and left the church, marvelling at his own contrariness. The churchwarden's warnings had elicited the opposite effect in him. He was more determined than ever to return to the grotto. Not that the recounting of terrible occurrences hadn't troubled him – they had. In fact, he didn't feel like rushing up the hill straightaway, there was no hurry; instead, he would stroll over to Ebberston Hall. Meanwhile, the wind might calm. The sight of the building would give him a better feeling for the man who had built the grotto. If he wanted to make a success of this venture, he needed to immerse himself entirely in the character and atmosphere of Ebberston.

SIX

EBBERSTON, NORTH YORKSHIRE, MAY 2019

WALKING AWAY FROM THE CHURCH, JAKE REFLECTED ON THE ambience of Ebberston. On the surface, he mused, it was a pretty little Yorkshire village, just one of many. But on closer scrutiny, everything about it was out of the ordinary, not least Ebberston Hall. He walked past the main entrance off the busy A170 for another four hundred yards, where a former drive was now a grass track flanked by horse chestnut and lime trees. He preferred this approach, as it gave less to the eye, and as he had discovered, whereas once the Hall was open to the public, now it was privately owned. As he only wanted to get a glimpse of the building, there was no need to present himself. He had read a leaflet for tourists about Ebberston Hall from among those supplied by Gwen.

He flipped open his notebook, found the entry and refreshed his memory. Built in 1718 for William Thompson, reputedly for his mistress – apparently, she found it beneath her station and refused to live there. Perhaps this was because it was constructed as a summer retreat or hunting lodge, without great pretensions. In fact, he had noted, it was called *the smallest stately house in the country*. One of its former owners, George Osbaldeston, had ruined himself by reckless gambling, and he, known as *the Hunting Squire of England*, had been forced to sell and move out. This fact added to the unsettling feeling Jake had about the atmosphere of the village. There was something about the place that disturbed him, and he was determined to get to the bottom of it.

Through the line of trees, he studied the attractive edifice. Right away, he realised how tiny the building was for a stately home. Nonetheless, it was charmingly constructed in Palladian style with a three-bay loggia with Tuscan columns on the first floor. No doubt the architect had planned it, Jake calculated, with an eye on the view along the narrow Kirk Dale. He wondered why Sir Charles had left it in favour of his newly built Dalton Hall. Probably he, too, wanted something grander to impress his aristocratic peers. Jake smiled. Personally, he'd be happy living in a gate lodge of a house like this. He turned away. This brief sighting was enough to give him a feel for the man who'd built the grotto, and it served to soothe his nerves after the nonsense the churchwarden had spouted as freely as a gargoyle in full spate. He chuckled at this image and muttered, "Poor Mr Hibbitt, his rubicund face is hardly that of a carved monster!" But then he thought of the hard eyes and the threatening voice, and his smile faded. Why should he change the subject of his novel? His mind was made up; Aldfrith it would be.

Having reached the main road again, he walked past the entrance to the Hall drive and took the hedged lane to the right, which he followed for a hundred yards. On the right of the lane, the hedging gave way to dry stone walling, and he spotted a wren bobbing on a capping stone, but the tiny creature, alarmed by his presence, darted into a hole where, no doubt, it had its nest. At the end of the walling, he crossed to turn left up a rough track, which in turn forked left, taking him on to a stony track between high bracken-clad banks overhung with blackthorn and rowan. They provided shelter from the wind.

Over years of country walking, Jake had learnt that walking quietly gave him a much greater chance of spotting wildlife. Today was no exception. He froze, for up among the trees, he caught a glimpse of the white belly of a fallow deer. A doe, judging by her size. Given how the mottled upper body camouflaged the animal, he congratulated himself on his sharp eyes for having spotted her. Uplifted by the gracefulness of the deer's movements, Jake followed the path as it curved right, ascending until he could see the circular stone monument that was Sir Charles's grotto.

His cheerful, edified mood evaporated at once. Something was wrong. In trepidation, he approached the structure. In front of the entrance, the acrid odour of charred wood pricked at his nostrils. Someone had lit a fire in front of the cavern. The hair at the nape of his neck stood on end. Where the entrance to the cavern should have been blocked by a large boulder and land-filled, now he gazed incredulously at the empty blackness of a cave entrance! Someone had removed all the obstructions, but as he gazed around him, there was no trace of the boulder or other obstructing rocks, nor of the explanatory board. Slowly, he approached the cave, heart thumping wildly. Two feet from entering, he heard a shuffling sound from within and cried out, at which silence fell, and he called, "Anybody in there?"

No reply, but a chilling sensation numbed him, and he felt malice emanating from the depths of the cavern. So strong was the sensation that without thinking further, he turned and fled the way he'd come. Twice, he glanced over his shoulder, but no one was in pursuit. Halfway down the track, he stopped to catch his breath, aware that he had been breathing badly because his heartbeat was too frantic. He leant against the bank and glanced fearfully back up the track – nothing, no one! He breathed deeply, sucking in air greedily. Had he imagined it all? Of course not! But how was it possible to clear away the boulder and rubble in so short a time and leave no trace? To do that they would have needed heavy machinery, but there was no sign of disturbance on the ground surrounding the grotto. Another Ebberston mystery! What was he to do? As his heartbeat calmed, he began to think coolly. Should he phone Mr Hibbitt and confess to ignoring his advice? If not, who could he turn to as a witness to the extraordinary circumstances? Nobody, so he'd better keep this to himself for the time being.

What a morning! He thought back on the day's events so far. First, the strange conversation with the churchwarden. The man himself had spoken of old wives' tales, but in fairness, it had been Mr Hibbitt who had put him on to Sir Charles's correspondence. That in itself was odd. Why hadn't he wanted to tell him about these occurrences until after he had read about Sir Charles Hotham-Thompson's *'mysterious and awesome occurrences'* for himself? Why not simply give him an outline and warn him off? Now, he had a mysterious and awesome occurrence of his own to contend with. He must go back and find an explanation. He straightened and took two steps back up the lane but stopped. He dared go no farther. Hadn't Mr Hibbitt spoken of dead bodies and raving madmen? For the first time, he didn't dismiss this talk as nonsense. Yet, he couldn't explain what had happened in any rational way – and it was this, rather than cowardice, that stopped him going back to the cavern. Even as he decided against going, he knew that he would have to return to the cursed spot – just that he wouldn't go right now. The feeling of malice coming from within Elfrid's Hole had been too strong, too diabolical.

He took two paces back to the spot where he had rested and leant there again, considering the events once more. Was there no rational explanation? He came to the dreadful conclusion that there was not. To calm himself, because he felt as though his head would explode, he thought about positive things like the jenny wren and the fallow deer he had seen. Basically, this was why he loved rambling. Since this was the case, why didn't he find another destination to kill time before lunch?

He had an idea. He could visit the site of the battle and the beck that flowed past. With this in mind, he took out his OS map and located his current position. There it was, to the west of Ebberston, adjoining the main road, written quite clearly, Bloody Close, and the gothic lettering used for historical sites indicated Ofwy's Dikes. Jake rifled in his rucksack and pulled out a leaflet he'd taken from his room, now folded and the worse for his rough handling, about the history of the area. He skimmed through the content until he came to: *The tradition is, that Alfrid was wounded in a battle within the lines of Scamridge, (either Six Dikes, or Ofwy's Dikes) near this place. The entrenchments at Scamridge near Ebberston have from time immemorial been known by the name of Oswy's Dikes, probably because Oswy's army encamped there, before engaging with the forces of his rebellious son.* He read on a little more: *There are many early earthworks in the area to the north of Ebberston and Snainton. Scam-ridge Dykes occupy approximately three square miles of moorland. They possibly date from the Stone Age. Here, over a century ago, a communal thatched dwelling was found among the mounds and ditches, and 14 bodies dating from 1,000 years BC.*

There was plenty to capture the interest of an archaeologist or historian in the area, he mused. His finger traced the route he would follow. First, he'd reach The Grapes, have lunch there again, and then proceed on the footpath near the pub on the left. That would take him to the Bloody Close, otherwise named Bloody Field.

After a most satisfactory lunch washed down by an excellent craft ale, good humour restored, Jake left the pub. He found the public footpath and followed it through the Bloody Field. He had feared he might be tormented by some peculiar feelings at the site of a slaughter, given his recent heightened sensibilities, but fortunately he felt nothing except his own historical awareness. He looked around the field, seeing nothing special in the surroundings, but the thought that a ferocious battle had been fought where he was stand-ing. He calculated swiftly – 1304 years before, men had died here. He wondered if a metal detector might find ancient weapons in the earth. With his final thought, he set off in search of the beck. Passing through and carefully closing three gates, he turned right, passed through the gate at the corner of the field, and strode on to a bridge crossing the stream.

There he stopped and placed the fingers of both hands against his forehead because a sudden feeling of dizziness had assailed him. He swayed, momentarily unsteady on his feet, and leant against the side of the bridge, clutching at it for support. As he leant against the structure, he glanced down at the flowing water and to his horror – he blinked and shook his head – the water was running red! This was the sort of thing he had been dreading. What was the matter with him? Had the accident made him insane? Dr Emerson thought not, but then, she wasn't staring at a beck known as Bloody Beck because the water had run red with the blood of the slaughtered...yes...but 1304 years ago...not now!

SEVEN

EBBERSTON AND EASTFIELD, NEAR SCARBOROUGH, NORTH YORKSHIRE.

When Jake returned to his bed and breakfast, Gwen fussed over him.

"My, my, you look as if you've seen a ghost! What's the matter, love? You look so pale. Come and sit down, and I'll make you a nice cup of tea."

In spite of her kindness, Jake didn't want to share his weird experiences and let her believe in the miraculous recuperative powers of her tea. Something she said had lodged in the back of his mind, and now he remembered.

"Mrs Mc...er...Gwen, remember when you told me about the strange events at the grotto? You mentioned two in recent times, but you only told me about the teacher. What about the other one?"

She gave him a peculiar look, hard to decipher—reproval, revulsion, or both?

"You really should forget about the grotto. It's unlucky, that place is. But I suppose you want to know for your book, don't you?" she said in a lighter tone.

"That's it," he encouraged her.

"It was before I came to Ebberston, you see. In the '70s a little girl vanished without trace. Then there was the finding of something of hers about twenty years later. I can't remember the details to save my life."

"I guess I might find out in the library in Eastfield. In any case, I need to go there for more information on King Aldfrith."

"I'll tell you what, love. I have to go to Boyes in Eastfield. I've been meaning to buy some curtain material for ages. The curtains in the back bedroom are getting so shabby. I'll give you a lift, and if you like we can meet up afterwards for a snack. What do you think?"

Jake leapt at the offer.

"It's very kind of you, and the least I can do is offer you lunch."

"Half-past nine all right for you, love?"

"That gives me plenty of time to get ready and to have breakfast. Fine."

Gwen dropped him off at the library on Eastfield High Street just below the main shopping centre at the bottom of the pedestrian area. She pointed to the shopping mall. "We can have lunch in there. What time shall I come?"

Jake glanced at his watch; it was already 10.45. He calculated two hours should be sufficient for the notes he needed.

"One o'clock would suit."

His landlady gave him a fond smile, and he thought, *There are people who are nice by nature.*

"I'll be here outside the entrance at one then, love."

He waved her off with a determined effort at a pleasant smile.

The library was staffed by volunteers, but it was a tightly run facility offering various services, such as photocopying and fax. He found a helpful elderly man, clearly a pensioner, with the efficient air of a former professional person.

When he explained his interest in Elfrid's Hole, the man initially seemed reluctant to help.

"That's a mysterious business you're looking into. Are you a journalist?"

Did he detect a note of suspicion and hostility in the old man's tone?

"Not at all, I'm a historian and researching for a novel about King Aldfrith. I just want to get a feel of the place."

At this, the pensioner mellowed and added, "Well, I don't rightly know whether what we've got on the cave will help with a novel about a Northumbrian king, but there's a whole file about the strange happenings at the cavern, you see, with it being of local interest and all. Of course, we've several books on the Anglo-Saxon kingdoms and in particular a very good article in a journal called *Celtica* you might like to look at. It'll give you a different angle to approach Aldfrith. I read it a couple of years ago – very well written."

"That's very kind of you. I like to see everything you've got, really."

Jake wasn't as interested as he should be in the king, not for a novelist wishing to write about King Aldfrith. In his present state of mind, he was more eager to delve into the box file about the curious events at the cave.

In particular, he wanted to find out about the girl who had vanished in the '70s. The file contained many articles dating from the earliest newspapers in the late eighteenth century up to the twenty-first century. Since the material was in chronological order, it was easy to find the 1974 article on the missing teenager. On holiday with her family and staying in Ebberston, fourteen-year-old Janice Pembleton went off in the countryside with her friend Claire Weekes, aged thirteen, but the latter obeyed strict orders to be home at 8 o'clock in the evening. Janice decided to stay out, and according to Claire, her last words were: 'I'm going up to the grotto.' She was never seen again. A large-scale search of the area began with hundreds of concerned volunteers scouring every inch of the countryside but failing to find a trace of Janice. Despite pursuing every available lead and interviewing dozens of people, the police were unable to get any closer to finding what had happened to the girl.

Jake sat back in his chair and realised how tight his throat had become and how his gut was sinking. These sensations were easy to explain. Would he have vanished like Janice if he'd entered the cave? The malevolence emanating from within the cavern was still impressed on his mind. What if Janice, like him, had found the entrance unsealed and had entered?

He resumed his reading and discovered that almost twenty years later, in 1992, a hiker following the track to the grotto had stumbled upon a small gold medallion. Janice's mother had identified it as a religious medallion she had gifted her daughter at her confirmation earlier in 1974. It had turned up not many feet from the entrance to the cave. Jake turned over the page but found nothing else on the missing girl.

The next article was about the schoolteacher who had died from a blow to the head. Reading it carefully, he could see why Mr Hibbitt hadn't been convinced by the coroner's verdict. The police had been unable to locate the place where the man had supposedly fallen and smashed open his skull. This missing but surely critical evidence left far too many questions unanswered.

Jake jotted down a few notes and sifted through the nineteenth-century reports. Two from the early part of the century dealt with lunacy. Although thirty years separated the reports, they bore a striking similarity. The two reporters referred to the incoherent babblings of the victims, both engaged in tending flocks, both raving about men with swords and axes come to steal their sheep. One thing in particular struck Jake: in the second case, the terrified, crazed man insisted that the thief had walked through the wall of the sheep pen. This, of course, was ascribed to the ranting of a madman, and the shepherd finished in the North and East Ridings Pauper Lunatic Asylum in 1849.

There was also an unsolved murder committed in 1888. The body of a visitor, mutilated by numerous deep wounds, inflicted according to the coroner by a long-bladed weapon, was found by a family on a day visit to the area who had decided to approach the grotto. The gruesome find ruined their pleasant day in the countryside.

Jake glanced at his watch. It was midday, and he'd gathered enough information about the cavern to understand that more than old wives' tales were responsible for its evil reputation. He really must begin some serious research about the king who had sheltered, wounded, in the cave. The hour before his appointment with Gwen McCracken flew by as he filled his notebook with details of the life of Aldfrith. The article recommended by the helpful pensioner gave him a real insight into the Irish parentage and education of the king who was to illuminate Northumbria with his learning and with the scholars he attracted to his kingdom. The only worrying gap Jake had left was what he needed to know most – how had Aldfrith died? It seemed that Anglo-Saxon scholars could not agree on that, and the contemporary records were too vague. It would make an excellent objective for him. If he, Jake Conley, discovered what numerous eminent Anglo-Saxonists had failed in, it would be quite a feather in his cap. Once again, it seemed that the answer lay in the mysterious Elfrid's Hole. Everything led him back there, and he knew that sooner or later he must overcome his fear and go back to the cavern.

The shopping centre boasted a fish and chips café, and seeing it was spotlessly clean, Jake suggested they eat there. Gwen readily agreed, and over the meal she enquired about his research. He thought he'd sound out her reaction. She wasn't locally born but had lived in Ebberston for fifteen years, long enough to be synchronised with local sentiments.

"Everything comes back to Elfrid's Hole," he said. "The mysterious occurrences in Ebberston are all associated with that place."

Gwen's fork hovered between her plate and her mouth, and she looked anxious.

"Which is why you must stay well away from it, Jake. Mark my words, something horrible *will* happen if you persist in your probing. Don't go back. There's something terrible about that cave. People in the village don't want to hear it mentioned, let alone go there."

"I believe you're right, Gwen." He wanted to soothe her. "And I'm sure I can write my novel without setting foot there again."

"Well, that's a relief, I'm sure. Oh, my, this piece of cod is so big, I'm not sure I can finish it all."

On the drive back to Ebberston, Gwen didn't mention the cave. Jake thought it strange she hadn't asked about Janice Pembleton since she claimed not to remember the details of the case. But he didn't refer to it and explained her silence as unwillingness to talk about the cavern.

Relaxing in his room, Jake wondered what to do next. He was in no hurry to return to Elfrid's Hole, and in any case, the idea of going there in twilight didn't appeal at all. He preferred to return

in the strong morning light. He read through the notes he'd taken and found his hand holding the small black book shaking. He wondered whether Gwen was right about *something horrible* and to warn him off his research. He'd never had occasion to combat evil in his thirty years of life. What on earth was he doing? Why not just let it go and write a straightforward historical novel like all the other sane novelists on the planet? But perhaps that was the point – he didn't really want to be like all the others. He was onto something eerie, and he couldn't let it go. As he mulled over the situation, it occurred to him that he had left one intriguing channel unexplored. To follow it, he would have to travel down to London.

EIGHT

LONDON, UK, 2019

Unsure whether he would be admitted into the august surroundings of the Society of Antiquaries of London, Jake visited the website and discovered that outside researchers were indeed welcome. There was one proviso:

'The Museum collections are held within closed stores, so prior notice is essential. Some of the Library collections and all the Society's archives are closed access or take time to retrieve, so researchers should give as much notice as possible if they wish to consult those materials.'

He decided that this was most reasonable and positive and to use the Enquiry Service, not the email but by phoning the number provided. Within minutes, he had stipulated his requirements to a helpful gentleman who replied and was thrilled to learn that material on the East Riding of Yorkshire by Sir Robert Wanley would be made available to him within forty-eight hours. This meant he would travel down to London by train from York to King's Cross the next day, stay overnight in the capital, and visit Burlington House the day after. The library opened at 10 am, so he made his appointment for 10.30.

Jake booked his ticket and accommodation online then went downstairs to inform Gwen of his plans. He needed to ensure his room here because he hadn't by any means finished his exploration of Elfrid's Hole. Whether Sir Robert Wanley's writings might cast more light on the mysterious occurrences remained to be seen.

He found her sitting at a sewing machine hemming a large piece of cloth. He told her the jaunt to London might be a waste of time and money, but he had to try since he could get no further with his research on Aldfrith. He preferred her to think he was researching the king, not the cave. She was pleased he was coming back to Ebberston but mostly that he wouldn't be going to Elfrid's Hole.

"That's a relief. You'll be much safer in London, love."

Originally a private Palladian mansion owned by the Earl of Burlington, the imposing façade of the house intimidated Jake as he approached the arched entrance. Just under the crown of the arch, a red flag rippled in the breeze, bearing the name Burlington House in yellow capital letters. The carved head of a goddess, Jake didn't know who, presided over the arch under golden lettering forming the legend Society of Antiquaries. If he had any doubts that the Society was a serious organisation, such ideas were dispelled by all this. Feeling unimportant and somewhat bogus as a researcher, Jake took a deep breath and marched under the arch, checked his watch – 10.25, perfect timing – and went to the entrance to be directed to the first floor, which housed the library.

The librarian who received him asked in a cautionary tone whether he had read the society's guidelines for outside researchers.

"Yes, as you see, I've only brought my laptop, no bags, and I won't be reproducing material, so no need for permission. I'm just here to read and take notes."

The librarian gave him a thin smile. "Very good, sir. If you would kindly step this way to the Reading Room."

He showed Jake to a table occupied on one side by a young woman, presumably a student, and laid on the other an ancient leather-bound volume with a serial number in gold foil embossed on the spine with a month and year.

"If you need any help, you can find me at the desk in the other room."

Jake thanked him and moved the volume to read the date: December 1784. He nodded to the fair-haired student, who'd raised her head to smile at him before re-immersing herself in her work. Jake booted his laptop and pushed it away to make room for the large volume. Gingerly, he opened its pages, yellowed with age, and his eyes swiftly ran down the contents until he reached the name Wanley. His heart fluttered as he read the title of the article: *On events both historic and otherwise concerning the mystery of ye cavern, named Elfrid's Hole, located in ye countie of York and more particularly within the bounds of Ebberston village. p. 127.*

The customary dull ache at the centre of his brow began, confirming he was on the right track. With exaggerated care, he turned the stiff pages of the volume, negating a fierce desire to flip them over at speed to reach the page he sought.

Page 127, after a few pompous lines in italics informing him of the qualifications of the writer, began with a long Premise. In other circumstances, Jake might have skipped an introductory essay and gone directly to the essential material, but a few words in Old English caught his eye, and he read:

The famous Anglo-Saxon poem The Ruin opens with 'Wraetli is thaes wealhstane', id est, 'Wraith-like is this native stone'. From this, we may deduce that within the stone of England itself lies the wraith: its being an emanation of England. Written testimony reaching us in this eighteenth-century suggests the Anglo-Saxons saw no ghosts, notwithstanding which, they knew themselves to be haunted.

Jake gaped at these words. Here was an eminent eighteenth-century antiquarian advocating the existence of ghosts, at the cost of exposing himself to derision from his contemporaries. He greedily read on.

Scientists, freethinkers and clergy discredit the existence of supernatural forces as superstition, but I wish to sustain, along with the great Doctor Johnson, who wrote on the subject of the existence of ghosts: 'All argument is against it; but all belief is for it'. I beg the indulgence of my long-suffering Reader to consider for a moment the impact of Protestantism upon our national psyche. The God of the Protestant is a God of Order and reason, interpreted by learned men in the form of systematic theology. This produces a coherent view of the world devoid of superstition, neatly and tidily parcelled for our consumption. But, Dear Reader, what of our national folklore that has deep roots in paganism? Are we also to sweep away a wider, older culture, the mentality of the supernatural in the name of scientific reason – or are we to believe the evidence of our own eyes?

This last rider made Jake's skin prickle into goose bumps. Had Sir Robert *seen* something supernatural at Elfrid's Hole? He continued eagerly.

Our nation has a long tradition of testimony, often committed to the printed word. Herein I shall cite the 1581 work of Stephen Batman.

Batman? Surely Bateman! Jake smothered an irreverent laugh and transformed it into a slight cough, not wishing to disturb the student opposite.

'The Doome warning all men to Judgmente: wherein are contayned for the most parte all the straunge Prodigies hapned in the Worlde'. Or again, Dear Reader, the 1682 volume of Nathaniel Crouch, 'Wonderfull Prodigies of Judgment and Mercy, discovered in above Three Hundred Memorable Histories. These, I sustain are not mere pamphlets suspended from stalls for the ignorant and gullible to gape at, nor almanacs or astrological compendia of the spurious kind, but serious, scholarly collections of testimonies various and unexplainable. In harmony with these authors, I eschew all reference to comets, eclipses, monstrous births, rainstorms of blood, lightning and the blast of trumpets. Nay, but I will return to 'Wraetli is thaes wealhstane' and unite my efforts to those of Robert Burton, who wrote less than one hundred years ago, 'Divells many times appeare to men, and afright them out of their wits sometimes walking at noone day, sometimes at night, counter-feiting dead men's ghosts.'

Jake sat up and ran his sleeve across his forehead. His 'third eye' was aching so hard he felt as though someone was drilling into his skull. This was a sure sign, he believed, that he was learning something of fundamental importance about the Ebberston cavern and its supernatural forces. He had reached the end of the Premise, and the writings of the long-dead Sir Robert Wanley had spoken to him about devils in the guise of men at Elfrid's Hole. What exactly had the antiquarian seen to age him and change his nature, transforming him into an irascible recluse?

Jake typed up some notes from the Premise but kept them short in his keenness to carry on reading. What came next was a measured account of the location and events of the Battle of Ebberston and Sir Robert's interpretation of the causes and the antagonists. He stored this away, too, for future reference. He also discovered, for the first time, the nature of King Aldfrith's wounds. Sir Robert had found a contemporary source affirming that the king had been struck by an arrow and subsequently received a wound to his thigh inflicted by a sword. Protected by his men, the king was carried to a cave on a hillside near to the site of the battle. They sheltered there, far enough away and unseen by the victorious foe. Later still in 705, the king's men took him to his palace in Driffelda, where he succumbed to his wounds and died. Much of this was known to Jake, but what followed astounded him.

Sir Robert began to talk about the location of the cavern and how his acquaintance, the esteemed Sir Charles Hotham-Thompson, had built a memorial to commemorate the site of Aldfrith's suffering and evasion. But he also referred to how the well-respected nobleman, for his part, not only shared the experiences he would now go on to describe but would also corroborate and endorse them. Jake gasped, causing the student across the table to stare at him quizzically. He pretended not to notice her interest. It was tiring following the ancient style of printing where the letter s was printed in a form similar to an f and the whole page of writing was dense and sloping to the right. But there was no question of resting his eyes; he had come for this and could scarcely believe his luck that the Society of Antiquaries had preserved this unique testimony.

I came to Ebberston Hall where lived the worthy Sir Charles, a distinguished war veteran of numerous campaigns. A colonel in His Majesty's Armed Forces is not the kind of person to be unduly disturbed or unmanned by the inexplicable. Yet I found him quite altered by his experiences at the place known to the local folk as Elfrid's Hole. So there it was in print; Sir Charles had shared his exposure to the supernatural with a fellow knight of the realm. *I must admit to surprise, nay, astonishment, when he first warned me of ghosts on his land and listed the mysterious occurrences associated with the cavern. My undoubted scepticism caused considerable tumult in the breast of my host, which was not quietened until I let him prevail upon me to visit together the site of the happenings. Whether it was the Colonel's insistence that we should each carry a hunting piece on our shoulder, which prevented any otherworldly apparition, the fact remains we saw nothing of the sort. However, the feeling of unmitigated malevolence issuing from the cave caused me to retreat on the instant.* "Exactly!" Jake exclaimed and had to excuse himself with the young woman opposite, "I'm overly involved in my research, I do apologise."

She smiled at him sweetly, and he inwardly promised to draw no further attention to his person. Irritably, he tried to find his place on the page. *The next occasion I visited the cave, I was, perhaps unwisely, alone and ask my Reader's indulgence if I return to Robert Burton's 'Divells' for there is no question of the evil emanating from the ghosts I chanced upon that day. Long dead they must have been, for they fought in the Battle of Ebberston one thousand one hundred and sixty-nine years ago as I write. I can only suppose the wraiths guarded the spirit of their king lying inside the cavern. Not that I can be sure, for I ventured no nearer but fled the unholy spot as the armed and helmed figures raised their weapons in an unequivocal gesture of hostility. I fell into the most confounded mental ague for several days and had to rest a sprained ankle procured in my hasty and unseemly retreat. Yet I thank the Lord I lingered not by Elfrid's Hole else I fear my quill would ne'er again have scratched on paper.*

Jake sat up and breathed deeply. He realised that with this last paragraph, he had ceased breathing – and now his head spun, and his heart fatigued to serve its purpose. He fully understood what it meant for a renowned eighteenth-century figure to lay bare his emotions and testify to such incredible events.

In the course of my recuperation, I had occasion to compare my sighting with those of Sir Charles and to devise a strategy to obviate further apparitions. Sir Charles, an old-fashioned Anglican, set his face against involving an exorcist, labelling it 'papist nonsense'. However, he was prepared to have the cavern filled with boulders and an especially large one, appropriately enough, placed in the style of that of Joseph of Arimatea's tomb, blocking the opening. The good Gentleman, aware of a disservice to an historical site, furthermore, settled upon the felicitous concept of commemorating the refuge of King Aldfrith with the construction of a stone memorial around and above the grotto. That the unfortunate deaths of two labourers should ensue in this operation may or may not be ascribed to unnatural presences. It is not for the writer to determine and beyond the scope of this article. The Reader will undoubtedly make his own judgments based upon the testimony herein...

Jake glanced farther down the page but could see little of importance to add to his research, just a prolonged justification of the veracity of what he already knew. Excited at this confirmation of his theory about Ebberston, Jake closed the volume and typed up a few notes. He closed his tired eyes, rubbed his aching forehead and pondered. What troubled him most was the unexplained re-opening of the Hole. How had it been achieved, and were innocent people at greater risk of a perilous encounter with ancient spectres? He realised he must find this out before another tragedy occurred.

NINE

BURTON AGNES AND EBBERSTON, NORTH YORKSHIRE

CONVINCING HIMSELF THERE WAS NO IMMEDIATE TRAGEDY TO worry about, Jake spent the next day rambling in the dales to the south of Ebberston. Deep down, he knew he was prevaricating about returning to the cavern for fear of what he might find there. Instead, he decided to visit an historic church in the region and chose St Martin's in Burton Agnes. It was an ambitious hike from Ebberston but well worth the effort.

The thirteenth-century church was tucked away on the hillside immediately behind Burton Agnes Hall and was well signposted. The first thing Jake noticed about St Martins was the approach to the entrance through a striking arch formed by the low branches of yew trees, so that he felt like he was walking down a long tunnel, back in time, as he approached the south door entrance.

He filled his notebook with details of the Norman elements in the building but most of all with details of a wall monument to Sir Henry Griffith – the tomb chest had reliefs of gruesome skulls and bones; perhaps it suited his gloomy mood. In any case, the long hike back to Ebberston cleared his mind, and by the time he arrived for a late meal at The Grapes, he had decided to walk up to the grotto the next morning.

After breakfast, his determination had vacillated. When he reached the main road, his conviction had returned, but when it came to taking the track, he again hesitated with a sense of foreboding. His thoughts kept returning to Sir Robert Wanley's reference to devils taking the form of ghosts. Was he being foolish to worry about such irrational matters? Whatever it was, he had to admit he lacked the courage to go on. He didn't know, he thought as he turned into the walled lane, which would be worse, finding the cave sealed off as before or gaping open as he had seen it the last time. Sealed would mean forces were somehow at work to move a massive weight or that he had imagined the cavern open. Open would mean, well...he dreaded to think. With these thoughts and this state of mind, he approached the grotto along the tree-lined bank until he could see the stones of the folly.

At this point he stopped. He moved neither forwards nor backwards. He hesitated, wishing there was someone he could send to see if the cave was open. He stayed like this for several minutes until, deciding not to be a weakling, he moved as silently as possible towards the grotto.

He had come to within three yards of the opening. Two things struck him: first, there was no obstructing boulder, and he could see the obscurity within the cave; second, there was a noise emanating from that darkness. The blackness could be hiding anything, and he could hear whatever it was. He strained, listening. No mistake – there was a noise: the sound of metal on stone. Inside the cave, a blade was being drawn across a whetstone. Jake took two steps forward, but then the sound stopped to be replaced by a low guttural growl. Not the snarl of an animal but of a man. He could sense the malice sweeping over him like a breaking wave. Jake's nerve snapped and he turned to flee into the undergrowth fringing the hillside around the grotto.

He pulled the branches and fronds tighter around him with a

whimper. His chest was tight and his stomach knotted. He dared not, would not, look. No matter how close the shuffling footsteps came, he would not look. He would not. Careful not to betray his whereabouts by rustling the branches, he searched for his mobile phone. Without looking, he'd snap a photo across the clearing. With shaking hand, he pulled it out of his pocket, held the phone up, automatically releasing the shutter with his thumb. The metallic click, so silent he usually failed to notice it, now seemed perilously loud. He prayed whatever was out there would not be alerted to his presence. With a shaking hand, he pushed the phone back into the pocket of his jeans, clenched his fist, swallowed hard and tried to ignore his pounding heart.

He glanced round over his shoulder for an escape route. There was something of a trampled trail, perhaps made by an animal, and he spotted what appeared to be a mushroom amid the leaf litter. He peered more carefully. No, it was not a fungus of any kind but a severed ear – a human ear. That did it! Jake panicked. Head down, he burst out of his hiding place into the clearing and, without looking, dashed straight along the downhill track. The noise of his boots running over the stony ground prevented him from hearing whether there was anyone, *anything*, in pursuit. It wasn't until he was safely down to the dry-stone walling that he dared to slow to a walk and look back. The track was deserted, so he leant on the wall to catch his breath and examine the photo he had snapped.

The picture was shaky. That was understandable. But even in spite of that, it was clear enough to show one remarkable thing – the clearing all the way to the grotto was empty! Yet, he would swear he'd heard footsteps approaching. Recent research into the paranormal had produced photographic images of ghosts, he was sure of that. He's seen some in the tabloid press. But here on his phone, the high-quality lens had captured *nothing*.

Jake swore. He was no closer to discovering the truth about Elfrid's Hole. It was his own lily-livered fault. He should have had the courage to peer through the foliage at whatever it was that was pursuing him. It was easy enough to say that down here, near enough to civilisation to call for help – up there was a different matter. Then there was the fact of the ear. Why only one ear? Was the rest of the body somewhere among the dense undergrowth? Should he report finding an ear to the police? Many people hated getting involved with the constabulary, and he was no different. For the moment, he wanted a chance to solve the mystery alone. But the ear troubled him. In solving the mystery of Elfrid's Hole, he wished to keep his own body intact.

With this as an overriding priority, Jake thrust aside the idea of returning to the cave and made his way to the main road. Again, he hesitated. Should he really return? Of course, he must. Otherwise he'd never know what was going on. Now? No, he couldn't face it at the moment. Maybe tomorrow. A pity he was alone. But who else could he take with him? Gwen? Well, she'd made her feelings clear on that score. No. Who else did he know? Only Mr Hibbitt, the churchwarden, and he'd warned him off the place.

Jake reached into his pocket and pulled out his phone to take another look at the photo. Had he missed something? Scrolling to the image, he almost dropped the phone in shock. Missed anything! In the middle of the clearing was a dark shape. It was blurred, probably due to his hand shaking when he'd triggered the shutter. But unclear as it was, it looked like a human figure wearing something on his head. A helm? The form was too dark and blurred to be sure, but Jake *knew* that it hadn't been there in the photo when he'd checked previously.

He switched off the phone and thrust it back. This confirmed two basic facts. Something *had* pursued him, and whatever it was, it was diabolical. How could it not be in his photo and later suddenly appear? Was this *thing* playing with his mind to tip him over the edge into madness?

There was one way to find out about his mental state. He could pass time by going back to the Bloody Beck and seeing what colour the water was. If it was flowing red again, he swore he'd go back to York and forget all about Ebberston.

Standing on the bridge over the beck, Jake didn't suffer any strange sensations and was relieved to see sparkling translucent water flowing past. He took this to mean he should continue his investigation in spite of the uncanny events. As an act of defiance, he took out his phone and looked at the photo. It had changed again! In the foreground, still out of focus and vague, was what might be the head of a person. The black shape had moved forward to fill most of the photo. Less like a face and more like a skull but with facial hair, the ill-defined features seemed to ooze malevolence. Jake hastily deleted the photo and rammed the phone into his pocket. Why had he looked at it, and just when he was feeling better because the beck was normal? Either there was something unusual about Ebberston or about himself. Which? He began to wonder if his car accident had done some irreparable damage to his brain. Figures cannot move forward in a still photo. The gurgling of the stream began to calm him, and idly he watched a small branch being tossed over some stones in the shallow water.

On calmer reflection, it couldn't be that he was crazy. His research in London had proved that others had discovered abnormal occurrences at Elfrid's Hole. If he was mad, then Sir Charles and Sir Robert also had been insane. Somehow, he doubted that two prominent men from high society would query their mental stability as much as he questioned his own. There was no doubt, though, that he shared with them the same aversion to the place where Aldfrith had sheltered. Sir Charles's repulsion for the cavern had been so strong he wished to seal it off forever.

Thinking about this, Jake frowned. He had no idea what had happened to the boulder and how it had been moved without heavy machinery or without mobilising half of the menfolk in Ebberston. He decided to go back to his bed and breakfast. Still tired from his exertions of the previous day and also from his earlier fright, he thought it best to rest and maybe research a little more on the internet about the reign of Aldfrith. He might even be able to map out the structure of a novel. These thoughts brought him back to his starting point. Who should be his main character, the king or a ceorl?

He pushed this quandary out of his mind temporarily because he didn't want to walk out distractedly in front of a vehicle. He had learned that lesson for sure.

TEN

EBBERSTON, NORTH YORKSHIRE

WELL-RESTED, JAKE ROSE EARLY, BREAKFASTED, AND WENT FOR a walk. The crisp, clear morning air invigorated him, so he decided to hike along a public footpath rather than the road. The only footpath he knew without consulting a map was the one he had already walked. It took him to the Bloody Field, and he followed it willingly. Afterwards, he reflected on this decision and wondered if there had been any element of choice or, more likely, some unnoticed compulsion.

Whatever the case, Jake strode along the footpath, his mind free of bothersome thoughts, enjoying the sweetness of the dew and the bird songs. At a certain point along the path, he spotted a small, white bone. He stooped to pick it up to verify whether it was from a human finger – he tried to remember his biology lessons at school. What were they called – phalanges, or something similar?

As he turned it in his hand, concluding that it was indeed human, out of the corner of his eye, he noted movement, nothing more than a shimmering in the air. Turning to identify the cause, he swayed under the effect of a dizzying faintness. The shimmering air began to transform into discernible shadowy forms. Jake wanted to shake his head to clear his vision but could not. Beset by an icy grasp, he could no longer see or think of anything but the spectral shapes. In a normal state of awareness, Jake would have gazed in disbelief; instead, he watched helplessly as the wraiths solidified into ghastly, gore-spattered warriors. Before his eyes, he witnessed the Battle of Ebberston in full swing.

Jake experienced no fear. It was cinematographic. He was in a place where nothing happened and therefore not in danger. He could not reason, nor analyse, nor think at all – just watch. He saw men in mail fighting with half-naked blue-daubed warriors. In other circumstances, Jake would have been aghast at the violence and bloodshed. He was a pacifist who abhorred warfare. Involuntarily, his gaze was drawn across to the far side of the field, where a banner of crimson and yellow stripes fluttered in the breeze. He knew it to be the Banner of Northumbria, but this was passive recognition. He saw a group of warriors fighting, densely ranked around one man. Could that be King Aldfrith? He would have asked himself the question if he'd had control of his thoughts. He only presumed it afterwards.

The onslaught around the banner was intense. The blue-painted warriors were among the defenders, hacking and stabbing, slipping and dying. The moment came during the most severe pressure from the mail-clad and be-helmed assailants when an arrow struck the King in the upper chest. Jake saw it clearly, as well as the subsequent confusion the incident caused. But then, as if the first spool in a projection room had come to an end, the figures faded, and Jake returned to twenty-first century reality.

Out of relief and superstition, he flung the small bone he had been clinging to as far away as possible. Had it been these remains of a fallen eighth-century warrior that had channelled the apparitions?

Badly shaken, but a privileged observer, Jake stood for a moment reflecting on what he'd seen. It was as if some uncanny force had intended him to see the moment the arrow struck the king. But why? What was happening to him? Was all of this pre-ordained in some way? The blue-painted warriors had been Picts.

But the history books didn't say they were allied to Aldfrith. He'd have to investigate that. Failing to reach a rational conclusion and not feeling at all well, he returned to his lodgings. A strong cup of tea was infinitely preferable to the return of the vision. If he delayed, there was the risk the air might shimmer again and present him once more with the horrors of Dark Ages warfare. *That* he did not want! His determined stride turned into a jog, and to his relief, he reached the signpost marking the beginning of the public footpath. He counted himself lucky that spears and arrows had not pierced his flesh, but maybe he'd been invisible to ancient combatants.

No sooner had he turned the key in the lock of her front door than Gwen McCracken appeared.

"My goodness, laddie, you don't look at all well! Coming down with a temperature, are you?"

"Something terrible has happened," he said, needing someone to confide in. "I don't suppose you could manage a cup of tea, Gwen?"

Her solution to any stressful situation being exactly that, Gwen went to put the kettle on.

"You sit yourself down, then you can tell me all about it, Jake. Back in a jiffy!"

As good as her word, Gwen arrived with a tray laden with tea and biscuits.

"You look pale. Has there been an accident on the road?"

"No, but I saw more blood than a thousand accidents!"

She looked at him in disbelief.

"What on earth are you on about, laddie?"

"That's exactly it, Gwen, I don't think what I saw had anything to do with this earth. Not today's, at any rate."

He had lost her and could see her confusion. He needed to explain as lucidly as possible.

"I was walking across the Bloody Field when..." He continued to explain the sequence of events, and the horror he had witnessed was writ so large on his face that Gwen never doubted it had occurred.

When he'd finished, emotionally drained, she said, "I can explain what happened, Jake."

He gaped at her. How could the simple, affectionate landlady of a boarding establishment explain such a phenomenon? She wasn't exactly Einstein in the intellectual stakes.

"My family are from the Highlands of Scotland, and our folk call this *an da-shealladh*."

Of course, McCracken. Is that Gaelic?

"That's Gaelic," she said, confirming his thought. "It means *the two sights* or *the sight of the seer*. It runs in our family. It gives you the ability to see apparitions of the living and the dead. I can't say anything like that's happened to me, but it did to my mam. It was in the War. She saw our uncle Jackie, who came to smile at her an hour before his death. There he was, as plain to her as I can see you, Jake. Standing in his naval uniform. He was on a minesweeper, blown up by a German mine, no survivors. So there you are, you see – *an da-shealladh*."

"I can understand that, but a whole battle, with hundreds of men?"

"If you think about it, it's even more likely. All those deaths all close together. You need a person able to channel his *per- per-*extrasensory powers!" She struggled to find the right words.

"I'll admit to you that I've been experiencing strange things since my accident."

"Aw, did you have an accident then?"

Jake told her about his coma and the after-effects and why he'd come away for peace and quiet with the intention of rambling and visiting a few historic churches.

"Oh, you poor thing! You're not exactly finding peace and quiet with these goings-on at Ebberston, are you?"

"It's not the quiet village I took it to be." He wolfed down another ginger nut biscuit, his favourite. "I have to fathom out this mystery, Gwen. It's not what I came here for, but it's a book in itself."

"I should be careful if I were you. You might not do yourself any good pushing on with this."

"The fewer people that know what I'm about, Gwen, the better. You won't tell anyone, will you?"

"My lips are sealed, I promise you."

He saw the stubborn determination and thought in that moment she seemed what he imagined a determined Scottish Highland woman to be like.

"Now, I want you to promise me something, young man." Her steely grey eyes bored into his.

"What?"

"You won't go back to Elfrid's Hole."

He shook his head. "I can't promise that, Gwen. Else how am I going to get to the bottom of this mystery?"

"Why don't you just make it up? I'm sure you can write a good enough story without risking your life."

"Do you really believe that could happen?" He crunched another biscuit. "Sorry, I'm eating them all."

"That's what they're there for. And, yes, I do think there's that risk. You wouldn't be the first to disappear or die, would you?"

"No, but if I solve the mystery, maybe no one else needs die. Think about that, Gwen."

She did for a moment, then said, "Why don't we go to the police? They could try again."

"We've nothing concrete to give them." Jake deliberately kept silent about the ear and the missing boulder. "Anyway, you just promised not to tell anyone."

She looked at him with a pitying gaze. "I don't want anything to happen to you, that's all."

"Would you like me to find different lodgings, Gwen?"

"Why would you do that?"

"I thought, well, if anything happened to me, people wouldn't associate it with your bed and breakfast."

"Now you're being silly!"

"Good, I like it here with you, Gwen. You're so very kind."

"One does one's best, love. Besides, nothing's going to happen to you. I'd have had a warning with *an da-shealladh*."

Jake considered this, smiled at her, and said the exact opposite of what he was thinking.

"I'm sure you're right. *Nothing* is going to happen to me."

ELEVEN

EBBERSTON, NORTH YORKSHIRE

A RETURN TO ELFRID'S HOLE HAD TO BE DONE, WHATEVER amount of courage, stupidity, or cussedness it took. Jake convinced himself that it was a personal crusade to be undertaken. Somehow, he would make the place safe forever. The problem lay in that one word: *somehow*. His only plan was to go there and poke his nose into the cavern to discover what resided there. This required no special equipment; he didn't even consider anything to keep him safe, and he therefore more than fulfilled the stupidity criterion.

The need for protection of some sort only occurred to him when he approached the cave entrance, the boulder still missing, and peered into the darkness. Conscious of his heart beating like an express train with its wheels pounding over the gaps in steel rail lines, he edged closer and closer to the opening. This time no sound came from within, which helped him keep his nerve. Even so, he detected a malign presence, but absurdly, he pressed on. He bowed his head to enter the cold, dank space. Cursing under his breath at the scrunching of pebbles or grit under his boot, he stepped forward. No noise at all would have been better. He reached into his pocket, pulled out his mobile phone, realising that switching it on might not have been his cleverest move because the home screen illuminated his face, but he wanted to use the torch option. Finding it, he tapped the icon, and suddenly the black hole was lit by a blinding beam. He directed it around the wall to his left – nothing. Then swung the beam forward into the depths of the cave – nothing. Then to the right. Was it possible? Again, nothing. But he could sense an evil presence. Was it invisible to him?

"I know you're in here, whatever you are!"

His voice sounded too high and frantic to his own ears. Then he heard it. The unmistakeable sound of a footfall from within the cave. He swung the beam around and lit up the depths in front of him. And there it was! The torch picked out the two eyes. Nightmare eyes! They shone unnaturally red and evil and were glaring at him from a skull-like head covered in long whiskers and capped by a steel helm. Then came the grin. Broken and missing teeth added to its baleful appearance. Unnerved, Jake had two choices: run or bluff. He chose the latter.

"Follow me outside. I'll be waiting for you in broad daylight."

He had meant to say this in a virile voice, but it came out squeaky. It's hard to do a macho impersonation when you are unarmed and concentrating on constricting your bladder. He slid the beam down over the rest of the apparition. It wore a mail shirt and leather leggings. Equipped for battle then, and he, idiot, had nothing to fight or protect himself with. But at least, he consoled himself, he had seen what occupied Elfrid's Hole – even if it scared him almost him to death.

He turned and re-emerged into the daylight, acutely conscious of the complete lack of other human presence. Facing the cavern once more, he stared at the opening until at last the dull glint of a helm signalled the appearance of the entity. It straightened up to its full imposing height, and Jake quailed. Here, quite alone, he faced his adversary, a stocky, muscular Saxon warrior in a mail shirt, with an axe swinging in his right hand. His fiendish grin and bright eyes issued the challenge Jake so much wished to avoid; he, Jake Conley, would-be writer, head-case – a domestic cat against a tiger! What death wish had driven him to return to the grotto?

At that point, he might have turned tail and run, but something weird happened. The dreadful figure in front of him shimmered and faded. Jake could see a shadowy form walking towards him slowly until this, too, faded. He blinked and still saw nothing. But he sensed a presence close to him. Then he felt it! The pressure of an icy hand on his chest. So cold it penetrated his sweater and the vest underneath. It was as if the entity was feeling for a heartbeat. It would have no trouble detecting it since it was pounding like a steam hammer. A fetid odour accompanied the gelid pressure on his chest: a stench of the grave. He could bear it no longer, but before leaving, he had to show defiance.

This was more than he believed himself capable of. He's seen the severed ear, and he'd seen the well-honed axe dangling from the skeletal grip. There was nothing to stop the Saxon wraith from chopping him to pieces here and now. Nonetheless, Jake took one step backwards away from the icy touch and cried, "Heed this, whatever you are! I'll not rest until I've sent you to Hell where you belong!"

He'd used the archaic 'heed' for effect. But the only effect it elicited was a diabolical shrieking from within the cave. The pure evil of the sound was too much. Jake turned, and with a self-control that hinted of insanity – he later reasoned – he walked steadily out of the clearing and down the track. He was certain that the spectre was following him apace because, although he couldn't see it, every time he turned to stare back up the track, he could sense its presence.

There was no reason to suppose that the malign being would shadow him only as far as the main road and not beyond. He supposed this, anyway, but was wrong. The unseen presence continued to dog his steps right up to the front door of his accommodation. Rather dramatically and foolishly, Jake put the key in the lock, opened the door and flung himself inside, slamming the door closed, all achieved in less than a second. As if a closed door could stop a spectre passing through.

Trembling, he leant against the hall wall. Gwen appeared, frowning, to see why he had slammed the door. Before she could say a word, Jake pointed.

"A ghost. The wraith of a Saxon warrior! It's followed me down from the cavern."

"Don't be daft! Ghosts don't come out in daylight."

"This one does, and it's got a battle-axe!"

Gwen scrutinised her guest. Many thoughts were going through her mind but not least that Jake had finally snapped. She just hoped this madman was harmless. She decided to humour him.

"Don't worry, love. I'll take a look outside and make sure it's gone." She made to turn the latch but found her wrist clamped and Jake begging her, "Don't!" His eyes were wild. "Leave it be! It'll go away when it's ready."

"Right."

She fell back on her reserve tactic, a cup of tea. After she'd calmed him down and heard his full account, Gwen, a level-headed woman, persuaded him to accompany her into the front garden. There, the absence of fetid smell, more than anything else, convinced him that the ghost had returned to its station at the grotto.

He speculated why there should be a ghost – or more than one, because he'd heard the fiendish laughter from within the cave whilst confronting the spectre. Ghosts were usually the tormented spirits of people who had met a tragic end. Back in 705, those Saxons were defending their wounded king. Could it be that some of them had died in the attempt? One thing was certain, he told Gwen: the spectres were still determined to defend the cavern against all comers forever, and they didn't stop short of killing. That, after all, was their profession.

"You're a damned fool, Jake Conley, and lucky to be alive to tell me this. I told you to stay away from that place. It's cursed, and knowing why doesn't change anything."

"You're right, Gwen, but I've got to find a way to rid Ebberston of these infernal beings."

He said this with a bravado that he certainly didn't feel in his timorous soul.

"And how do you suppose you're going to do that on your own?"

"That's what I have to work out."

He spent a relaxing afternoon browsing the Internet on his laptop and, between sessions on the social media, navigated to ghost-hunting sites but found little of interest and even less of practical use. He spent the evening in front of the television in the guest's lounge, and when he began to nod off in the comfortable armchair, he decided to retire for the night.

He fell asleep almost as soon as his head touched the pillow but woke up not long after, unsure of what had disturbed him. Almost immediately, he noted the fetid smell of earlier and stifled a cry. It was strong and near his bed. Jake became fearful. Something was not right. This was not how the universe was ordered. He had locked the door, but there was somebody, some*thing*, near the bed. The terror of the dark outweighed fear of what he might see, so he reached out and clicked on the bedside lamp.

"Where are you?"

His eyes adjusted to the light, and he saw a shadowy shape, one that shimmied and shivered. Then it attacked. More than seeing the dark form of the axe, he felt it swoosh through the air and rolled frantically to one side. The honed blade sliced into the pillow where his head had been a fraction of a second earlier, sending a cloud of white down into the air. Heart pounding, Jake leapt out of bed and rushed to the door, dodging another murderous black arc that flashed past his head. He screamed, flung himself out of the door, and plunged downstairs for the front door.

Alerted by his scream, Gwen came to the landing in time to see Jake dash out of the front door in his pyjamas.

"Wha—" Her cry was cut short as a hand in between her shoulder blades shoved her downstairs. She crashed to the bottom, banging her head and losing consciousness before arriving in a crumpled heap against the door.

Jake found her when he gathered the courage to return inside or, more likely, couldn't withstand the cold night in his thin pyjamas any longer. Relieved at the absence of the graveyard stench, he rang for an ambulance, got dressed, and accompanied his landlady to the A&E reception. She regained consciousness in the ambulance and found Jake holding her hand and looking concerned.

"It's my fault. I brought this *thing* on us! I should have taken your advice, Gwen."

She bit her lip, narrowed her eyes, and complained about pain in her arm. In hospital, they whisked her away for X-rays, and Jake waited outside a door with a red light lit above it and a warning about radioactivity on it.

When a woman in a white lab coat came out at last, he intercepted her with impatient questions but was brushed aside by a curt, "She'll live."

This was most unsatisfactory, and pursuing her, Jake was ordered to a waiting room. He'd been there for more than an hour, unable to extract information from anyone, when a policewoman he believed to be of middle-eastern extraction came to take his statement.

How could she realise that his hesitation to begin wasn't suspicious but just him trying to formulate the right words for her to take him seriously? The question was, how far back did he have to go? When he had completed his statement, the large brown eyes of the constable indicated she hadn't believed a single word. This became clear when she began to ask for his home address and name of his family doctor and pressed to discover where he worked and other personal information. Finally, she asked outright, "Mr Conley, did *you* push Mrs McCracken down the stairs?"

"How could I, if I was already outdoors in my pyjamas when she fell?"

"Well, she says someone pushed her, and you two were the only people in the house."

"Except for the ghost."

The constable snorted her disbelief, closed her notebook and said, "We'll be in touch."

"Just a minute. Are you going to check out Elfrid's Hole?"

"My superiors will decide that, sir."

With that, she walked away, but he heard her mutter, "Ghosts!" and saw her shake her head. He'd show them all. Ebberston was infested with them.

When, at last, he was allowed to visit Gwen, he found her sitting up in bed with a cast on her right arm. He'd had time to reflect and said straightaway, "Have the police questioned you, Gwen?"

She nodded.

"They more or less accused me of pushing you downstairs."

"*You?* I told them you couldn't have because I was watching you dash outside when I felt the shove. But who could it have been if you were down there?"

"The ghost, of course!"

"My God, you didn't tell them that, did you? They'll think you're a nutter!"

"I did. It's the truth, Gwen. I want them to investigate Elfrid's Hole. We've got to put an end to this once and for all before someone else dies."

"Ay, well, I could have broken my neck with a fall like that. You just won't leave well enough alone, will you?" Her grey eyes glared at him, but did he detect that she believed him and wasn't as angry as she pretended to be?

He spent an uncomfortable night dozing in the armchair by her bed, disturbed by the comings and goings of the night nurse. They would not discharge Gwen until they'd checked out her head for any after-effects of the blow she'd sustained. In mid-afternoon, he called a taxi, and it took them back to her house.

"Lucky I have no other guests until next week," she said on the way home. "I'm going to have to learn to cope with one arm."

"I think I should offer you dinner in The Grapes, Gwen. It's the least I can do."

The table booked, he fussed around his accommodation, making tea for his landlady, then slipped out to the shops with a list of purchases she needed. He had no idea that the local police were in contact with York, gathering information regarding his mental state. Perhaps he would have been relieved had he seen Constable Patel close the case as a domestic accident. He might not have been so pleased to read of his psychological disturbances following the road accident and the weeks in coma. The young policewoman dismissed his references to ghosts and Elfrid's Hole as post-traumatic delusion.

TWELVE

EBBERSTON, NORTH YORKSHIRE

Dinner in The Grapes didn't proceed as intended. It started well as Jake and Gwen clinked glasses of red wine with Jake gallantly cutting Gwen's steak into small bite-sized pieces so she could eat one-handed. He also showed interest in her upbringing in Scotland and chortled at her ironic sense of humour. The contrast when he became silent and pale and toyed with his food disturbed her.

"What's bothering you, laddie?"

He was staring over her shoulder towards the window, so she turned to look at what was troubling him. It could hardly be the two middle-aged women enjoying a companionable chat over their drinks.

"What is it, Jake?"

"You can't see him, can you, Gwen?"

"Who, love?"

"The Saxon warrior. Sitting to the left of the window. He's glaring at me, and his aspect is horrible; his face is more like a skull. I can't stand this!" He pushed his chair back. "I've got to get out of here!" He rushed to the door and out onto the main road.

Gwen twisted in her seat and looked back at the window. There was nobody to the left of the window as she expected, and to the right, the two women were looking at her curiously. They were probably speculating on what she had said to make her companion flee the room. She gave them a withering look and turned back, but as she did, she felt something disturb the air behind her and smelt a decidedly fetid odour that took away her appetite.

Jake's right. It's in here! Oh my God, what're we going to do?

There was also the detail of paying for their meal. She'd been invited and had come out without more than a few coins in her purse. She'd have to pay with a credit card. Gwen began a frantic search in her handbag for her PIN number. She couldn't remember it because she rarely used her card.

I'll have words with you, laddie, when I get home. You're nowt but trouble.

The laddie in question was running along the public footpath to the Bloody Field. There was no logical explanation for why he'd chosen to take the path and not follow the road to his lodgings. Other than blind panic. The Saxon ghost was more than his fragile nerves could handle, and he didn't want it to follow him home. Dusk was descending, and although he could still see around him well enough to run, the twilight distorted familiar objects like bushes and trees. This unsettled him further, and when he glanced back, he saw the Saxon chasing him, axe in hand. When he entered the Bloody Field, his situation worsened. Men in ancient armour were searching through corpses which littered the area as far as he could see. He was witnessing the aftermath of a battle that had taken place over 1300 years earlier! Almost hysterical, Jake spun round. Salvation! His Saxon pursuer was bending over a body. Might it be a comrade or a kinsman? Whatever the truth, Jake blessed its soul, turned in an arc, and tried to increase his pace back to the road. His pursuer was still absorbed in the cadaver, and all the others on the field ignored Jake and went about their tasks. He could see them through a veil of time, but they could not see him.

Only when he was back on the road did he think about his next move. Of course, the correct thing to do was to return to Gwen in the pub. It was only a few hundred yards away, and he had to pay for the meal. He found her offering a credit card to the barman.

"No," he said in a loud voice, causing everyone in the room to stare at him, "my treat!"

"Treat!" hissed Gwen. She lowered her voice to a whisper. "That's the worst dinner invitation I've ever been on, Jake Conley."

"I'll make it up to you, I swear."

He settled the bill and bought them each a single malt – a Cardhu. They both could use a strong tipple, he reasoned, and after all, she *was* a Scot. They sat down at their table, and she gave him a rueful smile.

"So, are you going to tell me?"

He did.

"The whole field was full, you say?"

She blew out her cheeks and looked at him levelly.

"Jake, I've no reason to doubt what you say. In fact..." And she told him about the stench she'd smelled when the ghost passed her earlier. "I didn't see him, but my God, he stank of death. Look, other people aren't seeing what you do. A battlefield full of ancient spectres! If people reported those sightings, Ebberston would be crawling with television crews and journalists. I think you'd better call it a day, Jake. This ghost is following you, and you must be in danger. I've got a broken arm and spent the worst meal of my life. Don't you think that's enough for anyone?"

He couldn't meet her eye. She was right, of course. He didn't want to give up on what had become a mission, a fixation, but he was scared. Back in the field he'd been totally unmanned. Where was the sense in this? He could be safe in his home in York, and, he felt sure, with him off the scene, Gwen would be safe in hers, too. He owed her that much.

"You're right. I've made up my mind, I'm leaving in the morning."

———

YORK, (THREE DAYS LATER).

JAKE SPENT a peaceful few days mostly in his room trying to sketch an outline of a novel that was forming in his head. This implied a little research, and he soon hit contradictions and lack of source material for the eighth century. Many historians maintained that King Aldfrith died of natural causes, but with his own eyes he had seen the king struck in the chest below the shoulder by an arrow. So he tended to believe the contradictory accounts that had the king dying of his wounds in Driffelda. Another matter that bothered him was the presence of the Picts fighting on the side of Aldfrith. He could find no reference to this anywhere. On the contrary, the constant warfare at the time between the kingdom of Northumbria and the Picts was well documented. In 698, in Aldfrith's reign, Picts slew Berhtred the *dux regis*, leader of the Northumbrian forces only seven years before the battle of Ebberston.

Jake spent considerable time sorting this out to his own satisfaction. Aldfrith had been a bastard child of Oswy, fathered to an Irish princess named Fina. By Irish law, he had to be fostered and brought up in Ireland. As a result, he became a Christian and a very learned one at that. When he became king of Northumbria, his accession was opposed by very powerful factions, not least the family of Berhtred. The king's background perhaps explained why he did not share the imperialist designs of his predecessors. It would explain why Picts rallied to fight by his side against potential invaders who first had to seize his throne. Jake decided he had seen a battle fought by rival factions against the crowned king.

After several days at home, he decided to walk out in the city and headed in the general direction of the Minster. Quite near the huge monument, his eye strayed to the façade of the Catholic Church of St Wilfrid. This splendid Gothic Revival building boasted detailed Victorian carving on the arch over the main door. He must have passed it countless times without lingering as today. Maybe it was the warm, low light bathing the carvings that made them leap to his eye.

He took out his phone and began to snap them, zooming in particularly on the archangel banishing Adam and Eve. The winged figure pointed, forefinger outstretched from his right hand, whilst from his left dangled a sword.

That was when an idea came to him: he wished he had St Michael and his sword to fight the Ebberston ghost for him. Jake wasn't a Catholic, but he reckoned that if he needed a priest to fight evil, the Catholics were his best bet. They believed in archangels, saints and the whole works. He hesitated outside the doorway. As a non-Catholic, how could he walk in claiming that he needed an exorcist?

The seed had been sown, and at home in his armchair, sipping a coffee, he found the Gallery on his phone to look at the photos he'd taken of the tympanum at St Wilfrid's. He dwelt on the image for a while, and the seed began to germinate in his brain. He decided he must make an effort to get an exorcist for Elfrid's Hole. With his thumb, he scrolled through the other snaps and almost dropped his coffee in shock. He'd swear he'd deleted that photo. But there it was, with its hideous, grinning, skull-like features of the Northumbrian Saxon warrior. How was it possible? Now he cancelled the photo again, switched off the phone, switched it back on, and double-checked that it really had gone.

He gulped down his coffee and wondered whether it was a coincidence that the horrible photo had reappeared while he was thinking about an exorcist for the ghost. Or had he been careless and distracted in Ebberston? Yes, more likely, he hadn't deleted it at all.

Convinced that this had been the case, he stood and walked over to the bathroom. His terror-stricken face peered back at him from the mirror where one word was written, probably by means of stick deodorant, in Old English. His knowledge of that language was minimal, but he translated the Anglo-Saxon for *DIE* without difficulty.

The ghost had latched on to him and followed him to York. He had provoked the spectre by thinking of St Michael and an exorcist; he needed one more than ever now. He had felt safe this far away from Ebberston, but he was still in danger wherever he went. He switched on his computer and began a search for exorcists, which is how he found the Sacred Order of St Michael the Archangel, with branches in more than 30 countries. This body specialised in exorcism of malignant entities. He read through the whole site and when he'd finished tried to find an exorcist in York. This search proved fruitless, or perhaps, he wondered, he hadn't typed the right words into the browser. He thought back to the site of the Order. They were quite clear on this: if a person felt he was being haunted, he should approach his parish priest for advice.

He went back into the bathroom. No, he hadn't imagined it. The word still menaced him from the mirror. He took out a bottle of cream glass cleaner and set about removing every last trace of the word. His anxious face peered back at him as he inspected his handiwork. There was nothing ambiguous about the chilling message. He would have to be careful. His mind went back to the bedroom of the bed and breakfast and how the axe had sliced through the pillow where his head had been an instant before. The danger was only too real. He wondered whether the ghost would leave him alone if he dropped his inquiries. Say he forgot about Elfrid's Hole and exorcists and the church? It was true the spectre had left him in peace for three days while he hadn't thought or done anything about Ebberston. He'd only researched the king they'd guarded at the cavern.

Yes, this has to be the way forward.

He breathed in and in a deep loud voice cried:

"Hark! It's over. I will let you be. Heed this, I will never return to Ebberston."

He stood there feeling foolish, speaking to an empty room and doing so in a kind of pidgin Old and Modern English. Then it arrived: the stench of decomposing flesh!

Jake yelped and dashed for the door. He was out and down the street, warily glancing over his shoulder and almost demolishing a small group of tourists in his panic. He threw them an apology over the same shoulder and headed straight for the Minster. There, he went into the visitors' shop and found what he was looking for – a crucifix – the largest they had. Maybe it had been produced for a church hall or a similar vast space. He bought it regardless of the price. It was large enough to hold in front of himself and cover his whole breast and more.

THIRTEEN

YORK

THE CRUCIFIX MIGHT HAVE KEPT HIM SAFE THAT NIGHT, OR IT might have been the deal he'd tried to strike with the ghost. Jake could not be sure, but the spectral presence hadn't returned to trouble him. Yet, he knew that making a pact with the Devil required much more than simply offering to back off. He wasn't particularly religious, but he knew about Faustus and other stories, and if he had a soul – he felt sure he had – he wouldn't barter it for anything.

A profound belief that the diabolical ghost would settle for nothing less than his death drove Jake back to St Wilfrid's in search of the parish priest. Jake was disappointed not to find him mid-morning, because it was Saturday and a parishioner told him, as usual, Mass was conducted at the Shrine of Margaret Clitherow, the martyr crushed to death for refusing to confess to treasonably practising her faith in 1586.

He waited inside St Wilfrid's and stood in front of the statue of Our Lady of York, reading its history with interest. Having no reason to do so, Jake had not been inside a Catholic church before, but now, in front of this statue, the strange aching returned to the centre of his forehead. It reassured him that he was embarking on the right course of action. To pass the time, he read more details from the explanatory notice. The statue, originally from a wayside shrine in Flanders, had been saved by nuns from French Revolutionaries who suppressed their convent. Thereafter, following various vicissitudes, the statue arrived in England and eventually in York, where the shrine was built. Jake stared up at the crowned and sceptred statue of Our Lady, Mother of Mercy, and understood why people might discover peace in devotion. At this moment of serenity, the co-existence of good and evil in this world had never been clearer to him.

Before his experience at Ebberston, he would have laughed at what he held to be nothing more than superstition. Religion to him, then, had been nothing more than a compulsion for sad people with empty lives. He now realised how arrogant and baseless his attitude had been. He'd really believed that God and the Devil were no more than fairy tales to get people to behave themselves. The evil of the Saxon ghost had touched him to his very soul. He was not a Catholic, but he made the sign of the Cross before the statue and mouthed a silent prayer of his own composition. This visit had brought him respite, some comfort. It had also given him an alibi, but how was he to know that?

The priest received him almost two hours after Jake's entry into St Wilfrid's.

"I'm not a Catholic," he blurted. "I've come for advice and help."

The middle-aged priest, a member of the Oratorian Community, had many years' experience of pastoral work. He smiled at this agitated young man benignly and sensed his spiritual agitation.

"You won't be needing the confessional, then. Since it's a lovely day, would you mind if we sat outside to take tea in the rectory garden?"

Taken aback but pleasantly surprised, Jake grinned.

"Y-yes, that would be perfect."

He followed the priest through a gate along a neatly laid flagstone path leading towards the rectory at the end of the long garden with its immaculate lawn. They sat at a table, and a gentle grey-haired lady hurried away to bring tea and biscuits for Father Anthony and his guest.

Ginger nut biscuits again – it was his lucky day. The priest, meanwhile, had extracted information almost imperceptibly about Jake's background, studies, and hopes. He had no need to be guarded and spoke willingly. The cleric's touching on his aspirations gave him the introduction he needed.

"That's what's got me into trouble, Father. I'm afraid my desire to become a writer has unleashed horrible forces, so that's why I've come to you."

"What's troubling you, son?"

Father Anthony stared over the rim of his cup at the suddenly grim face of the young man.

Jake plunged right into his tale, but he knew he had to explain his newfound sensitivity after his accident.

To his dismay, the priest picked up on this, and Jake began to worry that the cleric might believe what he had to tell him came wholly from within his ailing mind. But after a moment's quiet reflection, the clergyman said, "Jake, the Father created us, and only He knows what our minds are capable of. It sounds, from what you tell me, as though your unfortunate accident brought the blessing or curse, if you will, of spiritual awakening. Please go on."

"Then you believe what I'm about to tell you isn't the raving of a damaged head?"

"I'm making no judgments, Jake, just listening."

He smiled encouragingly and settled back with hooded eyes half-closed, enjoying the gentle breeze caressing his cheeks.

Jake resumed his tale, leaving out not a single detail. Only once did the priest interrupt to question him more closely about the aspect of the ghost. When Jake finished his account, he opened his eyes wide, and his guest saw the concern in their piercing, pale blue.

"It has appeared here in York, you say?"

"Yes, I had to buy a crucifix in the minster yesterday to...well...I thought it might keep it at bay. But I really don't know what I'm doing, and I'm scared."

"Of course, you are, son. But you've done the right thing coming here. Only God can combat diabolical presences."

"Do you think it's a demon, Father?"

"Quite possibly, one that has possessed an afflicted soul."

"Do I need an exorcist?"

The priest stared at him with a sceptical look.

"Not to be ruled out as a last resort, but we should move by degrees. I should come to bless your home...and your crucifix, Jake. I would come immediately," he glanced at his watch, "but pressingly, I have Mass at 12.10. Good Lord, I must dash! Would you knock on the door and get Mrs Fenwick to write down your address? I'll come around at about half-past two, with my gear!" He said this with a chuckle, bade goodbye, and hurried down the path to the gate.

Jake sat in quiet contemplation in such restful surroundings for a few minutes before easing himself out of the chair and complying with the priest's request. Later, he would think back on the serenity he had enjoyed in blissful ignorance of events elsewhere.

Sixth sense is not always a blessing. Sometimes it presages the horrendous as when Jake raised his latchkey to let himself into his flat. Negative energy enveloped him, and his skin prickled, but he ignored the warning and entered to see a ghastly sight: a bloodied corpse sprawled in the middle of his sitting room behind the remains of his coffee table. It was the body of a woman, but he didn't recognise her until he drew nearer and saw the swarthy skin of her lacerated face. Livie! He choked back a scream. His poor, intelligent, reliable Olivia. Victim of multiple cuts, and he had no doubt in his mind what weapon had inflicted them.

She didn't give back her key to the flat.

He immediately felt guilty that he hadn't bothered to ask her for it. She'd have been alive now in all likelihood. He tiptoed around the edge of the carpet to check the other rooms. He knew he mustn't contaminate the crime scene and would have to call the police and Benjamin, her father. He worked as a screenplay writer, had lost his wife eight years before and continued to look after Livie. How would Jake find the words to break this to him? The other rooms were in order, so he dialled emergency and asked for the police.

Within minutes, he heard sirens, followed by urgent knocking on the door. The police proceeded with their usual efficiency, photographs, examination of the body and so on. He had to make a statement of how he'd found the victim and how he knew her. From the start he had the impression that he was the main suspect. There had been no break-in, she was his *ex*-fiancée, and he was in police records, admittedly as the victim of a road accident, but he *had* been in coma for many days. The police considered there was no telling how that might unhinge a man's mind.

He glanced fearfully at Livie's body as the pathologist rolled her over and caught a glimpse of the tattoo of an aubergine on her left shoulder. Poor Livie had been obsessed with organic vegetables, not that her healthy eating and jogging had bestowed on her a long life. A sob escaped him, and he flopped down in an armchair. A woman PC came over to comfort him, and he mumbled that he ought to call Livie's father.

"We'll deal with it, sir. It's for the best." She noted down the number and proceeded to make arrangements to meet Benjamin without explaining why, just *a matter of urgency*.

They zipped up the body bag, and two paramedics in white uniform carried it out of his flat. At the sight, his resolve broke, and Jake burst into a flood of tears. He would never see Livie again. There was a time when he truly loved her. A series of regrets flashed through his head as he wept. He could feel a hand rubbing his back to comfort him and through a veil of tears looked up into the concerned face of the same policewoman.

"I'll make you a cup of tea, sir."

He nodded wordlessly, grateful, and after he'd regained some composure after his tea, a detective inspector introduced himself and said, "We have one or two questions, sir. Just a formality and simple routine if you don't mind."

His manner was measured and polite, not accusatory, but Jake wasn't fooled. He knew he had to be the prime suspect.

"Where were you this morning between ten o'clock and midday, sir?"

Jake struggled and failed to remember Father Anthony's surname, but what better alibi than a Catholic priest?

"He should be here in half an hour. We have an appointment for 2.30."

"If you don't mind, we'll wait, then." Detective Inspector Mark Shaw smiled at Jake's nodded consent before continuing.

"You said earlier that you and Miss Greenwood had split up, is that correct?"

"A couple of months back. I wasn't myself after a road accident."

"How long had you been together?"

"A little over two years. But I hadn't seen or heard from her after we broke up until I found her here ...like that...today."

"Did you let her into the flat?"

"No. I told you, the first time I saw her was when I got back from St Wilfrid's, and she was dead."

"How did she get in?"

"She never gave back her key."

"And you didn't ask her for it?"

The tone was definitely sharp for the first time.

Jake raised an eyebrow.

"Well, that would've been kind of definitive, wouldn't it?"

"So, you weren't reconciled to her leaving you?"

He could see where this was heading and would have to tread carefully.

"To be honest, I haven't had much time to work through my feelings. As I said, I've been researching a novel. It took me out of York for ten days or so. If you need it, I can give you the name of the person who put me up."

"All in due course, sir. First, I'd like your permission to search the premises."

"Is that really necessary?"

The reply came very sharp.

"This is a murder inquiry, and there'll be no problem obtaining a warrant, but I should tell you that if you *were* to become a suspect, a refusal now would not help your case."

"Am I a suspect then?"

The inspector gave him a cold stare.

"In this line of work, we have to treat everyone involved as suspects, sir. It's quite routine. Now, about this search?"

"You're quite right, of course. Go ahead."

"Very wise, sir. It's obligatory; unfortunately we have no murder weapon."

"The axe," Jake murmured.

"What was that?" The trained ear and alert mind of the inspector seized on this immediately. "How do you know?"

Jake stared in confusion at the policeman. How could he have betrayed his knowledge so easily?

"You won't believe me, but I know who killed Olivia."

"Try me!"

For the second time that day, Jake related the events that had occurred at Ebberston and provided enough details for the York police to verify. He was sure they would because occasionally the inspector stopped him to repeat and jot down something in his notebook. Only when he had finished did the policeman comment but not before exchanging a look of condescension with his woman constable.

"If I understand you right, Mr Conley, you're asking me to

believe there's a *homicidal ghost* on the rampage, which *only you* can see–"

"Yes, but I'm not the only one who can smell him."

"You do realise that this defies all rational, scientific explanation. I dread to think what my superintendent would say if I wrote this in a report."

He gave a sardonic little laugh, and Jake was only saved from an ill-judged indignant response by a knock at the door. He glanced at his watch: 2.30.

Father Anthony, punctual to a fault, stared in horror at the pool of blood on the floor.

"This is a crime scene, Father," the inspector said and added, "I'm afraid there's been no time to clean up."

"Oh, Good Lord, I hope it wasn't a killing, but judging–"

"Don't distress yourself, Father, but a murder took place here. Now, kindly tell me where you were between ten o'clock and midday this morning."

"Surely you don't think–"

"Please, Father, between ten o'clock and midday."

The priest looked at Jake and then at the inspector.

"At a few minutes past ten, I met this gentleman at St Wilfrid's. From there I accompanied him to the rectory garden, where we took tea and stayed together until midday, when I dashed off to celebrate Mass."

"So you were together the whole time?"

"We were, yes."

"Might I ask why Mr Conley had come to see you, Father?"

The priest looked at Jake, who gave him a slight nod, which did not escape the eagle eye of the inspector.

"I don't see why not. I'm not bound by the confessional. Indeed," and here his tone became disapproving, "I believe Mr Conley is not a practising Christian. He came to seek my advice concerning a ghostly apparition that is tormenting him. He asked me to find him an exorcist, and in fact," he pointed to a bag by his feet, "I came to bless this house...but sadly, I see–"

Detective Inspector Shaw, looking for a moment like a haunted man, exchanged a worried look with the WPC and said, "Yes, yes. Thank you, Father. Well, Mr Conley. That's all for the moment. Our investigation is ongoing, and I must ask you to stay in York until we authorise otherwise. I'll need your mobile number, sir."

FOURTEEN

NUFFIELD HEALTH, YORK HOSPITAL

Even a charitable soul like Father Anthony would have described the look given him by Detective Inspector Shaw as jaundiced.

"Well, well, we meet again so soon, Father," he said, "and once more in unfortunate circumstances."

"I do hope the young man is not too badly hurt. I came as soon as I could."

The policeman gave the priest a penetrating stare. He used this ploy whenever he wanted to unsettle his interlocutor so that he could catch an unguarded remark. The clergyman had irritated him at the perp's flat. It was blindingly obvious that Conley had killed his girlfriend and somehow roped the priest into giving him an alibi, but nobody was going to pull the wool over Inspector Mark Shaw's eyes. Nonetheless, he chose to reassure the clergyman:

"He was wearing sensible leathers and a crash helmet, so don't worry about him too much. On the other hand, the bike might take some repairing. The upper yoke looks in need of replacement, but he's sure to be insured."

"Excuse me, officer, I must see if I can find a doctor to reassure me that the poor fellow isn't too badly hurt."

"Of course, Father. I'll wait here for you. I need to take your statement."

With mixed sentiments, he watched the Catholic priest hurry away. Brought up in a family of agnostics, he had little or nothing outside the line of duty to do with the church. He had adopted his parents' scepticism willingly, but in his line of work, he encountered wickedness of every kind, and while the existence of God and the Devil remained so much mumbo-jumbo to him, he acknowledged the capacity for evil in almost everyone. Father Anthony represented the side of the angels as, he liked to think, so did he. But in his experience, goodness of heart was often accompanied by ingenuousness, so that darker forces, like the perpetrator, Jake Conley, were swift to exploit such weakness. This new case would give him the chance to put the priest straight and to find the chink in Conley's armour.

Unwisely, D.I. Shaw bought a coffee from a dispensing machine and sipped at something comparable to liquid boot polish. He needed a caffeine hit but not at the cost of his intestines. He dumped the plastic cup, coffee and all, in the adjacent bin. The sour taste in his mouth wasn't all due to the so-called coffee. The image of Olivia Greenwood was too fresh in his mind, and somebody was going to pay for the poor woman's brutal killing.

Shaw snapped out of his reverie. The priest was hurrying along the corridor towards him.

"Coffee, Father?" he offered with a sadistic smile. "No? Ah, well, perhaps we could sit over there and you can tell me what happened in your own words."

"I'm pleased to say the motorcyclist is all right, praise the Lord! Nothing worse than a sprained wrist and a stiff leg."

"That's good to hear. Take your time and tell me what occurred."

"It must have been around three o'clock, and I was returning to the rectory on foot."

"Twelve minutes past three, to be exact, but go on."

"Well, quite out of the blue, I felt my case wrenched from my hand and saw it fly into the road, right in front of the motorcyclist. What ill luck! It might just as well have been a truck or a van, but no, it had to be that poor young man! Of course, it unseated him, and you know the rest."

"So, you are saying, Father, if I understand correctly, your case was wrested out of your grip? You didn't throw it yourself?"

"Good heavens, no! Why would I do such a thing? Apart from anything else, the case contained holy water and other religious accoutrements. A priest does not treat such possessions with disrespect."

"I see. Did you catch a glimpse of your assailant?"

The cleric looked as if he swallowed back some remark, frowned, and said, "I was shocked and concerned for the victim. In fact, with another man, I hurried over to the motorcyclist and helped him off the road. The other fellow dragged the bike onto the pavement because of the traffic."

"So, you saw nobody?"

Father Anthony considered the detective and came to a decision.

"I'm going to be frank with you, officer, although I know you won't like it."

He paused to weigh up his next words – an interlude the detective used to encourage him.

"I wish you would, Father. I'm going to require all your cooperation and patience this afternoon."

"And you shall have it, to the best of my ability. Well, as I said, I was walking back from Mr Conley's house after I'd blessed it for him – just as well under the circumstances. The self-same diabolical entity that slaughtered Miss Greenwood must have followed me, and it flung my paraphernalia into the road."

"Are you saying Jake Conley followed you and committed the act?"

The priest gave the policeman the sort of chastising look he usually reserved for miscreant choirboys.

"Mr Conley? Good heavens, no! Why would he do that? No, I mean the ghost that's haunting him."

"Not more of this irrational nonsense, surely?"

The detective's tone revealed his deep exasperation.

"Inspector, one can't rationalise about the irrational. We are dealing with a diabolical presence in this case. The ghost is a tormented spirit and, for reasons to be established, has remained in our world, I'd hazard a guess, with unfinished business. This spirit has, in all likelihood, been possessed by a malevolent entity and is simply wreaking havoc to torment us."

The detective gave a hollow laugh.

"Can you not hear how absurd that sounds, Father? A ghost stalks you after a murder it's committed and knocks a motorcyclist off his bike because it doesn't like you blessing Conley's house. Is that what you're saying?"

"You're a detective, isn't it what you're paid to do? You look at the available evidence, try to decide what makes sense and then form your opinion and theories. But when it comes to the supernatural, we simply don't know, officer. Let me give you the good news, every one of us is going to learn the truth someday."

Detective Inspector Shaw snorted.

"What, beyond the grave, you mean?"

"Father, I have to deal with the here and now, and I have a murderer to apprehend."

The cleric shook his head.

"Have you stopped to think that Mr Conley is telling the truth? The man is obviously terrified; otherwise, why would he have come to me in such a state?"

"To create an alibi?"

"But surely, your forensic techniques are advanced enough to establish the exact time of death?"

Mark Shaw glared at the clergyman. The priest was no fool, and he'd touched on the crux of the matter. As things stood, Jake Conley's barrister would be able to get him off in a trice. But ghosts and demons! The police couldn't persuade any sane jury that a ghost was the killer. There was also the impossibility of catching such a being and bringing it to justice. No, if he wasn't dealing with a horrendous crime, he'd have burst out laughing, but this priest was totally sincere; of that he was quite certain.

"Tell me, Father, what did you and Mr Conley discuss after half-past two, after my colleague and I had left?"

Father Anthony wrinkled his forehead in an effort to remember.

"First, I explained the benediction procedure for the house and then went on to sprinkle holy water throughout the flat, but especially where the body had lain. After that we talked about the malignant entity and speculated on why the ghost could not find peace. You see, Mr Conley knows a good deal about the Ebberston ghost."

"So, he didn't speak about what you should tell the police during our on-going inquiries?"

"No, not a word."

"Think carefully, Father. Your reply is very important. Mr Conley is our only suspect at the moment."

"I can assure you, Officer, he did no such thing."

The policeman's eyes narrowed.

"How long does it take to bless a house, Father?"

"Not long at all. A matter of minutes."

"Exactly, and by your own admission, you didn't leave the premises until after three o'clock."

"And I stand by that. Mr Conley was in need of comfort and explanation. Don't you realise the poor man is traumatised? As I said, we discussed the nature of the haunting, and I taught him some spiritual defence."

"I see. For example?"

"A prayer: *I command and bid all the powers who molest me—by the power of God Almighty, in the name of Jesus Christ our Saviour —to leave me forever, and to be consigned into the everlasting lake of fire, that they may never again touch me or any other creature in the entire world. Amen.* Mr Conley has a quick mind, and he learnt it by heart at once – even if it's a bit rudimentary or, rather, truncated.

"I'm sure he has a lively intelligence, as you say, Father, but did you know he suffered a serious road accident, after which he had to attend psychiatric sessions?"

"Yes, he told me and was quite open about it. He attributes his psychic awakening to the accident. Who's to say he's wrong?"

"Who's to say that this lively mind isn't capable of creating this whole fantasy?"

The priest stood and leant over the detective, giving him a very severe look.

"How do you explain the invisible force that hurled my case? The street was busy, there must be countless witnesses who didn't see me throw it or who didn't see Mr Conley on the scene. Instead of chasing Mr Conley, Detective Inspector, allow me to suggest, without being facetious, that we work together to stop this malign being before it strikes again."

He stared at the policeman and noted how distracted he had become. The policeman wrinkled his nose.

"Can you smell that?"

"What?"

"Surely, it's vile!"

D.I. Shaw looked round, crossed to the vending machine, sniffed and pulled a face. He turned to see the priest, pallid, making the sign of the Cross and muttering a prayer. He caught the words *lake of fire* – the same prayer he'd taught to Jake Conley. Hadn't the suspect insisted other people could smell the ghost? That stench was one he, as a detective, was familiar with. The stench of decomposition. Impossible! The ghost couldn't be here in the hospital, in the twenty-first century!

FIFTEEN

FULFORD ROAD POLICE STATION, YORK

D.I. Shaw tried to keep any trace of satisfaction out of his voice as he recited the obligatory words:

"You are under arrest on suspicion of murder. You do not have to say anything, but it may harm your defence if you do not mention when questioned something which you later rely on in court. Anything you do say may be given in evidence."

Jake offered no resistance as a burly constable pulled his arms behind his back and cuffed his wrists. The situation struck him as unbelievable. How was he ever going to convince the obtuse detective of his innocence? Not that he blamed the policeman too much; after all, not many police officers anywhere in the world could claim to have encountered inexplicable supernatural forces as criminals. He needed a good lawyer, one who believed him.

In the interview room of the police station, Shaw and another officer Jake hadn't seen before sat opposite. As expected, Mark Shaw was hostile towards him, but the other officer came over as more relaxed and understanding. The usual interrogation procedure began with the detective announcing date and time to a recording device. Then came the bombshell.

"Do you know..." Shaw consulted his notebook for a name. "... Abigail Wells, Mr Conley?"

"Abi? Of course, she is –er – *was* Livie's best friend."

"So, you'd agree that they shared confidences, secrets, intimacies?"

"I suppose they did. They got on very well."

Shaw stroked his chin and stared hard at the suspect – his usual ploy.

"How would you react if I told you that the evening before the murder, Miss Greenwood confided in her friend that she was going to surprise you in your flat with the intention of starting over again with you?"

Jake swallowed hard. He hadn't expected this, and in reality, he'd have been delighted to start over with Livie.

The detective looked triumphant.

"But it wasn't a surprise, was it, Mr Conley? More of a nasty shock."

"I don't know what you mean, detective. The only *nasty shock* I received was when I came home and found Livie dead."

"You see, I believe you returned home, had a row with your fiancée, and attacked her with a sharp weapon. The pathologist reports seven deep wounds to the head and body."

Jake paled and turned to his lawyer, a young woman the police had provided for him.

"You're not obliged to say anything at this stage," she whispered. Then in a louder voice said, "My client has no comment."

"Actually, I have a question," Jake said. "I loved my girlfriend. Why would I kill her? And can you show me the murder weapon?"

The inspector glared at him.

"All in good time, sir. Perhaps you'd care to comment on Miss Wells's allegation that her friend confessed she was *scared* of your reaction to finding her in your flat by surprise."

"Oh, so that's what this is about! Abi hates me, always has, ever since I shunned her at a sixth-form dance. She'll take any opportunity to cast me in a bad light. Livie might have been a little frightened of my verbal reaction because, as I freely admit, I'd been *verbally* aggressive towards her after my accident. It was the reason we split up. But I never laid a finger on her, ever." His voice rose in indignation, sounding shrill to his own ears. "Surely you can find character references for me out there? I'm a pacifist, you know."

The fair-haired lawyer looked over her blue plastic-framed glasses.

"It seems a very thin case you're presenting, Inspector. Unless you have something more than the word of one witness against that of my client, I'll be applying for bail at once.

Shaw pursed his lips, stared at the table, cleared his throat, and said, "I think we're done here today. The interview concludes at eleven twenty-seven."

He switched off the recorder and glared at Jake.

"You're not going to get away with this nonsense, you know."

He gathered up his folder and notebook, marched to and knocked on the door, which a policeman opened from the outside. Jake's lawyer addressed the remaining policeman, "I'd like five minutes alone with my client, please."

The constable nodded and pointed to a glass panel, rather like a window, but opaque.

"One-way glass," he told Jake. "We'll be watching your every move."

With that, he knocked, too, and was let out of the room.

The lawyer, she couldn't have turned thirty, smiled at Jake. He noted the brace on her teeth and thought it a shame how it detracted from her decided prettiness. But her professional skills were what really interested him. He hoped she would be as clever as she was attractive.

She spoke in a low voice.

"I'll soon have you out on bail, Mr Conley. From what we've

heard so far, they haven't got much of a case against you. I presume you have no criminal record?"

"None at all."

"Good, that means I can press for a relatively low sum of money to be deposited. You understand, the judge sets it to ensure your appearance in court as and when required. No, the only problem is this." She puffed out her cheeks. "With the serious nature of the accusation, the police can hold you up to ninety-six hours, but I'll fight for thirty-six – maximum. One last thing – there isn't anything you aren't telling me, is there? You know, a lawyer can work better with all the facts. I'm not obliged to betray confidences."

Jake looked at her askance.

"Nothing. I've nothing to hide. The best thing, Miss – er–"

"Mack. Kate Mack.

"The best thing, Miss Mack, is for you to speak with Father Anthony at St Wilfrid's. Then you'll have a real grasp of everything."

"Why, are you Catholic, Mr Conley?"

"I'm not, actually, but I'd urge you to do it."

She gave him a strange look and held out a hand, which he shook.

"Very well," she said with a smile, "I will. By the way, I believe you're innocent."

These last words helped him ward off depression when he was confined in a cell alone. The police had removed his belt and shoelaces. Did they really suppose he was going to kill himself? They could think what they liked – they had as low an opinion of him as he had of them, apparently.

With nothing to do but think, to pass the time, Jake reflected on his plight. There could be no other arrest, nobody to remove suspicion from him and lead to his exoneration, because there was *nobody*. Unless the ghost confronted D.I. Shaw in a murderous attack on his person, the detective wouldn't believe a word of his story. Shaw was as adamant of his guilt as Jake was certain of his innocence. Something needed to shake the policeman's certainties.

That something might have come the next morning in the local newspaper, **THE PRESS**, given to him by Kate, who had come to tell him that bail had been granted and that he would be released no later than, she glanced at her watch, calculated, and said, "about seventy-two hours, at worst. Now you should read the article on page five. We'll speak later, Jake."

He noticed with pleasure her use of his first name and wondered whether...in a different context...but these were idle thoughts. He turned to page five of the tabloid, and his mouth fell open. The headline was PSYCHIC ENCOUNTERS GHOST IN CITY CENTRE. Jake sat down on the cold, hard bench and read.

Well-known York psychic, Muriel Dow, working name Mystic Mu, claims to have seen the ghost of an ancient warrior close to the Minster. "It was horrible," said the clairvoyant, "standing there with an axe dangling by its side and an expression of hatred on its face. I'm surprised it was out in the daytime. These troubled spirits usually come out at night." When asked about the appearance of the ghost, Mystic Mu described a warrior in a mail shirt and pointed to a similarity to the those seen in Anglo-Saxon re-enactments. "I believe I saw the ghost of a long-dead Anglo-Saxon warrior. The worst thing about the encounter was the aura of evil surrounding the ghost. I could detect a definite wickedness about him, and his axe head...well, it was caked with dried blood." Quite what a ghost might be doing outside the gates of St Wilfrid's Rectory the mystic lady could not explain. Jake clicked his tongue. He thought he could explain it. He read, *St Wilfrid's is not an ancient church but was built in the nineteenth century. Was the ghost familiar with the wooden church erected on the site of the nearby Minster in 627 for the baptism of Edwin, King of Northumbria? "York is a very historic city," Mu told our correspondent, "it should be no surprise that troubled spirits, mostly invisible to us, frequent the places once known to them. The more troubled the ghost, the more likely it is to manifest its presence. I suppose I was lucky to catch sight of him."*

"And to live to tell the tale," Jake muttered.

At this thought, Jake shuddered. Was the ghost stalking Father Anthony? He fervently hoped the gentle priest wasn't in danger. *If only he'd come and visit me, I could warn him.*

When the cell door finally opened, it was to admit the unsmiling detective inspector.

"Your lawyer's got you out on bail, Conley. You can collect and sign for your belongings at the desk in the entrance hall. You haven't got away with your crime, you know. I'm building the case against you."

Jake thrust the newspaper at the policeman.

"You should read this."

Did he detect a fleeting look of uncertainty in the hard eyes?

"I've read it. Tripe! Journalist a friend of yours, is she?"

There was no point in arguing. Jake knew that for the detective, he'd murdered his fiancée, and a lightweight newspaper article wouldn't make him change his stubborn mind.

As a priority, on his release, Jake went to speak with Father Anthony. Part of his motivation was to warn the priest against the lurking danger of the ghost; the other, more urgent part was a desire to learn how to open the eyes of the world to the truth, since he felt the clergyman would know.

Father Anthony was generous with his time and showed his visitor into his study. It contained a desk covered in books, papers trapped under paperweights with religious motifs, and an overwhelming bookcase crammed with aged volumes. The effect of the room on Jake was very sombre, as the Victorians, no doubt, had intended.

"I was dismayed when the police took you into custody." Father Anthony's expression certainly indicated dismay.

"The fact is, Father – and it's the main reason I've come to see you for advice – that I can't breach the Inspector's refusal to consider the existence of the ghost. How can I prove my innocence unless he accepts its existence?"

"Son, this is a battle the Church has been fighting for centuries. It's clearly stated in John 5:19.

We know that we are of God, and that the whole world lies in the power of the evil one. In Revelations, we read the heart of the problem, Jake." He paused to ensure that his words were being received in the correct spirit. Heartened by the look of concentration and no signs of argument or scepticism, he continued to quote:

"*And the great dragon was thrown down, the serpent of old who is called the devil and Satan, who deceives the whole world.*" The priest clasped his hands together and shook them gently backwards and forwards in a reassuring gesture of authority. "Do you see, Jake? It's in those last words. We're bound to come up against a wall of incredulity, of disbelief, when we try to refer to unseen entities. But listen, Saint Paul wrote to the Corinthians, *And even if our gospel is veiled, it is veiled to those who are perishing, in whose case the god of this world has blinded the minds of the unbelieving so that they might not see the light of the gospel of the glory of Christ.*"

The furrowed brow of Father Anthony unwrinkled, and with a serene expression, he regarded the younger man with an encouraging smile. "The fact is, my friend, there is only one way forward for you. Again, in the words of Saint Paul, *The very first step in arming yourself for battle against the devil is to gird your loins with truth. And when we engage the battle with God's weapons of warfare that are not of the flesh, but divinely powerful for the destruction of fortresses, we attack those lies and lay waste to them, destroying speculations and every lofty thing raised up against the knowledge of God...*"

"That's all well and good, Father, but I've been telling the truth, and it's getting me nowhere. People don't want to believe in demons and ghosts in the twenty-first century! How am I going to persuade a judge and jury that not only do they exist but that they are here among us, ready to commit terrible crimes?"

"What can I say, Jake? I'm a priest, and I believe you, but I'm only one poor cleric, so unless we draw upon greater forces, what hope is there? We must have faith. Listen, my last quote for today! It comes from an eighteenth-century Catholic priest: *Every attempt to disguise or soften any branch of this truth in order to accommodate it to the prevailing taste around us either to avoid the displeasure or court the favour of our fellow mortals must be an affront to the majesty of God and an act of treachery to men."*

Jake considered this for a moment. He looked into the hooded eyes of the priest and found them tired, gentle and concerned.

"So, what you are saying is that I must stick to the truth and somehow lay it bare for everyone to see and understand."

"It will require courage and persistence, son. But above all, you will have to ask God to help you. You are confronting dark and terrible forces."

"That's why you should be careful, too, Father. Did you see in today's paper...?"

He recounted the page five article as briefly as possible.

"I have no doubt this woman, Mystic...whatever she chooses to call herself, has the sensitivity to perceive spirits, and it can be no coincidence she described your ghost and located it at my door. We must proceed with caution."

The priest reached into a desk drawer and pulled out a pendant crucifix.

"Take this, Jake, wear it at all times around your neck, and *believe* in the power of the Lord. Now, you must begin your mission to expose the ghost or the malign demon it is!"

Father Anthony stood up and walked to the door.

"You know where to find me if you need help," he said as he opened it and waved Jake out.

"One last thing, Father. Should we need an exorcist, do you have a contact?"

"I don't. But I'll see what I can find. Keep me informed, and above all, pray and tread carefully!"

Walking down the neat path of the Rectory garden with renewed resolve, Jake slipped the leather thong of the crucifix over his head and dropped the cross under his T-shirt. The feel of it against his breast was comforting, but as a reflex, he pressed it to his chest under his sweatshirt as he walked through the rectory gate out to the street. He did it for defence against the lurking ghost whose unseen presence he sensed.

SIXTEEN

SKELDERGATE, YORK

Relieved to sense only positive energy in his newly blessed flat, Jake wondered how to set about clearing his name. He dismissed every plan that came to mind as inadequate until he settled on the idea of phoning the local newspaper and asked to speak with the reporter who had written the piece about the ghost.

"Is that Claire Heron?"

"Speaking."

"Uh, hello. It's about your report of the ghost by the Minster. Well, I think I can add considerably to that story."

When Ms Heron showed interest, Jake went on to describe his misadventures from the road accident to his release from custody earlier in the day. When he'd finished, there was a long silence, making him think he'd lost the line.

"Hello?"

"Yes, sorry. I was just pondering over what you told me. As I understand it, you're under suspicion for the murder of your fiancée and trying to accuse a ghost of the crime, and you'd like me to go public with this. It's highly irregular, Mr Conley. I doubt very much I can get it past my editor."

"Look, Ms Heron, I'm sure you can understand my problem. Nobody seems willing to take me seriously. But I swear to God, I didn't kill Livie; I loved her."

"I'll tell you what, there are some elements you've given me that we can run with. I'll have to check with my editor regarding the murder. You can understand it's complicated. There are the police to consider, not to mention the effect on the public of publicising a homicidal ghost in the city centre. Let me get back to you on this; I've got your number."

When the journalist had rung off, Jake cursed. He realised she wouldn't write what he wanted her to publish, but it left him to start over in a quest to prove his innocence. He decided to ring Abigail to find out more about Livie's last hours and to convince her of his blamelessness, but she kept declining the call, and he got nowhere. He called her every foul name he could think of but on calm reflection didn't blame her. If he'd been in her shoes, he'd have done the same. The rest of the day he spent idling, playing chess against the computer and losing, reading a novel about a Second World War fighter pilot, and finally watching a documentary about the origins of the universe.

The next morning, he went out early to buy some food for the next few days, and passing a newspaper vendor, he bought a copy of The Post. Having put his purchases in the fridge and cupboards, he settled down in an armchair with a glass of prosecco and turned to page five of the tabloid. The name Jake Conley leapt off the page at him. Claire had written an article headed THE MINSTER GHOST – ITS BACKGROUND.

Eagerly, he read: *Further to the sighting of the ghost of a Saxon warrior near the Minster by Mystic Mu, another York resident, Mr Jake Conley living in Skeldergate, has come forward with his own testimony. Some months ago, this unfortunate gentleman was the victim of a road accident that left him in a coma, as a result of which he claims to have undergone a psychic awakening. While researching his novel about an eighth-century Northumbrian king, Mr Conley did some field work, which took him to Ebberston, near Scarborough. Near the village, he visited a cavern known as Elfrid's Hole, where he says he saw the warrior and heard other tormented spirits within the cave. Local legend relates that King Aldfrith, protected by his men and lying wounded after a battle, sought refuge from his enemies there. "I'll bet my last twenty pence that they're still protecting him to this day," says Mr Conley, who swears the warrior spotted near the Minster followed him to York from Ebberston. "The ghost has attacked me twice, and I've had to have my flat blessed by a priest to keep him away," he says. The novelist insists the ghost of the Saxon warrior is no danger to the general public but adds, "He's giving me sleepless nights, I can tell you."* The article went on to give historical details about King Aldfrith, and Jake lost interest.

He drank his prosecco and refilled his glass. There was nothing in the article that helped his cause because there was no reference to the murder of Olivia. At this stage, Jake was indifferent to Ms Heron's piece, but had he known what effects it would have, he wouldn't have been so complacent.

———

SHEFFIELD, SOUTH YORKSHIRE

THE SAME MORNING, Dr Stuart Dow, self-styled Doctor, was reading a copy of The Sheffield Star. On an inside page it carried a synthesis of the two Minster articles published in The Press of York. Stuart Dow was fascinated. As a founding member of the Yorkshire ghost-busting outfit *Spook-a-Spook*, proud manager of his own Facebook group page, and organiser of various conferences at county and inter-county level, he was honour-bound to follow this up. He snatched up his mobile and tapped in Russell Leigh's number.

"Hey Russ! Have ye seen this on page eight of the Star? What do you mean ye wuz gonna ring me? I should perishin' hope so! Can ye call Veronica then? I'll get the van and load up the equipment. Sounds like we're onto a cracker here, matey. I'll get around to your place for midday. See that Ronnie's there, pal. It'll save me running around all the flamin' mornin'. Right-o, see ye later."

He unlocked a wall cupboard and took out a proton pack, with its hand-held wand ready to fire a controlled stream of protons to neutralise the negatively charged electromagnetic radiation of a ghost so that it could be held in the active stream. This was followed by an ECU – an Ecto Containment Unit – and three pairs of Ecto goggles. He swore when he grazed his thumb against the cupboard frame and reached deeper inside for the Giga Meter and the PKE meter beside it – the Psycho-Kinetic Energy meter. He surveyed the equipment with pride. They'd started out with nothing more than torches and night glasses, but now, through contributions and membership fees, they'd established a collection worthy of the most professional of units.

All right, there were sceptics who didn't believe in ghosts, but he, *Doctor* Stuart Dow, could prove their existence and had already rid several properties of unwelcome presences, earning himself a bit of brass and boosting his growing reputation as a serious ghost buster. Getting rid of the Wentworth Woodhouse ghost was still the finest feather in his cap. The poor tormented ghost of an eighteenth-century maid who'd died in front of the house under the wheels of a horse-drawn carriage had plagued unsuspecting guests for more than two hundred years, but Stuart Dow Esquire had dealt with her once and for all, make no mistake.

He gathered up as much as he could carry down to the drive and packed the equipment into the boot of his car, made a second trip for the rest, grabbed his jacket and their camping gear, then drove to Russell's place.

The unwariness born of a brash confidence in their own abilities, or perhaps the basic underestimation of the danger they faced, led Dow and his assistants to pitch camp in the clearing containing

Elfrid's Hole. In perilous situations, it is often the most timorous who pay the heaviest price. In this case, Russell Leigh expressed his concern, eying the black hole in the rock with unease.

"I don't think it's a good idea, Stu. We don't know what's in there. We should pitch the tents somewhere else."

"Don't be daft, lad. What's up wi' ye? I'm not carting loads of equipment backwards and forwards just because ye've got the wind up."

"He's got a point, Russ," Veronica agreed. "Come on, we've done plenty of places worse than this, and nowt's happened."

If Ronnie was all right with it, Russell thought, he could only acquiesce. So they pitched the tents, lit a fire, and brewed tea, a task he particularly enjoyed. Around the fire they discussed the relative merits of a night- or day-time reconnaissance of the cavern, and to Russell's relief, and surprise at his reaction, decided to do the recce in the morning. What was it about Elfrid's Hole that spooked him so much? He couldn't find a rational reason because he'd been on so many ghost-busting expeditions in places with a far creepier atmosphere and not been spine-chilled like this.

Normally a sound sleeper, also on hard ground, Russell lay restless and alert. After an hour, he strained his ears, a footfall? A fox, or a stray dog? Something was out there. Near their tent! He tried to control his breathing and steady his heartbeat. Why was he so jumpy? Then he heard it: a wheezing intake of breath. Not an animal, then. He glanced across the tent. Stu was sound asleep. Had Ronnie left her tent? Was she safe? Russell Leigh made the fatal decision to check on her.

He struggled out of his sleeping bag as silently as possible so as not to wake his companion, unzipped the entrance flap, and poked his head out into the cool night – and lost it. A single vicious axe blow beheaded Russell Leigh, former taxi driver, would-be ghost buster, at the age of twenty-nine.

In the morning, Veronica's insistent screaming was shrill enough to rouse Stuart Dow from a deep, refreshing sleep. His bleary eyes told his befogged brain that Russ should not by rights be lying half inside the tent door. Ronnie's screaming also told him something bad had happened. Quite how bad, he could never have imagined. Never in his life had he seen the horror of a decapitation. That the victim was a dear friend and that arguably he was to blame for his death for not considering Russell's qualms made matters worse.

With Veronica's help, he spread a groundsheet over the body, trying his best not to contaminate the crime scene.

"We have to call the police," he said, tapping 999 into his mobile, relieved that there was a strong signal in this remote spot. Having supplied the essential information, he concentrated on comforting Veronica, whose nerves were shattered. All thoughts of ghost busting at Elfrid's Hole he consigned to the past. All they could do now was wait for the police to arrive.

———

SKELDERGATE, YORK (TWO DAYS LATER)

JAKE'S MOBILE buzzed and vibrated on his coffee table. He'd set it on silent mode overnight. He snatched it up to see a number without a name.

"Mr Conley, hello. Claire Heron speaking. I'm calling to get your take on the Ebberston murder."

Jake sat up, interest afire. He'd not watched the news or surfed the web for a day or so, preferring to cloak himself in silence in an attempt to contemplate his personal problems.

"What murder?"

"Surely you must have heard? It's splashed over all the dailies with television covering little else. There's been a gruesome killing at that cavern you told me about–" a brief pause as she name-checked, "Elfrid's Hole. A member of a ghost buster team from Sheffield was beheaded there two nights ago. Don't you see, Mr Conley? This helps your case."

Jake *did* see, and after a series of excited questions and answers supplied to Ms Heron for a new article, he rang off, sat back, closed his eyes, and pondered his next move.

———

FULFORD ROAD POLICE STATION, YORK

DETECTIVE INSPECTOR MARK SHAW stared at his superintendent, who had deigned to visit his office.

"I'm sorry, sir, do I understand correctly that you wish to link the Ebberston murder to the Greenwood case? Of course, there is more than one element that links them. I'll get onto it at once, sir."

As good as his word, Shaw rang the doorbell of Jake's flat twenty minutes later and, not content, pounded on the door with his fist. One might as well make the suspect anxious, he believed.

When Jake opened the door, he pushed his way into the flat without ceremony.

"I'm guessing you'll know why I'm here."

"No idea, a social call?" Jake sneered. He'd formed a deep dislike of this ill-mannered policeman.

"Mr Conley, pleasant as your company is, I'm here on official business because our murder inquiry has become a double murder. I have to ask you, sir, where were you between six in the evening on Tuesday and the same time yesterday?"

Jake looked thoughtful but replied, "That's easy, Inspector, I was at home in the flat."

"And you didn't leave the building at all?"

"No."

"Is there anyone who can corroborate this?"

"I shouldn't think so, I've been alone all the while. Oh, except—"

"Yes?"

"Yesterday afternoon, a journalist rang me about what happened at Ebberston. But I suppose that's no good, I could have taken the call anywhere, couldn't I?"

"Don't underestimate police technology, sir. I'm sure the call can be located if necessary."

"Oh, I see," muttered Jake, as ever uneasy in the presence of the supercilious policeman.

"Equally, we'll find out if you were in, say, Ebberston, two nights ago."

"I wasn't!" Jack shouted, red in the face. "You can't pin a double murder on me. I haven't done anything!"

"I must say, this murder in Ebberston is very convenient. It looks like somebody is trying to make the police believe in ghosts, Mr Conley. Now, that somebody wouldn't be you, would it, sir?"

"I don't know what you're trying to imply, Inspector. All I know is that I was here, minding my own business at the time of the Ebberston murder. I didn't even find out about it until Claire from The Post rang me yesterday."

"Regarding your own business, sir, might I take a look at your computer?"

"I think you need a warrant, Officer...but as I've nothing to hide..." Jake rose from his armchair, strode over to his desk and switched on his laptop, typed in his password and pulled out the chair for the policeman.

Shaw looked through the browsing history, expecting to find the site of the Sheffield ghost busters. His search drew a blank, so he scrolled through the trash folder of the e-mail. Nothing incriminating. But then, knowing the criminal mind, he wouldn't be fooled.

"I'm going to ask you to let me take this computer to our lab for a day or two, Mr Conley."

"What for?" Jake's tone was aggressive.

"To rule you out of our inquiries, sir."

"Well, in that case, I suppose so."

He could always go into the Internet on his smartphone if he wanted to surf. It was connected to his router.

Having shown out the detective, Jake sat down to contemplate what had happened. One thing D.I. Shaw had said stuck in his mind. The Ebberston murder was convenient for him. It could prove that he hadn't lied about Livie's death. Whether the murderer was the ghost or a living person, Ebberston connected them. He should begin there, where he'd clear his name.

SEVENTEEN

EBBERSTON, YORKSHIRE

JAKE DECIDED NOT TO STAY WITH GWEN MCCRACKEN, AS MUCH as he wanted to greet his friend. He didn't want to bring more trouble on her, so he wandered around the village looking for accommodation. One or two places showed signs indicating vacancies, but it wasn't until he found one called The Elms that he decided to enquire. Jake had always loved trees, and the elm was his favourite, so when he saw the rough bark of its trunk in the garden of this property, he entered the gate. He remembered that, apart from the Tree of Life, the elm was one of the two trees mentioned in Genesis as appearing in the Garden of Eden. He preferred not to dwell on quite why his head was crammed with such useless information.

A short, thin woman with a busy air, introducing herself as Mrs Lucas, hair tied back in a grey bun, invited him indoors. The widow ordered him to take off his boots because she allowed nobody to wear outdoor footwear in her house. Obeying, he unlaced them and placed them side by side in a short row of female shoes.

"I'll have to buy a pair of slippers," he muttered.

She glanced at his feet. "What size do you take?"

"Forty-two," he said, unthinkingly giving her the European size.

"That would be an eight, then," she translated and bustled at once upstairs, from where she returned bearing a pair of tartan men's slippers.

"My Bert was an eight," she explained.

Jake pulled them on and followed her upstairs to a back bedroom, which he surveyed and uttered a few appreciative words for his host's benefit about the comfortable surroundings. He eyed the crucifix on the wall with appreciation. It might ward off demonic presences. Left alone, he settled down to consider what to do in Ebberston. He had no clear plan except to gather proof of his innocence to take back to D.I. Shaw in York. But how to go about it was the problem. Unfortunately, he didn't have much time to work out any strategy because after a few minutes he received a knock on his door.

"Come in."

With an apologetic expression, his landlady said, "Sorry to disturb you, Mr Conley, but there's a visitor for you in the guests' lounge."

"For me? That's odd," he said standing, "I wasn't expecting anyone."

A familiar but unsmiling figure greeted him in the heavily curtained sitting room with its large bay window.

"So, you've turned up again." The churchwarden's tone was hostile and his expression at odds with his usually benign features. "There's been nothing but trouble since you began poking around Elfrid's Hole. You, Mr Conley, aren't welcome in Ebberston, and I've come to tell you to leave."

"How did you know where to find me?"

"Ebberston is a small place, and we're a tight-knit community. In fact, Mrs Lucas is on the parish council. Word soon gets around. It's a peaceful place; leastways, it was until you started meddling and stirring up forces that don't concern you."

"Look here, Mr Hibbitt, I don't like your tone. And I'm telling you that they *do* concern me. I've come back to clear my name. The police in York have falsely accused me of murdering my fiancée. It was the Ebberston ghost that did it – surely, knowing what you do, you believe me?"

The churchwarden looked at Jake pityingly.

"Of course, I do. Didn't I warn you from the start to stay away from the cavern?" His voice took on an edge. "But you chose to ignore my advice. Look what you've unleashed! As I said, we're a peaceful community and want to keep it that way." He sighed heavily and pushed his glasses over the bridge of his nose with his forefinger. "We don't appreciate having microphones thrust into our faces and our everyday activities disrupted by swarms of journalists. Ebberston shouldn't be on the map for grisly murders. That poor man from Sheffield! They thought they could rid the ghouls from Elfrid's Hole – but if they've been there for more than a thousand years? Look, Mr Conley, I'm going to be frank with you: we want you out of Ebberston. Do us all a favour, pack your bag, and clear off back to wherever you've come from."

Jake gazed at the churchwarden incredulously.

What ever happened to 'love thy neighbour'?

"Just you listen to me, Mr Hibbitt. I'm not going anywhere. I've got too much riding on this. I could face a life sentence in prison for something I didn't do. Anyway, it's a free country, and you can't run me out of the village."

The churchwarden peered over his glasses, his eyes narrow and hard.

"Oh, can't I? We'll see about that! There's plenty of folk hereabouts that don't want you around. You've been warned." He pulled a flat cap out of his back pocket and rammed it onto his head. "Good day to you!"

Jake watched him march across the room and, on hearing the front door bang shut, crossed to the window and watched his new foe disappear down the long garden path to the road. He marvelled at what had just occurred. Tensions must be running high after the murder at the grotto. It was just as well to be forewarned. It meant he would have to tread carefully in his investigations. But he had no intention of leaving the village and certainly none of ceasing his *meddling*.

The first thing he would do with the rest of the afternoon was to call on Gwen; maybe she could give him a clearer picture of the mood in Ebberston. After that he'd go for a meal at The Grapes. Now, that was a pleasant prospect.

"I'm so terribly sorry." Gwen McCracken smiled sadly at her former boarder. They were sitting opposite each other at the kitchen table enjoying a cup of tea and, in Jake's case, munching chocolate digestive biscuits. "I read about your loss in The Post. Your poor girlfriend! How are you bearing up, lovey?"

"I keep thinking it's a bad dream. It's like...I mean...I know I'll never see Livie again...but every time my phone rings, I think it'll be her. I know it doesn't make sense—"

"It's the grieving. The mind can play funny tricks sometimes."

Jake looked at her kind, concerned face and felt a rush of affection for the Scot.

"The fact is, Gwen, I've come back to Ebberston to clear things up. You see, the York police are convinced *I* killed Olivia, but I loved her. I have to clear my name. I thought, somehow, I don't know exactly how, I could prove the Ebberston ghost killed her."

He could see he'd shocked her, and she was looking strangely at him. He pressed on.

"Maybe I should talk to the local police – kind of get involved in the case here."

"Oh, I don't know what to advise you. Except, don't even think about going up to Elfrid's Hole. They say it's all taped off, nobody's allowed up there. It'd only make matters worse for you."

They talked for some time. Jake failed to learn anything useful about the latest case, but Gwen confirmed the strong resentment in the village about all the press and media activity. She also explained that there was no police station in Ebberston but that the village depended on the North Yorkshire police; the Ebberston inquiry was being conducted from the station in Pickering.

"I'll have to get myself over to Pickering then and pay the police a visit."

But Jake was wrong; it would be they who'd come to him.

He left Gwen with a cheery wave and set off for dinner at The Grapes. Only after a couple of streets did he notice a person in an olive-green hoody following him. He turned to check twice and, on each occasion, saw that the youth was making a call on his mobile. It was with relief that he realised his shadow had followed him into The Grapes, for what was more natural than to be heading to a pub at this hour? Jake made his way to the area with tables, whereas the man in the hoody settled at the far side of the L-shaped bar, from where each had a clear view of the other.

There was nothing particularly unsettling about the young man. He didn't have the cropped hair or tattoos of a classical bully, no piercing and no heavy rings on his fingers. Jake told himself that he was too jumpy after everything that had happened in recent weeks. He watched the man in question take a draught of his beer and promptly forgot about him as the waiter came to take his order.

The food was to its usual high standard, and Jake washed down his tempura skate with curried mayonnaise with a cool lager. Satisfied, he went up to the bar to pay his bill. The man in the hoody studied him over his raised glass but looked away as soon as their eyes met.

Jake thought it strange that Mr Hoody drank two-thirds of his pint in a couple of greedy draughts and more unsettling still that he followed Jake out of the pub. Jake increased his pace to distance himself from his pursuer, if that's what he was, but when he glanced over his shoulder, the younger man was still only five yards behind him and making another call.

Every street that Jake crossed, the other man crossed, too. He thought about stopping and challenging him but thought better of it on the basis that it might still be coincidence. That illusionary thought dissipated as he approached The Elms. On the pavement before the gate lurked a group of five hooded youths and a rather more rotund figure with a flat cap and a scarf wrapped around his face in spite of the warm weather. Jake's heart sank, but if he turned to run, where would he go? He decided to brazen out the situation and, pretending nothing was amiss, headed straight for the gate opening on the garden of his lodgings.

When he approached the band, one of them detached himself from the group and strode up to Jake, stopping right in front of him so that Jake was obliged to move to his left to pass, but the other mirrored the action by moving to his right, impeding him. A series of reiterated moves in a preposterous dance made Jake lose his temper in the face of the provocative, taunting leer. He thought of punching that visage with all his might but didn't want to finish up in the wrong, so he settled for shoving his aggressor in the chest. That was enough to provoke an indignant cry of rage and bring the others to set upon him like a pack of beagles on a fox.

They hauled Jake to the ground, and a flurry of kicks from heavily booted feet threatened to crack his ribs. Mercifully, they didn't kick his face, and after more than a dozen blows, a familiar voice said, "OK, enough, lads, the meddler's learned his lesson." The voice drew nearer, and through the waves of pain, Jake made out the shape of a flat cap and a face covered by a dark-coloured silk scarf. "You were warned, Conley. We're not joking. Get out of Ebberston, and don't come back! You got off lightly this time..." Several of the yobs laughed. "You'd be wise to avoid an encore."

With that, they were gone, except for one, who decided to give Jake one last reminder to the ribs.

When they had really gone, Jake struggled unsteadily to his feet and staggered down the garden path, every breath agony, until he reached the front door. He let himself in and, unable to go farther, sat down on the carpeted stairs.

"Uh, hello there, I thought I heard somebody come in. Oh, my goodness, what's happened to you?"

Jake groaned and fingered his tender ribs.

"Beat me up. Six of them."

He was incoherent, but Mrs Lucas, a tender-hearted motherly type, had no intention of ignoring the matter. Efficient, she shepherded him up to his bedroom and insisted on baring his torso to examine his battered ribs.

"I don't think anything's broken," she said, "but I'm no expert. I think you'll need an X-ray to be sure. Does this hurt?"

"Ouch!"

"Mmm. Just a minute, back in a sec."

She returned clutching a bottle and a wad of cotton wool.

"Witch hazel, I swear by it. It'll stop the bruising and give you some relief."

She began to dab the liquid on his side, and he was grateful for the soothing effect. She helped him pull on his T-shirt, quizzed him on what had happened, expressed her shock at it occurring on *her* street, and wanted to know how many attackers had been involved. All this information she communicated to the police in Pickering, and within the hour a police car pulled up outside her gate and Mrs Lucas admitted an officer into her house.

The sergeant studied Jake with an experienced eye – not too much damage, then. But an unsavoury incident nonetheless, not designed to encourage tourism. What the veteran officer didn't expect was that a simple case of yobbish behaviour would take on such deeper significance. Incredulous, he listened as Jake told him about all the events from his first visit to Ebberston, Livie's murder and that night's attack. For reasons he didn't properly understand, he made no mention of the churchwarden, whom he had recognised as the ringleader of the assault.

The sergeant scratched his head in bafflement.

"Well, this is a turn-up, I must say. We had no idea that the York constabulary was involved. Up to now, nobody's linked the cases. This is quite an event! But are you seriously trying to tell me that the killer's a ghost? We'd put it down to a psychopath. This is going to ruffle a few feathers, sir."

Jake was relieved. On the face of it, the elderly policeman was the first officer to take him seriously, although he had a deep-lying suspicion that the sergeant might be humouring him. Whatever the case, the kindly officer insisted on taking him to the local hospital to check his ribs. Jake's protests that it was unnecessary were met with stonewall resistance.

En route to the hospital, he said, "I have to open a case here, sir. We can't have tourists being attacked by thugs on our beat. Also, I'll have to ask you to come to the station in Pickering, in light of what you've told me; I can come and collect you in the morning."

EIGHTEEN

PICKERING AND LITTLE DRIFFIELD, YORKSHIRE

At Pickering police station, a pleasant modern building, Jake was disappointed not to have the reassuring presence of the sergeant at his interview. Instead, consigned to a young, brisk-mannered officer, he immediately felt himself on the defensive. The inspector, a dark-haired swarthy character with a sizeable mole on his right cheek, by his own admission had been in contact with the York police. The thought of what D.I. Shaw might have planted in his brain made Jake edgy. His apprehension didn't escape the policeman, and the air of suspicion and incredulity this generated increased a vicious circle of unease.

Barely stopping short of an outright accusation, D. I. Smethhurst grilled him about his movements, alibis and motivations. Most of which, unfortunately for Jake, were either absent or unconvincing. The inscrutable brown eyes of the inspector considered the suspect before he settled for an honest assessment of the situation.

"I'm going to be frank with you, Mr Conley, no self-respecting police officer in the land would base a murder investigation on the non-scientific nonsense that you're trying to put across. To my knowledge, in the history of policing since the force came into being, there hasn't been a single murder attributed to supernatural forces. Behind cases of so-called black magic, there's always the hand of a flesh-and-blood criminal."

He had delivered his speech with the intention of provoking a reaction. When it came, it disappointed him. Instead of some unhinged rant, he received an apathetic sigh, resignation.

"I know. It'll be worse trying to convince a judge and a jury. That's why I came back to Ebberston. You must see, if I'm innocent – which I am – I have to bring the ghost out in public and have it splashed across the media. Otherwise, how am I going to clear my name?"

Smethhurst grunted, paying undue attention to the pen in his hand.

"By letting the police do their job," he murmured.

"With all due respect," Jake said, "how can you do your job properly if you close your mind to the truth?"

"If you want my opinion, Mr Conley, I think Ebberston is the last place on earth you should be. I think you have more substantial dangers than your ethereal ghost to deal with. By all accounts, you're lucky to have survived your visit unscathed. You might not be so fortunate next time. Our manpower is far too stretched to guarantee your protection. Consider this, you could lose teeth or even an eye in another assault, or worse, you could end up in a vegetative state for the rest of your life."

The policeman sat back and surveyed the effect of his words with bleak satisfaction. Jake hadn't really thought it through deeply enough, but the officer was right. There was no point in exposing himself to further physical punishment. He must leave Ebberston at once. But how could he if he hadn't found a way to prove his innocence?

As if reading his mind, D.I. Smethhurst reassured him.

"You don't strike me as a villain, Mr Conley. I can assure you, as officer in charge of this case, I'll do my utmost to bring the murderer to justice. We'll also be keeping a close eye on the comings and goings at Elfrid's Hole, supernatural or human. We have it under constant surveillance. The only thing I ask of you is to keep me informed of your movements as I might need to talk with you again."

"All right, officer. I'll take your advice and move out of Ebberston. I've decided to go to Little Driffield. I want to do some research there for my novel."

"Good. Here's my card. I'd appreciate it if you'd give me a call when you've settled on your accommodation there."

Jake phoned his Ebberston landlady about leaving his few belongings in her care until he could come to reclaim them. There were no vacancies where he had previously stayed in Driffield, which turned out to be a blessing in disguise. Jake found a convenient guest house in Little Driffield Village called Mill Cottage, run by a widower and his daughter, who was now at Leeds university, a post-graduate archaeologist. The gentleman, a tall, thin, curved figure with a hooked nose, was a local historian and delighted that his new guest was researching the area for an historical novel. He immediately made his collection of books and articles available to him and talked at length about the association of Little Driffield with King Aldfrith the Wise. His admiration for the learned monarch inspired Jake to find out more about the ruler.

His research took him back to the church, and in turn, this visit set him on the track of what he discovered to be a strange anomaly. The inscription, placed on the south side of the chancel, read:

WITHIN THIS CHANCEL LIES INTERRED
THE BODY
OF ALFRED, KING OF NORTHUMBERLAND,
WHO DEPARTED THIS LIFE,
JANUARY 18, A.D. 702,
IN THE 20TH YEAR OF HIS REIGN.
Statutum est omnibus semel mori.
(It is appointed for all once to die.)

But his discussions with Andrew, his landlord, had thrown up a series of contradictions about the King, apart from the variants on his name, including the manner of his death. There were those who maintained he died after a long illness in the royal palace, others who stated the monarch succumbed there to his wounds. The medieval chronicler, William of Malmesbury, stated that he died of a painful disease, which was regarded as a visitation of Providence towards the king for expelling Saint Wilfrid from his dignity and possessions. Jake ignored this as religious propaganda. Hadn't he seen the battle and the ghostly king wounded at Ebberston with his own eyes? But what intrigued him most of all were the extraordinary eighteenth-century events that Andrew pointed out in an article he'd written himself for a local history magazine. He read:

In the year 1784, the Society of Antiquarians in London sent a deputation to Little Driffield, to search for the body of the King. Somehow, they converted him into Alfred the Great, ignoring the fact he died 200 years after the Northumbrian monarch! The deputation began its labours on the 20th of September and finished with complete success. After digging some time within the chancel, they found a stone coffin and on opening it exposed the entire skeleton of the King with a great part of his steel armour.

Jake read this with mounting excitement only to be let down with a vertiginous crash. The antiquarians who searched for the remains of Alfred consisted of a party of gentlemen from Driffield, at the head of whom was a worthy baronet – Jake promised to find out who he was – but, Andrew wrote, the investigation terminated in entire disappointment: no stone coffin; no steel armour – in fact, no relic whatever of that monarch was found. The self-appointed delegation, probably to avoid the ridicule to which they would have been exposed, created this fabrication. Jake cursed under his breath. It seemed whenever he got close to finding Aldfrith, the ancient monarch slipped away from him. He turned the page.

In 1807, when the church of Little Driffield was demolished and rebuilt, the curate made another search, but in vain, for the remains of

Alfred. When the foundations were bared, it was found that the church and the chancel had both been contracted in size, and that if Alfred had really been buried near the north wall, upon which the words of the inscription were formerly painted in a fresco, his remains must now be in the church yard.

Jake sat up. This was a line of enquiry well worth following up. He would explore it with Andrew.

"Andrew, you mention the possibility that the tomb of Aldfrith now lies in the churchyard near the north wall. Has there been no serious investigation?"

"We have regular archaeological superintendence in Driffield whenever new building takes place. They keep a watching brief on the sites, but as to specific excavations, it's been a while. I should have my wife's material, did I tell you she was an eminent archaeologist?" His expression took on an infinite sadness. "My Heather is trying to emulate her mother, and I have no doubt she will succeed. Let me see, ah, yes..." He perused the shelves and selected a box file with a half-detached yellowing label on the spine. "This will update you on archaeological activity in the village, and there's been plenty of it. Regarding the churchyard, it's a tricky one because it will involve the diocese and permission from the Church authorities."

"Maybe we could start a non-invasive investigation. Passing a proton magnetometer over the ground would answer the question without any site disturbance.

"Good idea. I can't see anyone objecting to that. Leave it with me. I'll have a word with the vicar."

Rental costs of the magnetometer were too high for Jake's pocket, so he seized eagerly on Andrew's suggestion to contact the University of York's Archaeology Department only to be met with scepticism. The professor he spoke with on the phone gave him a very polite brush-off, maintaining that the grave, had it been near the nineteenth-century rebuilding foundations, would surely have come to light. Excusing himself with a series of other urgent commitments, the archaeologist rang off.

Jake swallowed his frustration, wondering whether this line of research had any bearing on his legal predicament. As this thought struck him, his eye fell on a list of excavations in Driffield, and as had occurred on a previous occasion, one line of print seemed to leap at him off the page. For some reason, a psychic phenomenon he didn't understand was directing him to the study of a medieval moated manor. Too trusting of his newfound mystic powers, Jake did not dismiss the line of enquiry as outside his period of interest, which had been his first reaction. Instead, he read with growing interest. The article was about an excavation performed on the Moot Hill Motte and Bailey castle, which still survived in good condition despite the nineteenth-century and 1975 excavations.

Jake decided to take a walk there, especially after he read on and his interest quickened:

Excavations at Moot Hill undertaken in 1975 demonstrated that the surviving mound was the motte of a Norman castle lying immediately to the east of the postulated site of the eighth-century Northumbrian royal palace, references to which, in connection with Driffield, are found in the Anglo-Saxon Chronicle for the year 705 AD. The Chronicle indicates that King Aldfrith, who ruled Northumbria after the death of his brother, Ecgfrith, in 685 AD, possessed a palace at Driffield. The excavations of 1975 also uncovered evidence of a Roman occupation dating to the fourth century AD beneath the motte. The surviving remains include the motte mound, which is up to 4.5m in height and 40m in diameter, partly surrounded by the remains of a ditch 15m wide and 1.5m deep.

This made Jake think. He knew there had been a Northumbrian royal palace at Driffelda and that Aldfrith's men had carried the wounded king there from Ebberston. Presumably he had died in the palace, but after his death, was he really buried at the Saxon church? The strange, dull ache in the middle of his brow returned with insistence. Did it mean that he was pursuing the right line of investigation? He straightened, stretched, and returned to the article:

The existence of buried remains of an extensive building was orig-

inally discovered during earlier works carried out in the nineteenth century. These remains included wall fragments and large stone steps. It was recorded in the Driffield Observer for June 1893 that 'an elongated rectangle for the castle' was found and that hand-made files and a chalk wall foundation surrounded by a moat up to 3m deep at its west side were revealed by the excavation of a drain. J R Mortimer, the nineteenth-century antiquarian, mistakenly identified the mound as a Bronze Age round barrow. The mound had been originally much larger, both in diameter and height, before part of it was removed during gravel quarrying operations in 1856-8. During these operations, Mortimer noted fragments of medieval swords, including what is described as an Anglo-Saxon sword – Jake gasped and put his hand to his forehead, which felt as if an unseen force was gnawing between his eyes into his skull – *and spears, a bronze celt and English silver coins. It was also believed by Mortimer to have been at one time an Anglo-Saxon Moot Mound, although there is no direct evidence for this other than its name.*

He was definitely on the right track if his spiritual indicators were to be believed. The finding of Anglo-Saxon artefacts at the moot hill excited him. Jake began to formulate a theory that would have long-reaching effects on his case, although that day, standing dizzily with aching head in front of the untidy documents scattered across Andrew's desk, it was still too vague to provide him with much hope. His immediate concern, however, was to take a taxi to The Elms to reclaim his belongings. About this time, WPC Siobhan Reardon fell downstairs in her house in Ebberston, cracking two vertebrae in her neck and breaking the radius in her right arm.

NINETEEN

PICKERING, YORKSHIRE

A PARTITION WALL SEPARATED THE TWO MEN. IN THEIR OWN way, neither wanted to be where he was at that moment, and each was studying the other before their first meeting. Doctor David Richardson glanced through a sketchy report on his soon-to-be patient, PC Daniel Collins, provided to him by Chief Inspector Harveer Singh, and it took only a few words to pique his professional interest. He read:

PC Daniel Collins is a 33-year-old who enjoys praying, spreading right-wing propaganda and drone photography. He is intelligent and reliable but can also be nervy and a bit untidy.

He is a Christian who defines himself as straight. He started university but did not finish the course and entered the force instead. Physically, Daniel is in good shape. He is average-height and carries no excess fat.

He grew up in a middle-class neighbourhood and was raised in a happy family home with two loving parents. He is currently single. His most recent romance was with a receptionist called Letty Starr Burns, who is 19 years older than him. They broke up because Letty accused Daniel of being too materialistic.

Daniel has two children with two different partners: ex-girlfriend Cara and ex-girlfriend Dottie: Isabel aged 10 and Sylvia aged 16, respectively.

Daniel's best friend is our forensic scientist, Nancy Lambert. They are inseparable. He also socialises with PCs Gerald Benson and Kelby Glenn. They all enjoy jigsaw puzzles in their off-duty time.

Doctor Richardson shrugged. This report told him almost as much about Chief Inspector Singh and his prejudices as it did about the constable in question.

At the same moment the psychologist finished reading this brief outline, the constable was edgily surveying the framed certificates on the waiting room wall. He didn't want to be there, but he might as well know what manner of person would be checking on him. He read that the doctor was a *Chartered Psychologist by the British Psychological Society (C. Psychol.),* and another parchment inside a heavy gilt frame informed him he would meet an *Associate Fellow of the British Psychological Society (A.F. B. Ps. S.)* very shortly. Although it didn't mean much to him, his eyes continued their perusal of the doctor's qualifications: *Member of the Division of Clinical Psychology of the British Psychological Society* and *Registered Psychologist with the Health and CARE Professions Council (H.C.P.C.).*

Not that Daniel was impressed – he was only here because the chief inspector had given him a direct order. The constable wasn't sure it was a psychologist or a long holiday, or both, he needed.

The call came, and he entered to find Doctor Richardson sitting in a comfortable swivel chair with a notepad on his thigh.

"Constable Collins, pleased to meet you. Now, I see your chief inspector has referred you to me; although he's furnished me with a few details about you, he makes no mention of why he feels in need of my professional services. Perhaps you would be kind enough to enlighten me?"

"I'll do my best, Doctor, but it's all rather strange. May I begin by saying I probably wouldn't have come to you of my own accord?"

"Mmm."

The psychologist expected some kind of resistance. He had worked with policemen all over the United Kingdom, most of whom suffered from compassion fatigue. Attending road fatalities, knife attacks, school shootings and other unspeakable horrors took its toll of even the most independent, self-reliant, macho-like policeman. Collins looked exactly like the sort of tough individual who would suppress all emotional expression. But he would not pose a problem.

"The reason I'm here is for something that never usually happens in our line of work. I'm afraid I might seriously be cracking up."

Doctor Richardson sat up and paid attention. This was promising from a clinical point of view.

"Go on."

"Well, you'll know about the beheading up at Elfrid's Hole, I suppose?"

He looked at the doctor for confirmation. The psychologist studied him with a concerned expression and nodded before hastening to a wrong assumption – it was compassion fatigue, after all. The sight of a decapitated body and a severed head might destabilise the hardiest individual.

The constable continued, "We were put on a surveillance rota to guard the site, keeping ghouls, the press and ramblers away. A doddle, really, but that's when strange things began to happen."

"What kind of things?"

"I began to hear voices. Voices that came from the cavern. But when I went to investigate, of course, there was nobody there. It was empty. Probably the wind. The next day, I started to see things – like shifting shadowy shapes near the cave. Look, I don't believe in ghosts and suchlike, but there was something definitely *not right* about those figures. At first, I thought it was the light and my imagination fooling my eyes into filling gaps between the gloom and the rock. I also felt an icy cold grip me, and I'll admit I became fearful. You see, people don't just appear and fade – these, well, I can't really explain, they were, like, misty figures that flickered and dimmed. I got the feeling they were something that belonged to the earth, but at the same time had left it long ago. I've never run off the job before, but I couldn't stay there! I was totally and utterly scared out of my wits."

"So, now you've convinced yourself you've seen ghosts. Is that it?"

"How was I supposed to explain any of that to my colleagues and superiors?"

"But you did, didn't you? Otherwise you wouldn't be here."

"Not exactly. It was my mate, Gerry – Gerard Benson, another constable – he knows me really well, and he dragged it out of me. He was fed up of seeing me mooching around with a long face. In the end, he winkled it out of me. Gerry knows me well enough to take it seriously and knows that I'd be the last person on earth to invent some crackpot story. That's why he went to the Chief, and that's why I'm here. There are ghosts up at the grotto, and I've seen them!"

A look of desperation came over his countenance.

"I'm telling you, I'm never going back up there! I'd rather lose my job."

The psychologist jotted down a few notes but then looked at the policeman and spoke in a calm voice.

"And yet, going back there might be exactly what you need to overcome your anxiety. What if you were right all along? Might it not have been a trick of the light? And there's another thing, Dan, – may I call you Dan?"

"Yeah."

"I was saying, there's another thing. Statistically, more than eighty-eight percent of the police admit to experiencing stress, and you wouldn't believe how many suffer from poor mental health. It's quite possible that the mind can induce the most unusual delusions when overtaxed. No," he held up a hand, "hear me out. I'm not saying you're crazy or a gibbering wreck. I'm saying that the kind of accumulative stress involved in policing could lead even a strong man, like yourself, to have a *minor blip,* let's call it that."

"I'd like to believe that, Doctor, but how does it account for the icy feeling that gripped me at the same time?"

"The power of auto-suggestion. You'd probably read somewhere that people feel cold in the presence of ghosts. But let me assure you, as a man of science: ghosts don't exist."

Daniel Collins looked and felt embarrassed. The doctor was saying what he'd wanted to believe deep down all along. Only, he *had* felt cold, and he'd seen what he'd seen. He hadn't invented it all by the power of his mind, and as a matter of fact, he hadn't been stressed before going up to the damned cave. Daniel Collins decided the best course of action was to play the doctor along.

"You're quite right, doctor, I reckon I knew all this and suppressed it. It was just my imagination. I'm sorry to have wasted your time."

"Ah, but you haven't, my dear fellow. If I've been able to reassure you in that way, then I've done my job and can conclude my report for your chief. I'll recommend he sends you back up there at the first opportunity.

Daniel paled but did not surrender to his desire to plead and cry aloud his fear of returning to the cavern. Somehow, he'd find a way of dodging out of it.

On his way to the station from the surgery, Daniel thought about the power of auto-suggestion and accepted that it might well be a way of creating self-delusion. Then he rejected the possibility as far as his own case was concerned. Surely, he thought, self-limiting programming as practised by Doctor David Richardson was worse. Why should he accept the word of one man, however specialised and highly qualified? He, Daniel Collins, knew himself better than any shrink – and he *knew* he had seen ghosts.

Back at the station, he found Gerry struggling with paperwork, the part of the job his friend liked least and which generally led to outbursts of bad language. This evening, the constable appeared calm and good-humoured.

"So, did you drive the shrink to drink, buddy?" Gerry laughed and put his ballpoint pen behind one of his prominent ears.

"He did his best to convince me that I spooked myself by the exceptional power of my massive brain."

"Humph! I'm no psychologist, but I'll go on record as saying that your brain ain't that massive, pal. I'd go as far as to say–"

"Better not, Gerry, if you value the straightness of your nose!"

"Oooh, officer, the nasty bogeyman threatened me!"

How long this banter might have gone on Daniel would never know because Kelby came in, and as to Gerry as calcium carbonate is to camembert, he brought a serious tone to proceedings.

"Well, the good doctor tried to convince me that my ghosts were all a figment of my imagination. That I'd invented them by the power of auto-suggestion," Daniel answered his enquiry.

Kelby stared at his friend, whom he had always admired for his stoical level-headedness. It was not possible, and besides...

"I'd have a word with the sergeant if I were you, Dan. He had a chap in here the other day, and I was there when he took his statement, who swears his girlfriend was murdered by one of your ghosts. It turns out one of them's stalking him. Just saying..."

"You're serious, aren't you?"

"Oh, yeah. The guy seemed quite regular too, not one of your head-cases. I'll bet the serge can put you in touch with him."

"I'll get on to it. It'd be handy. Thanks Kel-lad!"

TWENTY

LITTLE DRIFFIELD, EAST YORKSHIRE.

JAKE SAT AT THE DESK IN ANDREW'S STUDY AND STARED BLEAKLY at the untidy trail of cuttings and photocopies he had spread across its surface. He had wasted more than an hour trying to establish where King Aldfrith was buried and had got no nearer to solving this self-imposed puzzle. He ran through what he knew. Prior to the Victorian reconstruction, the medieval church with Saxon and Norman elements was in poor condition. In the Middle Ages, a fresco proclaimed that the king was buried in the chancel. Excavations disproved this. The king's grave might be outside the north wall, but he had no way of establishing this.

Quite why he was so set on finding the royal burial, he was unsure, but the nagging feeling persisted that if he could find the king, he might end the hauntings at Ebberston. This was a wild theory without any fundamental proof, pure instinct, and in any case, finding the burial wouldn't clear his name, which surely must be his priority; nonetheless, he pressed on.

Both elbows on the desk, he put his head in his hands and sighed. When reaching a dead end, what did he usually do? After a while, the answer came to him. Usually, he applied a 'what if?' approach. So in this case, what if the medieval fresco was wrong? Maybe the king never had been buried in this church. What if the King had been buried near his palace? In another church? Why not? Jake thought about this. Saxon churches were often built on the site of a Roman temple. He began to scrabble through the papers. He needed any reports on Roman excavations in the area. Luckily, he had time to research as much as he liked because he couldn't go to Ebberston for the time being and would have to pass the time usefully until the police hauled him in.

Discouragingly, his first efforts revealed to him that there were more than 140 indications of Roman occupation in immediate proximity to Little Driffield. These were gathered from old maps, tithe maps, field names, excavations, crop marks, aerial photographs, field walking, detectorists, and historical documents. Jake sighed. What a task! He began by ruling out any references more than three miles from the village, which made his reading more manageable. He glanced at and picked up a photocopy of an old newspaper article dated June 1893 from *The Driffield Observer*. This referred to the excavations on the Moot Hill in nearby Driffield by the local archaeologist, J.R. Mortimer. He read, *Previous to 1856, when the west side was removed, it had been circular, about 90ft diameter, and of considerable height, and had a ditch and rampart, part of which remains, close round its circumference. It was apparently formed mainly of chalk.* Reading on, two things captured Jake's interest: firstly, Mortimer had found pieces of Saxon swords, spears, and axes, but secondly, he discovered traces of fourth-century Roman occupation farther down. A rusting paperclip held another article behind it, referring to the 1975 excavations there. This stirred his curiosity; he read that the Northumbrian royal palace was presumed immediately to the east of the Moot Hill. In that case, he would have to concentrate his research around that area. But what would he find there today, houses? Industrial development?

There seemed to be no alternative – he would have to take a stroll to the Moot Hill, but first, he'd check out what he could find out about it. It was the site of a Norman motte and bailey castle. The builders had used a much earlier chalk mound for the construction of a keep. Archaeologists had found traces of a bridge over the foss separating the motte from the bailey. As he suspected, but didn't care, housing developments had encroached on the bailey area. It didn't bother him because his real interest lay farther afield.

Having checked the location on a map, Jake headed out until he came to Gibson Street in Driffield. From there the motte was freely accessible, and he stepped over a stile and across the tufts of rough grass towards the raised mound of land covered on one side by entangled bushes and small trees. His impression was one of abandonment. Standing on top of the hill, he had the sense of past times and could peer through the leaves at the houses and network of roads below. Sadly, he didn't see the hoped-for fields.

The situation became more favourable when he went down to street level and took Allotment Lane before striding along Northfield Road – its name was more promising – as far as Long Lane. This led onto the main A614, but interestingly, it was flanked by endless open fields. He would now have to find out who owned the land and obtain permission to field walk. Andrew would be able to help, he felt sure.

He was mistaken. Andrew seemed in awe of landowners.

"Great Kendale Farm? I hardly think Mr Beal would appreciate you trampling all over his land."

The name of the farm was enough for Jake. He'd find out for himself.

Andrew had been mistaken. When Jake found the number and phoned, Mr Beal could scarcely have been more jovial.

"I don't see why not, old chap. Although quite honestly, I don't know what you'll find of interest for your research. You won't be using a detector, will you?"

"Just my hiking boots, Mr Beal."

Having reassured the farmer that all he wanted to do was walk the fields, the farmer became more expansive.

"If you're lucky, you might find the odd coin ploughed up. Do you know, back in the eighties, I turned up a statuette? I sent it to the British museum because it looked old to me. They were very good and sent me whole page of explanation. A seventh-century portrayal of Saint Peter, they said. You can tell it's Peter by the keys at his belt, apparently. Tell you what, if you'd like to see it, come around to the farmhouse tomorrow about five o'clock, and I'll show it to you."

His bright red sweatshirt probably saved Jake from disaster the next afternoon. He had been walking around the field nearest the busy main road when suddenly he felt as though his head would explode. He blinked and shook it several times, but an unaccountable dizziness made him totter and fall onto the ploughed field. He lost consciousness, but for how long he couldn't say. When he came round, he was staring into the smiling face of a man in his thirties.

"Mr Beal?" he croaked. "I'm Jake. I spoke to you on the phone yesterday."

"Not to me," the young fellow said cheerfully, "my dad, it was. He said he was expecting someone this evening. But look here, what's happened, then?"

"I-I'm not sure. I came over dizzy. Next thing I blacked out."

"We should get you to a doctor."

"No need, it can happen, they say. After my accident. I got hit by a car."

"Good job you weren't crossing the road." He jerked a thumb at the cars flashing by. "Doesn't bear thinking about."

"No, you're right," Jake concurred, but he knew *why* it had happened. He struggled to his feet, and the young farmer gave him a hand. Jake looked around him, pulled out his phone, and took two or three photographs.

"You're a rum 'un, mister. There's nowt interesting in this 'ere field."

Jake knew better, but he wasn't going to betray the secret, not yet; it was the only way he had of creating an 'X marks the spot.' He simply muttered, "A kind of souvenir."

"Let's get back to the farmhouse. I think you could do with a drink, and the old man's expecting you."

In the farmhouse, sitting beside a warm Aga, gratefully swigging a glass of beer, Jake let his saviour do the talking.

"Lucky Mr Conley was wearing that red top, else he could have spent the night under the stars, and no one would have been the wiser."

There followed a discussion about Jake's *condition* and general agreement that all's well that ends that way. The genial elder Beal waved an object wrapped in a grimy white cloth.

"You'll be wanting to see our saint, I expect?" he said with a grin and unwound the cloth from a carved stone statuette about ten inches tall. On inspection, Jake found the artefact delicately carved but artistically crude. The head was out of proportion to the body, but even at first glance, it was clearly Anglo-Saxon. There was no doubt who the statue represented. Equally disproportionate keys hung from the saint's belt.

"Blimey, the saint would need to be a weightlifter to let people through the Pearly Gates!" Jake brought a smile to his host's face.

"It's seventh-century. They carbon-dated it. See here." The farmer unfolded a yellowing sheet of paper and passed it to Jake, whose eye immediately settled on 630 AD ± 40. That placed the statuette prior to Aldfrith's reign, but not much. The question he was burning to ask came a little too anxious to his own ears, but his hosts seemed to notice nothing.

"You said you ploughed it up, Mr Beal. Which field would that be?"

Quick as a flash, he trotted out a name that meant nothing to Jake. That much was obvious because his son said, "That's the name of the field I found you in today, Jake."

Why didn't that surprise him?

"Near the road?" Jake asked, affecting an air of nonchalance.

"Naw, about a hundred yards in – if I remember rightly – but it was a long time ago."

"Well, thank you for letting me see it, Mr Beal. It's a fine piece."

"Do you think it's worth much?" The farmer's tanned and lined face contrasted with his white teeth, shown by his grin.

There was nothing rapacious about the farmer's expression or tone, it was just a simple request.

"I should think a collector might pay a good price, Mr Beal, but I'm no expert. You could photograph it or get it valued by an auction house if you want to sell."

"Naw. I've grown fond of the old fellah." His grin was engaging, and Jake felt emboldened.

"Have you ever thought of having an archaeological inspection of the field?"

"Can't say as I have. I wouldn't want loads of folk digging up my field. It'd interfere with my crops."

"Don't you rotate? I mean, doesn't it lie fallow every so often?"

"Oh, you know about farming then, my lad?"

"Not a lot, sir. Just what they taught us at school."

"As a matter of fact, it's scheduled to lie fallow next year." He looked at Jake shrewdly. "Why do I get the feeling there's something you're not telling me?"

Jake felt himself reddening but knew the time wasn't right to be completely frank.

"My research isn't complete, but I think I'm on the right track. You know, a preliminary archaeological survey wouldn't involve any digging. You wouldn't know they'd been there."

"So, you *are* on to something, then?"

"Maybe," Jake admitted, "but it's too soon to say. I'm just going to ask you one question, Mr Beal. Let's say I found something really important that lay in your field. Do you think you might be prepared to allow an investigation?"

He wondered at once whether he'd made a mistake by revealing his hand on this, their first meeting.

But to his relief, the affable farmer said, "That would depend on how important it was and what proof you could furnish. I'm not over keen on having another one of them." He pointed to the statuette on the table. "He's grumpy-looking enough for two!" He chortled.

"I haven't any proof yet, but if I get it, would you mind if I troubled you with it?"

"I don't see why not. But you'll have to promise that you won't go keeling over again. Gave us all a fright, you did, my lad. Don't want no bodies in my field."

Jake bit his tongue. A body in that field was exactly what *he* wanted.

TWENTY-ONE
LITTLE DRIFFIELD, EAST YORKSHIRE

JAKE SAW AN EMINENT ARCHAEOLOGIST'S NAME BY CHANCE IN an academic magazine...an article entitled *A study of Settlement on the Yorkshire Wolds: Anglo-Saxon Buildings and Associated Finds,* but, nonetheless, within Jake's sphere of interest.

His landlord looked at the open page of the magazine on the dining room table and couldn't resist interrupting Jake's peace.

"The woman who wrote that article is related to me."

"Really?"

"Sure – she was my wife!"

"I'll give your daughter a call and see if she's interested in helping – Lord knows I can use help no matter where it comes from!"

Jake phoned the number Andrew supplied him, and a softly spoken voice answered. After a few pleasantries, Jake explained to the woman that her father had prompted him to contact her. He arranged to meet her at the university with her father.

Heather Poulton proved to be as gentle as her telephone manner had indicated, but the shrewdness in the green eyes did not escape Jake as she weighed him up. They were taking coffee in the modern union building, and Jake appreciated the relaxing ambience. He particularly liked the idea of a post-graduate mixing freely and natu-rally with the undergraduates. The

stylish wooden chairs also pleased him, old-fashioned as they were but gaily painted in coral or lime green.

Not wishing to waste the archaeologist's precious time, he plunged straight into what he hoped would prove irresistible to her, the chance of associating her name to *the find of the century* in her home parish. Overcoming her foreseeable scepticism turned out as difficult as he'd imagined. What proof had he to convince her that Aldfrith's grave lay in a ploughed field, other than his strange headaches and mystical sensations? The passion of his pleading and the plausibility that a Roman temple might have been located in that vicinity convinced her to speak with her professor of archaeology.

Heather sat opposite him, giving him an encouraging smile accentuated by her bright red lipstick. She was very attractive, Jake noted. Strawberry blonde wavy hair gathered from a central parting and pulled back into a ponytail set off her oval face, high cheekbones, and deep-set, large olive-green eyes. He found it difficult to reconcile this cool, well-posed young woman with his set ideas of unkempt semi-bohemian excavators in woolly jumpers caked in mud, scrab-bling around in fields.

"My professor's not an Anglo-Saxonist, but as you say, it would be the find of the century, and all we're asking, to start with, is the loan of a proton magnetometer to test for soil disturbance. I think he'll give us the go-ahead."

Jake rubbed his forehead and fervently hoped so.

Three days after this initial meeting, a white van pulled up, unseen by Jake, outside his lodgings. Andrew's cheerful call summoned him from his bedroom.

"Jake, Heather's here with her equipment!"

He rushed downstairs and almost collided with the archaeologist at the foot of the stairs as he swung around the newel post in his rush.

"Steady on, Jake Conley! We've got all day, you know. A cup of coffee before we set off wouldn't go amiss."

"I'll see to it," Jake offered.

"Too late," came a voice from the kitchen, "Dad's already on the job!"

Heather smiled. "Dad's nothing if not considerate, bless him!"

Jake studied the archaeologist. Certainly, she'd changed appearance radically. Gone was the impressive professional woman-about-the-lab appearance of the other day, exchanged for practical jeans, sturdy boots and, oh, yes – woolly jumper, although there was nothing hippy about Ms Heather Poulton.

After coffee, they drove to Great Kendale Farm and parked the van as close to the field as possible. Jake thought it best to inform Mr Beal of their presence from the outset.

The farmer greeted them with his usual cheerful grin. "So, you're Lucy Poulton's lass, then? I remember your mother, used to beat me and my wife at mixed doubles badminton. A sad loss." He shook his head and stared into space, lost in memory. He snapped out of his reverie. "You're most welcome, Ms Poulton. So what does your inspection entail?"

Heather launched into a technical explanation of how a proton magnetometer uses the principle of the Earth's field nuclear magnetic resonance to measure very small variations in the Earth's magnetic field, allowing ferrous objects on land to be detected.

It is used in archaeology to map the positions of demolished walls and buildings or, in this specific case, they hoped, a grave.

"And what if you find what you're looking for?" The farmer smiled roguishly. "What's in it for me?"

Heather patiently explained the current laws on Treasure Trove and smiled charmingly at him when he said, after hearing her out, "I really don't care about personal profit. I'm just thrilled to think that we might have a Northumbrian king buried in my field. You'd best get on, then. Do you need a hand with your equipment?"

It wasn't necessary. The equipment consisted of a light rectangular metal console, a cable, and a sensor.

"What's inside this box?"

Jake was genuinely intrigued.

"Basically, a battery with eight hours autonomy, a microprocessor, proton-rich liquid, a couple of copper coils, a GPS system, and see the slot on the top? That's for the memory card. Pass me the console, Jack. I'll connect the cable to the back." She screwed a connector to the plug point. Meanwhile, Jake took out his phone and scrolled to the three photos from several days ago. He squinted at the screen and tried to assess the exact spot from where he'd taken his bearings. *A little farther ahead*, he thought.

"Are you all right?" Heather gazed at him in alarm.

He'd grown pale and was clutching his head in both hands.

"This is the place." His voice was shaky.

"Sure you're okay?"

"Don't worry, I told you, it's the strange effect of my accident, but it confirms we're on the right track."

"I hope you're right." She powered on the device and began to walk over the ground indicated by Jake, sensor outstretched.

"I'm using this as a horizontal gradiometer. I've set it at a depth of six feet. Oh, my God! Jake! You exceptional individual!"

He hurried over to stand beside her as she pointed with a trembling finger at the LED graphics onscreen.

"We have a rectangular cluster of anomalies. See here in blue, it's a clear signature, a high-amplitude signal quite consonant with gravestones."

Jake felt terribly dizzy and sank to his hands and knees on the ground.

"Jake, Jake, what is it?"

"I-I'll be all right in a minute. I probably need to move away." He staggered to his feet and marched off ten yards towards the field boundary. Instantly, the dizziness passed, and he breathed in deeply.

We've found King Aldfrith. I know we have!

"If you're all right, I'll just move a little farther away. I've marked this spot. I'm getting other readings. There's much more down here!"

When they'd finished the magnetometer survey, on the way back to the farmhouse, Heather was exultant.

"Jake, you know what you've done, I suppose? You've led me to an important complex. Only excavation will show if it's Saxon – or should I say, more correctly, *Anglian*? Of course, it might pre-date that period. I suspect Aldfrith's palace would have been where the bailey of the Moot Hill lies. It's been built over, so this is something else. Whatever it is, it's going to be big! Let's hope Mr Beal doesn't change his mind."

Jake looked at the archaeologist bubbling with excitement. There was something girlish about her enthusiasm, and he liked her like this.

"Heather, how soon do you think excavation can begin? Will it cost much? Can you get a team together?"

"What a lot of questions, Mr Conley! We can use second-year students. The university has just finished the excavation of what was probably a Norman chantry. My professor is casting around for a suitable new project. If you're right about this being Aldfrith's grave, he'll probably leap at it and make funds available."

They spoke with Mr Beal and impressed the need for secrecy upon him. Work, she told him, should begin within the month. She suggested using a JCB digger to remove four feet of topsoil over a contained area, which would expedite the excavation without compromising the site. Everything now depended on the go-ahead from Heather's Professor.

Another couple of days passed by until a call came through to Jake, but it wasn't the one he was expecting.

"Good morning, Mr Conley? My name is Collins, Daniel Collins. I'm with the North Yorkshire Police. I wonder whether I might call at your accommodation. Strictly speaking, it's not police business, sir, more a private matter."

Jake could not begin to wonder what the police officer wanted to talk to him about but agreed to receive him the next morning. When he opened up to Jake about his experience at Elfrid's Hole, it became clear to him how disturbed the policeman was by the whole affair.

"They tell me you made the statement that a ghost from there killed your girlfriend, is that right, sir?"

"My fiancée, yes. There's something unholy going on at that cavern, constable."

"I'll say there is! So, let me get this right, you've actually seen the ghost?"

"Yes, more than once. In fact, you might find this hard to believe, but I've seen a whole army of them near the Bloody Beck."

"Bloody Beck?"

"Yes, a stream that runs along the field where a battle took place in 705 AD. The ghosts you saw at the cavern were some of the defeated army who carried away their wounded King. At the moment I'm searching for his final resting place."

"I see. I really came to get confirmation that it isn't me who's going crazy. My superiors and the police psychologist are trying to convince me I imagined everything."

"Oh, they will do that; it's easier than broadening their minds to what they've shut out. How can they understand that there is a veil between this world and another and that you and I have peered through it?"

"My chief wants me to go back to the cavern. I-I can't do that."

"Don't go there!"

Jake said it with such feeling that the constable widened his eyes and nodded his head

"I'd rather leave the force," he said.

An idea, a hope, came to Jake.

"I don't suppose...I mean, if it comes to a trial, would you be prepared to testify that you saw those ghosts? I need a credible witness to back me up."

"Credible? You'd better hope they don't kick me out of the force for disobeying orders, then. But yes, I'd be prepared to do that, Mr Conley."

They conversed more generally over a cup of tea, and Jake outlined his new theory of busting the ghosts by arriving at their king. Collins promised to keep this information to himself. Jake discovered he quite liked the bluff policeman, so he saw him off warmly enough. The thought of having corroboration for the ghost sightings cheered him immensely. He was not to know he would never see PC Daniel Collins again.

The other phone call came the next morning when a very excited Heather Poulton said, "Jake, great news! Prof. Whitehead's said yes! He's so keen on the idea that he wants to be present and involved, and he's going to put out an instruction sheet for our second-year students. I should warn you, he's a little bit eccentric. He's given me the go-ahead to move on the excavator. Can you ask dad to sort it with Bill Wyatt? His firm does all the earth-moving around Driffield. As soon as he's booked, I'll come over and make sure he works in the right place and settle the bill. We won't be able to organise the students for a couple of weeks, but I'd like the topsoil off before they're on-site."

They exchanged some other conversation, especially Jake, who was fixated on the possibility of a Roman temple at the site, and they had greeted each other when Heather remembered, "Ah, by the way, can you slip over to Mr Beal and ask him where we can set up a campsite for the students? We'll be supplying those portable loos for them and the camping equipment. Jake, can you see if there's a local fast food place, too? Sorry to burden you, but the students will have food vouchers from the university. I've been away from Driffield too long, but if there's a burger place, that would be ideal. But they'll need to accept the vouchers; see what you can do."

"Will do, but there's a price."

"Oh, what's that?"

"You have to agree to a meal out with me. My treat."

He picked up on the smile at the other end.

"Sounds lovely. It's a deal."

He saw Heather five days later when she came to pay the earth movers and organise their work. Jake tagged along out of curiosity and a sense entitlement based on the whole show being down to him. Heather had brought the GPS coordinates furnished by the magnetometer, so they located the place in the field down to the last square inch. The archaeologist spoke to Mr Wyatt, who had decided to do the job himself.

"My main worry is the weight of that beast, Mr Wyatt. If, as I think, there's a sarcophagus down there, there's the risk of damage under the crushing weight of your machinery."

"How accurate is your positioning, miss?"

"*Very* accurate."

She paced out a rectangle to show him.

"Get some twigs and mark it out," the digger driver ordered a surprised Jake brusquely. He obeyed at once, hacking at an elder bush in the nearby hedgerow with his pocketknife. In a few minutes, he had stripped back a dozen short branches, and he carried them back to the pair, who were talking and pointing at the ground. Jake tossed the branches to the ground so that he could sharpen the end of one and proceeded to do the same with the others. Heather took them from him one at a time and dug them into the ground until a rectangle of ten by six paces was marked out.

"Right then, to work!"

With that, the owner climbed into his cab and turned on the engine, sending a cloud of black exhaust fumes into the air. The digger creaked forward on its caterpillar tracks and stopped, halting the track pads only a foot away from the marked area.

That thing must weigh ten tons!

Even as he thought this, Jake understood what Wyatt intended to do. He would extend the long boom over the site and lower the excavator stick so the bucket could dig up the earth without extra weight bearing down on it. This could work well if done carefully. Down into the earth dug the teeth of the bucket, and like a mechanical hand closing in a giant fist, the hydraulic arm raised it up, swinging round and releasing its grasp, tipping the soil onto the ground: the beginnings of their spoil heap. Jake looked at the hole the machinery had dug and calculated that it was a wheel-barrowful. If he'd had to dig it himself, it might have taken him a quarter of an hour, while the excavator had done it in an instant. Out came another huge steel fistful so that after half an hour, an acceptably neat rectangular hole scarred the field. Indifferent, unawares, the traffic beyond the fence whizzed by, and it seemed that no one had paid their activity any attention.

"We're done here," Heather told Wyatt and paid him from a roll of notes she'd kept in a buttoned pocket of her denim jacket. They shook hands, and the lumbering machine clanked its way back to the lane.

The archaeologist surveyed the hole.

"That's literally saved several days' work with picks and shovels, not to mentioned blistered hands." She smiled knowingly. "Our students aren't used to heavy manual work. Even so, the boys will still have some digging and barrowing to do."

"Let's hope all that weight didn't compromise anything important."

"It was a risk worth taking, Jake. Mr Wyatt certainly can handle that excavator, can't he? He's done a great job here. If we go back to the car, I've got a ground sheet in the boot and some pegs. We should peg it over the hole in case it rains and to stop busybodies with fancy ideas digging farther down."

"That's not very likely, is it?"

Heather smiled. "Well, I'm guessing you and dad haven't told anyone, but who knows how much Mr Wyatt talks?"

"Oh, I see! Let's get it done then."

When they'd finished, Heather clapped her hands and looked pleased, then with a coquettish grin said, "You know, Jake, about that meal? I don't need a fancy restaurant where you need to book or anything. Just straightforward pub grub would do just as well."

"I'm hungry, too. Why don't we go off the beaten track and find a nice little country inn? Maybe we could ask Mr Beal for suggestions."

Mr Beal Junior was the knowledgeable one about pubs. He came up with three suggestions before dismissing them by remembering a fourth – *a brilliant place* a bit off the beaten track, but wasn't that what they wanted? A romantic setting? He ventured to suggest it, risking Heather's wrath, but instead, she smiled shyly and pressed for directions.

TWENTY-TWO
LITTLE DRIFFIELD, EAST YORKSHIRE

THE LAST PERSON ON EARTH JAKE WANTED TO SEE APPEARED AT his lodgings the next morning. Andrew's deep voice, so at odds with his slight frame, calling up the stairs, alerted him to a visitor. In the guests' lounge stood the swarthy-featured inspector from York.

"Detective Inspector Shaw! To what do I owe this honour?"

"Let's say to ongoing investigations."

The reply was deliberately laconic, the dark eyes scrutinising him intensely, as hard as jet.

"Oh, yes? Have you caught Livie's killer?"

"Don't mess with me, Conley! I'm on to you, remember?"

Jake glared at the police officer but swore to himself he wouldn't let his dislike get the better of him. Instead, he spoke suavely.

"So, what can I do for you, inspector?"

He even managed a forced smile.

The policeman drew a small notebook from a breast pocket, flicked it open, and took a pen.

"Let's work backwards, shall we? Begin with your movements yesterday."

"I was here in Driffield with my landlord's daughter, Dr Heather

Poulton. I'm helping with a dig on nearby land. I can provide you with a number of witnesses. In the evening we went to a village with a pretty name, Cherry Burton, to eat at The Bay Horse. It serves good food. Dr Poulton was very pleased because she's vegetarian, and they catered for her. As for me, I found a decent pint of real ale: Cocker Hoop. Do you know the village, inspector? I can recommend you take your wife there."

"I'm not married, Mr Conley."

Why doesn't that surprise me?

"And the day before, on Sunday?"

"Here in Little Driffield. As a matter of fact, I had a visit from one of your colleagues – from Pickering."

Was he mistaken, or had he piqued Shaw's interest?

"A colleague?"

"Yes, a Constable Collins. Nice chap."

"We know about him coming here. We traced his phone calls to you."

Jake glared at the Inspector again.

"Can a man have no privacy?"

"Not when he's the chief suspect in a murder investigation."

"But why trace Constable Collins's calls? Surely you don't suspect him of anything?"

The detective inspector stared at Jake, eyes boring into him.

"You really don't follow the news, do you, sir? Or else you're a consummate actor."

"I beg your pardon?"

"Daniel Collins hanged himself yesterday."

"My God, that's terrible! What...w-why?"

"That's what we're trying to find out. He left a note..." Shaw flicked back a few pages in his notebook. It said:

He keeps following me. I can't go on. I don't want him to hurt my girls. Conley knows. Ask him.

Jake gaped at the inspector. What nightmare was he conjuring out of nothing now? He immediately denied any involvement.

"It's impossible. I hardly know – *knew* the man. We met the once and chatted, he was very friendly–"

"Isn't it strange how the people you know meet unfortunate ends? Your fiancée, your former landlady nearly breaks her neck, now PC Collins."

"It's no coincidence!" Jake couldn't stop his voice from rising. He hated to sound falsetto: it wasn't manly. With a great effort of self-control, he lowered his tone.

"There's a connection. Daniel Collins is telling you so – do you doubt a doomed man's last words, inspector?"

"Of course not; the connection is *you*, Conley."

"It's not *me!*" Jake shrieked. "It's the bloody ghost!"

Shaw bunched his fists and looked for all the world as if he might strike Jake Conley.

"Don't start with that nonsense again! I've had enough of you and your so-called ghost. Somehow you got into Collins's head and drove him to suicide. He leaves two young daughters. You do know that, don't you?"

Jake didn't. He found it distressing, and it showed on his face.

"Aw, spare me Conley!"

Jake looked at the inspector with loathing mixed with despair.

"Why? Why would I want to drive the constable to suicide? I barely knew him. Tell me that, great detective."

He could no longer hide his dislike and contempt for the obtuse police officer.

"It's my guess he was on to you, and you found a way."

"In that case, you'd be long dead, inspector."

The detective took one menacing step towards Jake, thought better of it, and glared.

"Are you threatening me?" the policeman growled.

"It's the other way round if anything. I keep telling you, I've done nothing. I'm a pacifist, yet here you are harassing me instead of getting rid of that ghost."

"The ghost is in your head, Conley. That's what's driving me to distraction. I'm going to check out your alibis. You're as slippery as an eel, but I'll not let you get away with your crimes."

Jake let him leave the room before calling, "Oh, inspector!"

The policeman's swarthy face reappeared around the doorframe, wearing an inquisitive expression like a mask.

"What?"

"I just wanted to say, you should spend as much time at Elfrid's Hole as possible."

The only reply was an indignant snort.

Jake stood at the window and watched the car drive away.

Will this nightmare never end? Unless, of course...

———

HE'D FALLEN into a deep depression after Shaw's visit and desperately needed something to take his mind off his woes. He consoled himself that he'd be locked up if the police had a shred of proof against him. Still, it was only natural to worry. Two days later, Heather appeared at her father's house. This was exactly what Jake needed. Who better than the attractive archaeologist to distract him?

"Jake, Professor Whitehead will be joining us this afternoon. Don't be put off by his curious behaviour. He's a lovely guy, really, just slightly eccentric. The students are coming by minibus. We've got fifteen of them, ten women and five blokes. I'm going to get them to pitch camp while the girls sift through the spoil heap; it's not heavy work. James – Prof Whitehead – will never forgive me if we miss a coin or a shard in the topsoil. Ten of them should get it done by mid-afternoon, when I expect him."

Jake soon became aware of the sniggering and whispered comments directed towards himself and Heather by the female students. He was flattered because Heather was so very attractive, and a part of him wished it were true; the more realistic part told him that when she found out he was the main suspect in a murder trial, she'd have nothing more to do with him.

The sifting of the spoil heap produced a basketful of objects of little interest: some clay pipe stems and bowls, probably dropped by eighteenth- or nineteenth-century ploughmen, similarly a couple of small earthenware bottles, which when cleaned up might make reasonable ornaments, Jake thought, and some sherds of post-medieval pottery. But now with the spoil heap sifted, the professor would have no excuse to criticise Heather for lack of scrupulousness. He watched on with interest as she jumped down into the hole and began stretching twine and fastening it to small wooden stakes, so that the area was divided into smaller squares. Each of the ten squares was provided with a card bearing a block capital letter of the alphabet in a sequence marked from A to J.

"Ladies, food vouchers!" she called when back at ground level. She plunged a hand into a tapestry bag slung from a shoulder to her opposite hip, withdrew a wad of long, narrow vouchers, and handed them out to the eager recipients. Then she asked Jake to explain where they could be presented. It wasn't a long, complicated walk and as such easy to explain the streets they had to take. They were given an hour's break, but before they went, Heather impressed upon them not to talk openly about their work on Great Kendale Farm.

"What about us, Doctor Poulton?"

One of the young men, a red-haired, rather pugnacious type, indicated the men.

She laughed. "You guys have to work up an appetite first! I want you to take two letters each." She pointed to the cards A - J. "And go down exactly another foot. You've done it before, so you know the ropes. Picks, barrows, and shovels, chop-chop!"

One of the young men lingered, and Heather was quick to respond.

"Yes, Mark?"

"Sorry, prof. But will it be like this every day? I'd hoped to spend lunch with my girlfriend."

"Oh. Who is she?"

"Jenny, Jenny Holt."

"Ah, Jenny... a lovely girl. Don't worry, it's only for today. I'll sort it differently tomorrow."

She smiled at his shy, mumbled thanks and turned back to face Jake as the youngster jogged to catch up with his mates.

"They're a good crowd. They mostly are on these digs. But I remember a difficult bunch a couple of years back. It's a sociometric phenomenon. Strong leaders can be either positive or negative characters. The group tends to follow like sheep. Luckily, this year, Anton's very positive."

"Anton?"

"Yes, the red-haired guy. Looks can be deceiving, he's as nice as ... I was going to say pie, but I need to coin a more appropriate cliché – how about as nice as a bulldog?"

"Sorry, Heather. It simply doesn't work for me!"

They both laughed but stopped short as a voice behind them cut in.

"Really, can this be? Scenes of hilarity at a sacred burial site?"

Heather flushed and spun round.

"Oh, James! Professor Whitehead!" she corrected herself in a trice. "May I introduce Jake Conley? It was his intuition..."

"Yes, yes, I know. Pleased to meet you, young man."

Jake gazed at the long grey sideburns, moustache with waxed extremities à la Poirot, and red spotted bowtie and groaned inwardly. Then he remembered Heather's warning and gave the Professor a gracious smile.

"Honoured to meet you, sir."

That gained him a fulsome smile and got them off to a good start.

"Doctor Poulton tells me you believe this to be the grave of King Aldfrith. May I ask how you arrived at this conclusion?"

"It's complicated and non-scientific, professor. I'd like you to get to know me better before I make my confession."

"By Jove, you've really whetted my curiosity now." His sharp eye shifted to the students who were parking barrows laden with tools. "Laddie!" he barked at the nearest, who happened to be Mark.

"Professor?" The respect was evident.

"Can you lads ask the driver to remove the planks from the bus so you can fetch them to create a barrow run?"

He turned back to Jake.

"Is this your first dig?"

Jake admitted it was.

"The planks are for the spoil heap. The young and athletic can take a run at it with a soil-laden barrow, and they tip out the contents at the top, hopefully without mishaps." He chuckled at some recalled misadventure. "Never place a spoil heap near a perimeter fence." The chuckle deepened. "One of my students knocked an octogenarian lady off her feet. The poor dear was innocently returning to her sheltered housing. By sheer good fortune, no harm done, just a little shaken. It was a Roman fort on the Ermine Street, that one." His mind wandered into the past. "There was a light drizzle, the barrow slipped, he lost his footing, and the soil, which could have gone anywhere, sailed in a perfect arc right over poor Violet. I remember her name; she was such a treasure! Made the most wonderful carrot cake and brought it to the dig every day."

Jake couldn't help but like the professor. He was sure they would get on well.

He soon got bored of watching the students removing their allotted layer of soil and took the shovel off Mark in middle section F and set to, hurling soil into a barrow. Soon, Professor Whitehead called to him.

"Jake, do me a favour, would you? Could you clear about a one-foot square hole right next to the earth wall? Take it steadily. I need to study the stratigraphy. Just a minute!" He took a tape measure and asked Jake to take the free end and hold it on the exposed ground. "Mmm. You're already down five feet. The next foot is the crucial phase of soil removal. Can you do that, then? One foot square and steadily, mind you."

Even working with extreme caution, Jake completed the task in ten minutes. The soil was compact but not difficult, being a light clay

– ideal for arable farming, Mr Beal had said – so when he struck stone, Jake was excited. Excitement gave way to dizziness, and he swayed. Now he was certain he had struck the edge of Aldfrith's grave. He breathed deeply and shook his head to clear it. To no avail. He staggered to the short ladder and climbed out to gain relief and find the professor.

"I've hit it, professor! I'm sure the stone I struck is the grave."

"By Jove! Let's see."

Agile for a man in his sixties, the tweed-clad figure climbed down into the hole.

Jake stood as far back from the excavation as possible whilst still being able to see the professor's face. The whirling sensation behind his forehead eased, and he took two tentative paces nearer.

"By Jove, this is the cat's whiskers!" the jubilant scholar cried. "You are right, young fellow. One foot down exactly to the tomb." He worked a little with the shovel. "It's limestone; we'll have to proceed with care. It's easy to damage the material otherwise."

Under the attentive surveillance of the two archaeologists, the soil was removed until a creamy-yellow limestone sarcophagus was revealed. Professor Whitehead organised the young women with trowels and brushes to remove the last of the soil and expose the coffin lid. With ten of them around the sarcophagus, the task was swiftly performed. Their work revealed a carved, scrolled border around the lid.

"That's enough for today, ladies and gentlemen. Now gather round for a word. Of course, you are free to spend your evening as you see fit. I must impress upon you the importance of keeping today's find an absolute secret. No loose talk in pubs – alcohol is the greatest tongue-loosener known to man. Tomorrow, we'll reveal the sides of the stone coffin, too, but not until I've passed a portable 3-D scanner over it. We need to know the precise nature of the contents and how delicate they are before attempting to raise the tomb. Doctor Poulton, I charge you with bringing the Artec Eva 3-D scanner first thing in the morning. I have a meeting this evening and will have no time to go back to the laboratory."

"Good as done," Heather said with a smile.

The students made their cheerful way back to the campsite, and the professor roared off in his Jaguar, leaving Jake and Heather to contemplate the stone coffin protruding like a tooth from the hungry earth.

"This tomb's been there undisturbed for more than 1300 years," Jake said, his voice awed.

"Tomorrow we'll know for sure whether you were right and it's Aldfrith, Jake," said Heather, linking her arm through his as they walked back towards the farmhouse.

"Do you think we ought to cover the site with that tarpaulin?" he asked.

"It's not going to rain, but it might deter people or animals. Yes, have you got the energy?"

"Of course."

The real reason for his concern was that he wanted to stay close to her for a little while longer.

TWENTY-THREE

DRIFFIELD, EAST YORKSHIRE

Jake spent a troubled night trying to work out why the Northumbrians had buried Aldfrith in unconsecrated ground. It was mystifying, especially since the sarcophagus suggested the tomb of a wealthy and powerful individual. As he tossed and turned in bed, he even questioned whether the tomb might not be Aldfrith's. Then he remembered the effect on him when he exposed the limestone. Surely that would not have happened if the tomb belonged to someone else.

The next morning, on site, Professor Whitehead gathered the students around him to explain the technology of scanning. Jake stood next to Heather and listened with keen interest.

The archaeologist was wielding a handheld device and began his explanation.

"This little beauty is a fully-charged Artec Eva 3-D scanner, which gives us six hours of autonomy. It'll enable us to 'see through' this ancient coffin, which, if it is filled with artefacts, as I suspect, means we cannot open it *in situ* without damaging the contents. As you can see, ladies and gentlemen, the device is very light, weighing only two pounds, but this little chappie rattles along at sixteen frames per second and can capture and process up to two million points a second with a resolution of 0.5 millimetres. I hope you're taking notes – I'll be expecting some exceptional projects at the end of this dig!"

Jake's sideways glance revealed that several students were recording the professor on their mobiles.

"...one hundred microns accuracy, too, an indispensable tool for any archaeological laboratory or, indeed, any museum..." The professor droned on with other specifications and particulars. He recaptured Jake's interest only when he connected the device by cable to a portable computer.

While the archaeologist climbed down next to the sarcophagus lid, Heather ordered the disappointed students to stand back from the computer she was holding and summoned Jake next to her. "You'll all get plenty of chances to see the scans later."

She clicked on a screen several times, and Jake, from the corner of his eye, saw the elderly professor pass the scanner systematically over the limestone lid. Jake gasped as the computer screen displayed first the leather-booted legs of a skeleton wrapped in finely woven textile. The images were high-resolution, and he could see every detail of the crafted pommel of a sword laid alongside the corpse. The colours were vibrant, too. The scan reached the cranium, and Heather whispered excitedly, "We'll be able to make a facial reconstruction in the lab, Jake. You'll see what your Aldfrith really looked like."

"Can you do that?"

"Of course, I'll do it myself. Oh, look there," she squeezed his hand, "by the left arm of the body, there's a pouch of coins. Silver coins. I'll bet they're sceattas. Mind you, they didn't call them that at the time – for them, they were *peningas*."

Professor Whitehead climbed back out and issued instructions for digging around the rest of the sarcophagus before indulging his curiosity regarding the scan. A cursory glance and he spun round to beam at Jake.

"The find of the century, without a shade of doubt! Well done, young fellow-me-lad! I'll see you get all the recognition you deserve.

The next challenge is to raise the sarcophagus and transport it to a laboratory without damage. We can't just open it, you know, unless the air conditions have been adjusted to optimum for preservation of the contents. Bradford, I think, Heather! Archaeology has changed in my lifetime, it's so technological now. It's all right for you youngsters," he beamed at them, "...but an old dog like me, well..."

Heather took out her phone.

"I'll ring Mr Wyatt. He'll have a mobile crane or know where to hire one."

Within minutes she concluded the call.

"Done! He can do it. He'll be here mid-afternoon."

"Professor! Look here!" Anton called, a huge grin transforming his usually belligerent expression into a friendly gargoyle impression. "There's an inscription on this side. It's definitely writing."

Less nimble than before, Professor Whitehead still managed to join the red-haired student with some alacrity.

"By Jove, so there is! Maximum urgency, gentlemen! Get the earth away as quickly as you can so that the ladies can remove the soil from the incisions. This is of exceptional importance! Hallelujah! We are truly blessed!"

Jake almost expected the eccentric scholar to dance a jig, such was his enraptured state.

An hour's steady work, and the young women had done a marvellous job with their trowel points and brushes. They'd revealed a scroll-framed panel with incised writing in Old English. Heather pronounced herself satisfied with the cleaning and moved the students out so that she could photograph the panel.

"Look at this!" She showed her photo to the Professor and to Jake, who eagerly bent over it.

He saw:

Ar-fæst nergende crist gewrite alfriþes nama in þe boc þe ece lifes and ne letaþ his nama geswice hwætre þurh þe ure drihten gemanan bið.

. . .

"WHAT DOES IT SAY?" Jake looked desperately from one archaeologist to the other.

"I'm no expert in Old English, dear boy, but I can get by," the professor said. "But first, congratulations! You were right from the start." He pointed to the fifth word. "Aldfrith! This is his epitaph. Forgive my rough and ready translation. I believe it reads:

Merciful Saviour Christ, write the name of Aldfrith in the book of eternal life and never let it be obliterated, but may it be held in remembrance, through you, our Lord."

"Yes, but why, Professor? Why bury their King here in unconsecrated ground? It's been bothering me all night."

The professor shook his head.

"Good point, dear boy. Perhaps we'll only find the answer when we've excavated the entire site."

Jake nodded, but he wasn't satisfied. For some reason, he believed the answer to his question would reveal the whole mystery of Elfrid's Hole, and he was determined to fathom it out.

———

JAKE WAS able to watch the raising and removal of the sarcophagus, a delicate operation involving a hydraulic crane, chains, and a flatbed truck. Professor Whitehead fussed to such an extent throughout the operation that it concluded without the slightest damage to the exterior of the stone coffin. Once the massive find disappeared from view, destination the Archaeology Laboratory at the University of Bradford, which boasted a well-equipped and renowned forensic archaeology department, Jake spoke to the professor on a matter close to his heart.

Unfortunately, he was only able to form a vague preamble and unable to discuss it to any extent because at that moment a police car drove into the lane with its blue light flashing. Jake stared at it dispassionately until the familiar figure of D.I. Shaw, leading two other policemen, strode towards him. His heart sank.

Professor Whitehead, still in fussy mode, marched forward to meet them, whilst Heather drew close to Jake.

"I wonder what they want," she whispered.

"Me. They want me," Jake said bitterly.

"Officer, we have every right to be here," Professor Whitehead declared. "We have all the necessary authorisation."

"I don't doubt it, sir. We are not here for you." Shaw cleared his throat, set his jaw, and in a solemn, self-satisfied voice stated, "Jake Conley, I declare you under arrest on two charges of murder, two of attempted murder, and one of actual bodily harm."

Beside him Doctor Heather Poulton gasped, then murmured, "Jake, tell me it isn't true!" She clutched at his arm as Shaw proceeded to recite Jake's rights.

"Of course it isn't bloody true!" Jake hissed venomously. "Whatever you hear or read about me, Heather, I beg you not to believe it and to trust me."

"Cuff him!" The order came crisp and smug.

There was no point in resistance, so Jake meekly cooperated and allowed himself to be led away while memorising the taut, distressed features of the lovely archaeologist. Mortified, with a sinking feeling, he considered that his bright plans to win her affection would be reduced to a glimmer even if he managed to clear his name. As a burly officer marched him with occasional pushes to the waiting car, he wondered what trumped-up evidence Shaw could produce, since he knew he was innocent of all charges.

The ride to Pickering was conducted in total silence. Not even the police exchanged words, although occasionally the short-band radio coughed into crackling life on police business. Jake was hustled into an interview room where Detective Inspector Shaw, with ill-concealed satisfaction, said, "At last we have the proof against you we required. You're a slippery one, Conley, but the game's up."

Jake stared at him and with a confidence he didn't feel, drawled, "Highly unlikely, detective, in view of the fact that I've done nothing."

"You call attempting to murder a woman police officer nothing?"

Jake gaped and noticed the policeman's obvious scepticism at his surprise.

"I don't know anything about a woman police officer."

Shaw flipped open his notebook and flicked through the pages.

"No, eh? So how do you account for the fact that four witnesses have testified to seeing you entering and leaving WPC Siobhan Reardon's house in Ebberston on the evening of 29 May at exactly the time she was pushed down the stairs, fracturing the vertebrae in her neck? Tough cookie, Reardon; you'll be saddened to know she's survived."

"Four witnesses, you say? I'd hazard a guess at who at least one of them is. They're lying. I've never heard of this policewoman, but I'm glad she's going to be OK."

"Magnanimous of you, Conley. You're a dab hand at pushing women down stairs, aren't you?"

"I'm saying no more until I speak with my lawyer. I believe I have the right to make that call."

The inspector smiled grimly. "You do, indeed. You can make it from your cell before we relieve you of your personal items, sir. But then, you know the ropes, don't you?"

His conversation with the brisk Ms Mack when she arrived was brief and to the point.

"I had hoped, without offence, not to be your client anymore, Kate, but it seems I'll be needing your assistance after all." He went on to outline the charges against him and concluded, "They haven't got a shred of proof except these contrived accusations, which will be easy to disprove. I'm relying on you for that – a little investigation will do it if you're up for it."

"Explain yourself." The lawyer was cool and professional without a trace of the previous friendliness Jake had hoped for. He regretted having used only her first name; perhaps he'd been over-familiar.

"Well, Ms Mack, this is the number of Doctor Poulton. She's

an archaeologist at Leeds University. She found me the taxi that took me to Ebberston and back to Little Driffield on the night of the assault on the WPC. I had the driver wait outside whilst I collected my belongings from Mrs Lucas. I was less than ten minutes there, just long enough for a polite chat with my former landlady. Find him, and he'll confirm that he took me straight back to Little Driffield, and of course, Mrs Lucas will back me up, too. So, you see, I couldn't possibly have been at the policewoman's house.

Kate Mack at last allowed herself a smile.

"I don't know what it is about you, Mr Conley, but you certainly seem to have rubbed Inspector Shaw up the wrong way." She peered over her blue plastic-framed glasses exactly as he remembered, adding, "Can you tell me why?"

"Sure, he needs a conviction and doesn't believe in ghosts, so he'll never get one."

"Then you still maintain a ghost killed your fiancée?"

"It's the truth, Ka – er – Ms Mack."

The blonde smiled and tilted her head. "It's fine, you can use my name, Jake. But it may be wiser not to in front of the police. It seems they aren't very impartial when it comes to you as it is. I'll be on my way. The sooner I find your taxi driver, the better."

Jake would have felt much better had he been able to listen to the telephone conversation between Kate Mack and Heather Poulton because both women expressed themselves convinced of his innocence. And since Little Driffield was a small village and not exactly teeming with taxi drivers, it was a simple task to confirm the truth of Jake's statement. The fellow in question agreed to meet Kate at the Pickering police station the next day. She reassured him that his time and petrol would be compensated. She felt sure that Jake would not begrudge that as part of his lawyer's fee. She also arranged for Mrs Lucas to be present. The bed and breakfast proprietor, having taken to Jake, was only too pleased to help. As for the prisoner himself, not having the benefit of this information, he, deprived of all personal items, passed the time lying on his bunk, trying to work out the mystery of Aldfrith's burial.

From his earlier research, he remembered that upon the death of the king, civil war broke out over the succession in Northumbria. He recalled that Aldfrith had at least two sons. The eldest was old enough to rule, but a noble unconnected with the royal house was able to seize power for a few months in 705. The effort to remember the name of the noble – it was on the tip of his tongue – helped him pass the time until, suddenly, he said out loud, "Of course, Eadwulf!" This man disputed the succession, supported by Aldfrith's old enemy, Bishop Wilfrid, with the supporters of the king's young son Osred.

Lying there, thinking of the death of Aldfrith, the familiar dull ache came to the centre of Jake's forehead. This startled him because it seemed out of context with him locked up in a police cell, but it made him wonder. Was he onto something important? Did it confirm the soundness of his plan? How he regretted the untimely arrival of the blundering inspector! A few minutes later and he'd have been able to outline it to Professor Whitehead. He had enough to worry about now without tormenting himself about how the eccentric professor might react, so he decided to force his tired brain to dredge out all he knew about the death of Aldfrith, especially in light of the burial.

Normally speaking, he thought, the king would have been laid in state and pomp in the nearest church dear to him, which in this case should have been Little Driffield's St Mary's. Clearly, the medieval fresco was wrong. Maybe its assertion that Aldfrith was buried in the chancel was based on logical supposition, without any proof. So, he wondered, what had made the king's loyal followers bury him in that particular spot? Had they faced resistance and opposition? Would the archaeologists' ongoing excavations provide an answer? Would they find, for example, traces of a church surrounding the burial spot? He hadn't seen the wider magnetometer survey and wrapped up in the excitement of finding the tomb, hadn't thought to ask Heather.

"Ah, Heather!" he moaned, and thought about his feelings for her and the possible consequences of his incarceration. Would it destroy any hope he had of winning her? He cursed Inspector Shaw and invoked the wrath of the pre-Christian Anglo-Saxon gods upon him.

Then, he remembered that he ought to be thinking about the death of Aldfrith. What had happened in 705? Immediately, the dull pain returned to his forehead as he recalled the political confusion of the time. Osred, who began to reign at the age of eight in 705, was regarded by the illustrious Saint Boniface as a worthless youth who led an evil life and violated the ancient privileges of the Northumbrian Church. Jake remembered reading an early ninth-century poem in which Osred appears as a wild and irreligious young king who killed many nobles and forced others to seek refuge in monasteries. Few mourned his murder in 716. Was it any wonder, then, that this monarch showed no interest in retrieving his father's tomb? At this thought, a blinding silvery flash disturbed his vision, like the onset of a migraine, except that Jake didn't suffer from that particular ailment. It passed instantly but was enough to serve as warning to him that his conjecture was correct.

He stared at the soulless, cream-coloured cell wall, bit his lip, and reflected that he needed to get out of there to talk to Professor Whitehead about his scheme and, *ah, yes,* plead his innocence with Heather.

TWENTY-FOUR

PICKERING, NORTH YORKSHIRE.

"I want to be completely clear on this, Mr Gregory. You waited in your taxi outside this lady's house for how long?" Detective Inspector Shaw knew his case against Conley was crumbling as he spoke.

"As I said, officer, no more than ten minutes."

"That's how long it took him to collect his belongings and to have a little chat with me, Inspector," Mrs Lucas interrupted and added, "Such a charming man!"

Kate Mack smiled at the policeman. "In the light of this evidence, Detective Inspector, I'm formally requesting the immediate release of my client."

Shaw had to admit defeat and tried not to betray his conflicting thoughts. Conley, he considered, had not pushed WPC Reardon but sure as hell *had* murdered his fiancée. All he said was, "The charge of attempted murder and actual bodily harm is dropped. Conley is free to go."

The pleasure and relief on the three faces before him irritated the inspector so much that he determined to make one last effort whilst he still held his man.

"Ms Mack, come with me, please. There's one last formality, and I think you should be present." He turned to the other two. "We're finished here. Thank you for your time and cooperation, madam, sir."

He led Kate to the interview room and invited her to take a seat. Within minutes, Jake came and sat next to her.

"You're free to go," she whispered. "Apparently there's a final issue...I've no idea what."

After some minutes the inspector returned with a woman police officer wearing a neck brace.

"This is WPC Reardon. She had an accident recently."

Jake rose and extended a hand. "Pleased to meet you." He smiled, and more to irritate Shaw than for innate elegance, and asked, "How are you? I hope there's no lasting damage."

"Shouldn't be, thanks for your concern."

"I wanted you to meet Mr Conley, constable, to ask whether you'd seen him before."

The policewoman studied Jake's face for a moment.

"This is the first time I've seen this gentleman."

Her expression changed suddenly from one of friendly curiosity to one of terror, the look of someone remembering a nightmare.

"Just a minute! Aren't you the person who saw the ghost at Elfrid's Hole?"

"And not only there, officer."

"You see!" She turned on Shaw with a belligerent expression. "I told you! It was the ghost that pushed me down the stairs. I could smell the stench of the grave on him. That place is infested. I saw more than one of them when I was on duty. Thank God somebody else can back me up!" She spun round to face Jake again. "They'd all taken me for a hysterical female," she said bitterly.

"It should be me thanking God." Jake stared hard at the detective. "They'd all taken me for a murderer."

What passed across the face of the inspector was hard to decipher. Finally, he said, "It looks like I'm going to have to take this matter of ghosts seriously after all. There are too many reliable witnesses—"

"Including my client, inspector," Kate Mack interrupted.

"Well, I admit I was thinking more of WPC Reardon and PC Collins, not to mention that Catholic priest in York."

"Father Anthony?" Jake said. "Why don't you contact him, inspector, see whether you can get an exorcist up to the grotto to rid Elfrid's Hole of ghosts once and for all?"

Jake said this despite its being in direct conflict with his master plan. But, he considered, it wouldn't do any harm.

"Yes, sir, why don't we do that?" WPC Reardon latched onto the idea eagerly. "That place, or rather what inhabits it, has caused enough woes over the years...centuries..." she added lamely.

D.I. Shaw thought for some moments. He could do that, but against his better judgment, whilst now reluctantly accepting some supernatural presence at the cavern. He could not help but think that Conley had in some cunning way used it for his own ends: to construct an elaborate scam in which to cloak the murder of his fiancée. He decided to play along with it for the moment until he could finally pin down the slippery eel.

"Very well," he said, "I'll get on to that. Meanwhile, you, Mr Conley, are free to go, but I'm going to ask you not to leave the country."

"Leave the country," said Jake. "Just when I'm about to become famous? No way. In fact, inspector, I'm thinking of going back to Mrs Lucas's place in Ebberston for a few days."

"Is that wise, sir? Given what happened to you?"

"It's a risk I'm prepared to take. I have unfinished business there."

The detective frowned at his own evil thoughts. As an upholder of law and order, he wondered why part of him hoped that Conley would be beaten up again. It was only human, he told himself, since a murderer deserved far worse. Instead, he allowed the hypocrite in him to come to the fore, stretching out his hand, which Jake took in surprise. He said, "Well, take care, sir."

Having retrieved his personal effects, Jake stepped outside to the pleasant surprise of finding Mrs Lucas and the Little Driffield taxi driver.

"What are you two doing here?"

His lawyer filled in the missing details and added, "Don't worry, I'll be sending the bill."

Jake thanked her warmly and looked at Mr Gregory. "If you're free, perhaps you could take us to The Elms. If you have a vacancy, I'll be staying a couple of nights."

"Oh, lovely, of course, my dear. You're always welcome."

"I'd better ring Doctor Poulton, then," the taxi driver said.

Jake's heart skipped a beat. "Heather? Why?"

"Because I'm supposed to be taking you straight back to her."

"Don't worry, I'll ring her."

From inside the cab, he rang the archaeologist and was delighted by her pleasure at his release and the dropping of the charges. She insisted she knew all along that he was innocent, and he was even more delighted at her disappointment that he would be staying in Ebberston for some days. Not one to miss an opportunity, Jake invited her for a meal in The Grapes, where he was certain of buying her a good meal. To his delight, the archaeologist accepted. The next evening, he would tell her of his plan. He decided it might be tactically shrewd if he left it to Heather to suggest it to James Whitehead – always supposing he could convince her first.

Across the table from Jake the next evening, Heather Poulton, wearing an elegant, figure-hugging black dress and large gold hoops at her ears, stared incredulously at him.

"Let me run back over this to see if I've understood you," she said. "Basically, you suggest that because of civil war, King Aldfrith's tomb could not be transported to its destination at St Mary's in Little Driffield, right? So it was buried presumably temporarily – which turned out to be permanently – in unconsecrated ground. As a result, the king's spirit has remained troubled along with those of the men who succoured him at Elfrid's Hole. But isn't that a bit fanciful, Jake?"

"Not if you consider all the apparitions over the centuries, causing even prominent and well-esteemed people to risk their reputations by testifying to the presence of ghosts there. That brings me to my solution, Heather, and this is where you come in. You surely remember the finding of the remains of King Richard III in Leicester in 2012?"

"Of course, it was a national event. Wasn't he reburied in Leicester Cathedral three years later?"

"Yes. Now listen, Heather. That was in keeping with British legal norms, which hold that Christian burials excavated by archaeologists should be reburied in the nearest consecrated ground to the original grave. See where I'm heading with this? By rights, King Aldfrith should be buried where he was meant to be all along, in St Mary's, Little Driffield. I measured it on a map; it just beats All Saints at Driffield, though not by much. I don't expect there'll be any objection from the Queen. She was consulted over Richard and refused any involvement of the royal family."

"So, where do I come in, Jake?"

"I need you to convince Professor Whitehead that when they've finished with Aldfrith in Bradford, he should arrange for a ceremonial re-interment, similar to King Richard's, but in Little Driffield. Do you think you can do that? Obviously, it may take a year or two to finish all the archaeological examinations. You'll know more about that than me. But I'm convinced the interment in consecrated ground will bring an end to the troubles at Elfrid's Hole."

She smiled at him, raised her glass of red wine, and said, "You're an odd bird, Jake Conley, full of weird ideas and theories, but you grow on a girl. I'll do my best with James, but I doubt he'll swallow all your theory. He should go along with the legal norms. I don't think he'll want to court controversy similar to York's challenge to Leicester over Richard III."

"Did I ever tell you I've been diagnosed as a synesthete...?"

This statement led to a long explanation and to Jake finally pointing to the window seat, where two young women were engaged in close conversation.

"...and he was sitting right there, axe in hand, a skull-like face, and I ran for dear life out into the countryside until I came to the battle-field and saw the conflict that took place in 705–"

"Wait! You actually *saw* the battle taking place? Can synaes-thesia really achieve that?"

"I'm telling you, Heather, I even saw Aldfrith wounded by an arrow."

"We'll be working on his cause of death, by the way, but there's one thing I'm not clear on. If you were in the middle of a battlefield, how come you weren't hurt?"

"I've thought about that a lot. My guess is that all those warriors, dead now for centuries, have found eternal rest or eternal torment, whatever you believe in. The only one that could hurt me was the ghost, probably possessed by a demon."

"If I didn't know you better, Jake, I'd ring for a couple of psychi-atric nurses with a straitjacket and a syringe. Hey, if you look at me like that, I might do it anyway!"

"I know it's a lot to take in, Heather, and it overturns all our assumptions about time, the afterlife and everything. But believe me, no one wants to put an end to the horror of Elfrid's Hole more than I do."

"Well, Jake, synesthete, or whatever, you're a very privileged person. Can you imagine what an archaeologist would give to stand in the middle of an eighth-century battle as an unharmed observer?"

"It really should be enough that I've provided you with the tomb of King Aldfrith. Ungrateful wench! You'll be famous now."

"*Wench!* Watch your step, or I'll rearrange that pretty nose."

"Pretty, is it? Does this mean we're an item, Heather?"

Nothing ventured, nothing gained!

She smiled at him.

"Why do I get the idea you're nothing but trouble, Jake Conley? Lucky for you, I'm an adventurous sort."

"Is that a yes, then?"

She raised her glass and smiled enigmatically. "You're the synesthete, you should know!"

He leant across the table, and they shared their first kiss.

TWENTY-FIVE

EBBERSTON AND PICKERING, NORTH YORKSHIRE

THE NEXT MORNING, FEELING LIKE A MAN WHO'S JUST WON THE prize of an Aston Martin in a lottery – such can be the power of a first kiss with the right woman – Jake strode out of the gate of his lodgings, intent on quite a different interaction. Assuring himself that there were no lurking hoodlums, he hastened to the church at Thornton-le-Dale. Twice he stopped to admire an attractive floral display among the gardens. One in particular appealed to him where the house-holder had concentrated all her efforts on blue flowers of many different kinds; it was very eye-catching.

At the church, he entered the number of the churchwarden, which he hadn't memorised on his previous visit, and made an appointment to meet in front of the house of worship. Jake decided not to take any chances and explored the graveyard. He was in search of a vantage point from where he could see up and down the lane leading to the building. He couldn't afford the risk of Mr Hibbitt bringing his band of bully boys. If he saw anyone approaching with the churchwarden, he would hide. As he walked through the head-stones, one in particular caught his eye. It was dedicated to a long-lived soldier and bore the legend that this infantryman had been a guard over Napoleon Bonaparte on St Helena and one of the bearers accompanying that emperor to his grave. Jake gasped at the good fortune of having stumbled across such a monument to a man involved in an event of international history. He took a photo to show to Heather.

He saw a grove of trees near the boundary fence, which over-looked the raised pavement, itself overlooking the road. Here was ideal cover from which he could espy anyone coming towards the church. He didn't have long to wait before the figure of the church-warden appeared, marching at a pace that did credit to his advancing years. Jake wondered why someone who could stride out in military style was so portly. Perhaps he had other vices apart from organising the beating of innocent visitors. He didn't dwell on worthless suppo-sition but hastened to the church door so that he'd be found in a more natural place.

Mr Hibbitt surveyed him with apparent dislike.

"I thought I'd been clear about you staying away from Ebber-ston." His tone was hostile.

"I won't be bossed around by anyone like you."

"Don't say you haven't been warned."

"Lucky for you, I'm a pacifist, else I'd take great delight in dealing you a bloody nose. Whilst we're on the subject of warnings, I wouldn't repeat your bully boy tactics. You should know that the press will be very excited about my discovery of King Aldfrith's tomb in Driffield. Anything to do with Jake Conley in the coming days and weeks will be national news, Mr Hibbitt. How will that look for your precious Ebberston if I'm beaten up here for the second time? No, sir, you'd do well to steer clear of me unless you enjoy being hounded by tabloid journalists."

With great pleasure, Jake watched the fellow's face pass through a range of unpleasant emotions, ending with a look of resignation.

"Why should I believe that you've found Aldfrith's tomb?"

The sneer was as unpleasant as the rest of the personage. Jake could hardly believe that he'd found the man friendly and benign on their first encounter. He quickly tapped a few images on his mobile, and a series of pings came from the churchwarden's smartphone.

"I've sent you some photos. Take your time and ask me any questions you have."

With glee, he watched the amazement grow on the visage of the lay church representative, who pointed to a photo of the crane setting the tomb on the truck.

"Where is the sarcophagus now?"

"In the Archaeology Department of Bradford University for scientific study."

"And *you* claim to have found it?"

"I *did* find it, as you'll discover soon enough from the morning papers. For the moment, the whole business is being kept under wraps to prevent sightseers and the curious from overwhelming the site. If you'd be kind enough to keep this between us, I'd appreciate it. You see, Mr Hibbitt, I've decided to trust you and appeal to your better nature."

The churchwarden stared hard at Jake and at last allowed himself something approaching a smile, more a twist of the side of the mouth. "How do you know the sarcophagus was Aldfrith's?"

"I've sent a picture of the inscription on the side if you scroll through the images. It's in Old English, but his name is quite legible."

"Good Lord, you're right! Maybe I misjudged you, Mr Conley."

"I think *underestimated* is the better word, Mr Hibbitt."

At this point, Jake made a mistake he was to regret later. He continued, "I believe this discovery might help to put an end to the woeful occurrences at Elfrid's Hole. When the king is re-interred in consecrated ground–"

"You mean you want to bury him here, in our church?"

"No question of that, I'm afraid. There's the law that states he must go into the nearest church to the point of exhumation, which would be St Mary's at Little Driffield. A pity, really; there's something appropriate about here, where he was mortally wounded.

Anyway, I'm thinking of bringing to an end the horrors of Elfrid's Hole before the re-interment of Aldfrith."

"What do you mean?"

"At my request, the police are organising a Catholic exorcist to perform the ritual up there."

"Over my dead body! A Catholic here, in our parish. I'll put a stop to that!"

"Don't be ridiculous, Hibbitt. King Aldfrith himself was a Catholic, was he not? And a far more learned one than either you or I."

"I don't give two hoots! I'm not having it, and as for you, meddler, do us all a favour and get out of Ebberston once and for all. I don't care about your warnings." He had regained his former snarling aggression. "Just get lost!"

With that, he spun round and headed out of the churchyard. Jake watched him go and began to worry. Had he said too much? Would he regret confiding in this confrontational, self-important individual?

Back at his lodgings, he shed his trainers, parked them neatly beside his boots, and slid his feet into his tartan slippers. In his room, he lay on his bed and considered what to do next. His idea to come back to Ebberston was largely through a desire to see an end to the malign presences in Elfrid's Hole, and inasmuch he had told Hibbitt the truth. The problem was that he didn't know when the exorcist would come to Ebberston, but he would like to be there when he conducted the ritual. If for no other reason, he wished to ensure the efficacy of the exorcism. He wrestled with the problem for some time before drifting off to sleep. When he awoke, he shivered because he had lain uncovered for six hours, exposed to the cold draught from the window he had forgotten to close. He rose and pulled back the curtain to shut the window and saw to his amazement that it was night-time. He should not have been surprised, of course; the bedside alarm clock confirmed it was 04.08.

He slipped into bed, dressed as he was, and lay soaking up the warmth, thinking once more what to do in Ebberston. As is often the case, clearer thinking comes to a brain refreshed by sleep. It occurred to him to pay a visit to his nemesis, Detective Inspector Shaw. The detective would know when the priest was due to come to Ebberston, always assuming that the cynical policeman hadn't changed his mind. It was worth going to Pickering if only to find out about the arrival of the exorcist. At the same time, he would inform Shaw of the church-warden's threat. That could do no harm and would put the police on their guard for the safety of the priest. Hibbitt had obviously never heard of *ecumenical detente*: he probably didn't know the meaning of either word. Jake smiled grimly under his blanket. Satisfied with his plan, he again fell asleep.

The next morning in Pickering, D.I. Shaw called Jake sharply into his office and that made him suspicious. In fact, the detective greeted him with, "Ah, Conley, come to make a confession, have you?"

"I keep telling you I haven't done anything!" he replied. "I've come to ask whether you've called in an exorcist."

"I'm expecting a call. Father Anthony put me in touch with a Father Sante. He's of Italian extraction, apparently, a Jesuit. He's coming tomorrow morning. It should be interesting." The policeman looked hard at Jake and with a sneer, added, "He should be your cup of tea, Conley, he had the gall to lecture me about the devil being real and not just an abstract concept, but here among us!" He pointed an accusatory finger at Jake as he said this.

"He's right, of course; demons have possessed the ghosts of Anglo-Saxon warriors at Elfrid's Hole, and they're capable of all kinds of evil. The sooner Father Sante casts them out, the sooner we can all live in peace."

"Just listen to the nonsense you spout, Conley!" The detective had grown red in the face. "Well, you don't fool me. You're using this mumbo-jumbo to cover your crimes, but I can see through you."

"Detective, I think you should concentrate on real wrongdoers, like the churchwarden at Ebberston."

Shaw sat back in his leather swivel chair. "What are you talking about?"

"He threatened me again, but more specifically, he said he would never allow a Catholic priest in his parish."

"So, you've been stirring up trouble again in Ebberston. You are bad news, Mr Conley."

"I think you are obsessed with me, Inspector. Maybe you should ensure Father Sante has extra protection."

"Sir, I think you had better leave now and let me concentrate on my job. There are criminals at large who need to be apprehended." He glared at Jake. "Good day to you."

Jake left the police station dejected but consoled himself that the Jesuit priest was coming the next day and that he would be present to watch. He glanced down at his feet. The lace on his trainer had become untied. He bent down to fasten it in a tight bow. The significance of this simple gesture did not cross his mind.

TWENTY-SIX

EBBERSTON, NORTH YORKSHIRE

While Jake was engaged in his unpleasant conversation with D.I. Shaw, churchwarden Hibbitt had paid a visit to his lodgings.

"So, you see, Mrs Lucas, not only is he suspected of murdering his fiancée, but he's also planning on bringing a Catholic priest here to exorcise our grotto. I have to put a stop to this. We can't have papists sticking their noses into our parish affairs."

"But Mr Hibbitt, Jake seems such a nice person."

"Dear lady, it's your own pious character that sees only good in people. There's been nothing but trouble since Conley came here."

"But he told me he wants to put an end to it."

The churchwarden could see that no good could be obtained by losing patience with the widow. She was a fellow member of the parish council, and he'd appeal to her in that way.

"Mrs Lucas, my dear, this is our parish, and we must all work together to sort out our own affairs. Left in peace, Elfrid's hole is no bother. Just occasionally something *inconvenient* happens there. But it's only since Conley began stirring things up that the situation has got out of hand. Please trust me, I have a plan to restore peace and quiet to our village."

"Oh, yes, that would be lovely. How can I help?"

"First of all, nobody, especially the police, must know I've been here with you today."

"Oh, I don't know if I can lie to the police, Mr Hibbitt."

"But you must, Mrs Lucas, don't you see? Conley is manipulating the police. We must thwart him even if it means breaking the principles of a lifetime." He took her hand and looked her in the eye, smiling benignly. "I'm afraid I have to do the same. It's for the best, believe me."

"Oh, well, in that case..."

"Good. Now the second thing is, I have to take one of Conley's boots. If he notices it missing, play-act a bit, I know you can, you made a *wonderful* Emilia in Othello. Plead surprise and ignorance. I'll get it back when the moment is right."

"Oh, did you really like my acting, Mr Hibbitt? I thought you made a splendid Iago, by the way."

"Even if I had to act quite out of character, Mrs Lucas. Now, that Conley fellow, *he'd* make a natural Iago."

"Consider it done then, Mr Hibbitt. Oh dear, what a state of affairs!"

"Now don't you fret, my dear. You know it's for the good of the parish, and I'll look out for you."

He left the house some minutes later carrying a plastic bag containing Jake's right boot. He dropped it off at his home before inveigling Mrs Holmes, another member of the parish council, with the same reasoning he'd used on the Lucas woman to give false testimony to the police. She agreed, like the widow, only after much scrupulous soul-searching, but Hibbitt got his own way and continued to plot his conspiracy.

Jake came back to his lodgings in the afternoon, distracted, head full of thoughts. He didn't notice the missing boot and simply placed his trainers in line with all the other shoes. In his room, he sat on the bed and phoned Heather.

She was excited.

"Jake, we've had the results of carbon dating for the contents of the tomb. The bones, like other materials, returned a date of 700 AD plus or minus forty years. That's further confirmation, if it were needed, that our remains are those of Aldfrith. The coins, as I supposed, are from his reign. They are silver sceattas bearing the name *Aldfridus* on the obverse. You know, Jake," she could barely contain her enthusiasm, "they are the earliest coins in the land to proclaim they are royal, and until now they were quite rare. There's a horse-like creature with a triple-forked tail on the other side of the coins. They're all in excellent condition, fellow-me-lad, as James would say."

"How is he?"

"Tickled pink, as you'd imagine – he'd say that, too! Jake, when are you coming over to Driffield? I miss you."

"I miss you, too. Dunno, I've some unfinished business here in Ebberston."

"The other evening was wonderful. Thank you. Remember, we've got unfinished business, too, Jake."

His heart beat faster; surely, he wasn't reading too much into her words?

"As soon as I can, I promise."

He asked a few general questions about the continuing excavations and learned that the isolated base of a Roman column had come to light, but while she expected further Roman artefacts, nothing more of an Anglo-Saxon nature had emerged, which seemed strange to both of them.

It wasn't until the next morning when he needed his boots to go up to the grotto that Jake noticed one missing. He grilled Mrs Lucas, who denied all knowledge of the missing item. Jake stared at her unbelievingly – a boot can't just disappear.

"What about visitors, Mrs Lucas? Did anyone call when I was in Pickering?"

A consummate actress, his landlady said, "Not even the postman came yesterday, Jake. Oh dear, I really can't think what's happened to it. I imagine it'll turn up."

"On its own little legs, you mean?"

He stared at her intensely, but she didn't betray any emotion other than bewilderment. It took him in. The mystery of the missing boot remained. There was nothing for it; he would have to wear his trainers to go up to the grotto. He'd have to be careful not to turn an ankle. That was all there was to it.

"I'm going up to Elfrid's Hole, Mrs Lucas."

What emotion did her expression betray?

"Is that a good idea, Mr Conley? Those shoes aren't suitable, and that place is getting a nasty reputation."

"Don't worry, we'll soon have it sorted," Jake said with confidence, "and I'll tread carefully."

"Yes, that'd be as well."

There was something decidedly odd in her tone, but Jake thought no more of it and set off somewhat unsettled from his lodgings. Mrs Lucas, as instructed, phoned Mr Hibbitt with that information.

It had rained during the night, so the trail up to the grotto, although largely stony, also had places where mud and puddles prevailed. Jake did his best to avoid stepping into any of these, so he kept a close eye on the ground before him. That was how he saw a crisp £10 note, one of the new plastic ones, lying in the mud. Never one to walk away from such an opportunity, he stooped to pick it up. As his fingers closed over it, the world seemed to explode inside his head in a sheet of yellow flame. He just had time to realise someone had struck him. The flame faded to purple, and then to black. Jake pitched forward on his face and lay still.

When he opened his eyes, he saw daylight filtering through slats in a ramshackle wall. He had been placed with his back against such a wall, and the floor was simply beaten earth, dusty and scattered with plant pots and the occasional implement. Clearly, a shack for an allotment or suchlike. For a while he lay still, trying to remember what had happened. The banknote was obviously part of a trap to make it easy for someone to put him out of action. But why? And why wasn't he bound and gagged? Clearly his permanence here was of no importance to his assailant. Whoever had hit him simply didn't want to leave him on the open track for some reason. With an effort, he tried to stand, only to bury his face in his hands, as if they might steady the throbbing in his head. As full consciousness returned, he looked about him again, seized a hoe, and used it as a walking stick to lean on as he struggled to his feet. His head ached, and he touched his scalp at the crown of his head. His fingers came away wet and sticky. He needed to bathe the wound as soon as possible. The door was locked on the outside when he tried it, but Jake knew it would not resist a determined blow. The pity was, he didn't have his heavy boots, and he didn't fancy kicking with his trainers.

Once more, his eyes settled on the hoe. He wedged it between the doorframe and the flimsy wooden door. Putting as much weight as he could muster against the beech handle of the tool, despite causing his head to thump worse, he heaved, hoping the handle wouldn't break. Instead, with a splintering crack, the door swung precariously open, looking as unsteady on its hinges as Jake was on his feet. He saw that his supposition of a padlock had been correct, and the splintering had been where the lock gave way.

A glance showed him that the shed was standing near a dry stone wall beyond which the track ran to the grotto. With calculated slowness, Jake climbed over the wall. His every strenuous movement was accompanied by silvery flashes behind his eyes. He decided therefore not to overexert himself under the circumstances and to head back downhill at snail's pace. The sooner he reached The Elms and could bathe his head, the better.

Letting himself into the bed and breakfast, he didn't notice that his missing boot, somewhat muddied, had returned. The oversight was understandable given the explosion in his head when he bent to untie the laces of his trainers. He still didn't notice when he placed them beside the boots and put on the slippers. His main priority was clean water to rinse his wound, after which he'd ask Mrs Lucas for some aspirins.

She fussed over him and insisted on disinfecting the wound with antiseptic, which stung and caused him to breathe out through clenched teeth. She pressed to know what happened, and when he told her, she offered to call the police. Whether he should have accepted troubled him only in hindsight, but he refused. Yet the police arrived of their own accord to arrest him.

They also seized Jake's boots, which were a pair, he noted with surprise. Once again, they drove him to the Pickering police station and began the interrogation only when Kate Mack arrived. She wanted to know what her client was charged with this time.

"Assault on two police officers and a Catholic priest, occasioning grievous bodily harm."

"It's a lie!" Jake blurted. "I was the one who was assaulted. Take a look for yourselves." He bent his head forward and pointed to the general area of the wound under is thick hair.

"So why didn't you report this so-called assault?" D.I. Shaw's tone was sceptical.

"Because I'd only just struggled back to my lodgings, and Mrs Lucas washed and medicated it. There wasn't time before the police car arrived, you can ask my landlady."

"Oh, we will, no doubt about that."

Shaw reached for his phone and made a call.

"A quick inspection of a superficial head wound for you, doctor. Yes, now! It's urgent. Yes. In the interview room."

Moments later, a doctor in a white laboratory coat pulled on latex gloves and inspected Jake's wound. He grunted and said, "That must have given you quite a headache, young man."

"It did, doctor. I was worried that they might have fractured my skull."

The doctor resumed his poking around, and Jake winced.

"Nothing broken, but you have some serious contusions around the cut, which I presume has been well cleaned."

"My landlady used antiseptic on it."

The inspector cut in, "What caused the blow, doctor? Could it have been self-inflicted?"

"In that exact spot? I'd say self-inflicted was impossible."

Shaw looked disappointed. "Would a blow like that be hard enough to cause the victim to lose consciousness?"

"Absolutely. It was delivered with great force using a blunt instrument, like a baseball bat or similar. The assailant was right-handed and, you'd assume by the force used, tall and male."

"I see." The detective looked anything but discouraged. "Thank you, doctor. That's all for now."

Jake looked at the satisfied expression on the inspector's face and said, "Do you mind telling me if this is about the exorcism at Elfrid's Hole? Did it take place? Was it successful?"

"You tell me, Conley. After all, you were there, I wasn't. And by the way, you don't fool me. That blow to the head came after your crimes. All it means is you had an accomplice who carried out your orders to strike the blow. But you made a couple of mistakes, slippery as you are. Criminals always do."

"I don't know what you're talking about, as usual. Perhaps you can enlighten me?"

"Willingly. Allow me to recreate the scene for you. Father Sante, with his religious stuff, enters the cave. You lurk among the trees, realising that the moment isn't right to strike because the priest is protected by two male and one female officer."

"Just a minute," Jake interrupted. "Why exactly would I want to strike the priest? If you remember, officer, I was the one who wanted him to come and perform the ritual."

"You'll have a chance to explain that in court, Conley. Most of what you do would baffle the keenest criminologist. It's enough that we've got proof against you this time."

"Amazing, since I was never there."

"Oh, but you were, and this time, we have incontrovertible proof."

Jake had a terrible sinking feeling.

Of course, the missing boot.

"Allow me to proceed with the reconstruction. From the cavern comes an infernal screeching and wailing. WPC Reardon loses her nerve and flees down the track, seen by two witnesses as she rushes past them. From among the trees, you realise this is your chance, and you strike the nearest officer a mighty blow that brings him down. The other policeman, horrified and distracted by the hellish noises from the cave and concerned for the Jesuit, hurries over, stealthily followed by you. You repeat the deed, felling the constable. It's my guess, Conley, that the unfortunate priest simply chose the wrong moment to emerge from the obscurity of the grotto. You, not wanting to be identified subsequently nor wishing to harm a man you'd been instrumental in bringing here, delivered a similar but less violent blow to the poor fellow."

"I can't have done any of this because I was lying unconscious in a dilapidated shack farther down the track."

"Don't try my patience, Conley, we have you this time. There are two witnesses who testify to seeing you run away from the crime scene, your T-shirt bloodied – I see it is – and there's the little matter of your boot prints in the mud tying you to the scene of where each officer fell. Our laboratory has already confirmed the precise match of the sole pattern, and now they are analysing the soil samples."

"Can't you see I've been set up? They framed me. I warned you two days ago that this might happen."

"The plea of a desperate man when he knows the game's up. Except that your own fall-guy, and I mean the churchwarden, has a rock-solid alibi for the time of the crime."

"Of course, he would have. He's had days to plan this. I have myself to blame for telling him an exorcist was coming."

"Right, Ms Mack, take note. I'm now going to formally charge your client for today's crimes, and I don't exclude adding further charges for previous misdemeanours at a future date."

The inspector proceeded to fulfil the statutory requirement and when he'd finished magnanimously offered the lawyer time alone with her client. He felt secure with the evidence he'd gathered that he'd finally entrapped Conley.

Kate Mack accepted and, once alone, asked Jake to relate the day's events. He began with his conversation of the previous day with Hibbitt and the churchwarden's threats, proceeding to the missing boot and added the relevant detail that only one boot was soiled. He then told her about the banknote and the blow sustained to his head and his movements after he'd regained consciousness.

"It's looking bleak, Jake, I have to tell you, but not impossible. I'm off to do some police work of my own.

TWENTY-SEVEN

PICKERING AND EBBERSTON, NORTH YORKSHIRE

KATE RELIEVED JAKE OF HIS T-SHIRT, ADMIRING HIS TONED pectorals, meaning he now had to pull on his denim bomber jacket for indoor wear. He looked cute, she thought, and felt a pang of jealousy for Heather's relationship. She then mentally rebuked herself, remembering her professional dignity. For purely investigative purposes, so she told herself, she snapped a portrait photo of her client before hurrying to the police laboratory with more serious matters on her mind.

She met the police doctor, an old acquaintance through being a friend of her father's, with a familiar greeting and a smile.

"Good morning, Bryan, it's about the attacks at the grotto. I'd like you to analyse the blood on this T-shirt. My client, Jake Conley, maintains that it is his. I say Inspector Shaw needs to prove otherwise; I believe my client's word. Can you do it?

"Easily done, but we'll have to take a pinprick of blood from Mr Conley to compare the results."

"There should be no problem with that – oh, by the way, there's another thing–"

"There always is with you, Kate." Doctor Blanch chortled.

"There's something very strange about those boots you're working on."

"I'd noticed myself."

"Are you thinking what I'm thinking?"

"You are referring to one clean and one dirty boot, I presume."

"Well, I believe it has great bearing on the case against my client who tells me *one* of his boots went missing."

The doctor whistled between his teeth.

"And you think someone's trying to frame him. It doesn't exclude the possibility of him cleaning one boot himself, of course, if he's a cunning individual."

"True, but I assure you, my client is a model citizen."

"Aren't all your clients saints, Kate?"

"Humph!"

"Don't worry, I'll be sure to put this anomaly in my report, so that you can play upon it in your lawyerly way."

"Thanks Bryan. Love to Agnes, is she well?"

"Breathing fire and brimstone as usual, so she must be."

Her business at the laboratory concluded, Kate drove to Ebberston to try to solve the mystery of the missing boot. Mrs Lucas showed her into the guests' lounge. Kate hesitated in the hall and glanced meaningfully at the row of footwear. "Shouldn't I kick off my shoes, Mrs Lucas?"

"Oh, that's all right, my dear, come on in. It's different with my guests. I insist with them. You know, many go rambling and return with muddy boots."

"Of course, quite right," Kate said soothingly, "which brings me to the purpose of my visit." She outlined the police case against Jake and how it hinged on the missing boot.

"What really happened to that boot? It couldn't just disappear for a day, could it? Are you holding something back, maybe protecting someone, Mrs Lucas? You know that Jake could go to prison for many years for something he didn't do, don't you?"

The lawyer studied the widow's face, especially the eyes, and what she saw there confirmed her hunch: the woman was evasive.

"Oh my, Mr Conley's a lovely man. I wouldn't like anything like that to happen to him."

"So tell me what really happened to the boot, Mrs Lucas."

"I have no idea. I-it vanished and reappeared the next day."

Her eyes were shifty, and Kate didn't believe her. Nonetheless, she said, "Of course, I believe you, Mrs Lucas, a lady of spotless character like yourself." Her sweet tone, without a hint of sarcasm, brought a brave smile from the woman. Kate handed over her card. "If anything comes to mind that might help my client, Mrs Lucas, please give me a call. Lovely house you keep here, by the way. I'd better be on my way, I've a lot to do."

As she walked along the garden path Kate pursed her lips. She hadn't finished with the old cat, by no means. That she had lied, the lawyer had no doubt. Sitting in her car, she moved on to plan B. She rang Heather, and a rapid run-through of her plan soon convinced the archaeologist.

"Are you clear on this Heather? Use the excuse of collecting Jake's things, pay his bill, and I'll reimburse you, naturally. And lay it on thick, remember."

Two hours later, Mrs Lucas answered the doorbell and stared into the pretty face of the archaeologist.

"Good morning, madam, I'm Jake Conley's fiancée, and I've come to collect his belongings and settle his bill."

"Oh, how very nice to meet you, my dear. My word, what a lovely couple you make."

If Mrs Lucas was a good actress, Heather was a better one. Somehow, she made her eyes fill with tears.

"A-all this," she stammered and sniffed, allowing a tear to roll down her cheek, "is going to ruin our *wedding plans*." She wailed the last two words.

"Oh, my dear, come through here and sit down. I'll make a nice cup of tea." This was just what Heather had hoped for, the chance for an extended conversation. When the landlady returned with her laden tray, Heather snivelled in a low voice, "We were going to get married in Beverley Minster on July 25. It's a Thursday, it's always been my lucky day. Whenever I had an exam on a Thursday, I always passed with flying colours. But now it's all in ruins." She wiped an eye with a hand-kerchief. "Something's so wrong, Mrs Lucas, Jake's a lovely person! He would never do those horrid things they've accused him of!"

She watched the woman's reaction. Was it guilt? That was definitely a furtive expression, and she wouldn't meet Heather's eye. So she went in, all guns blazing.

"Did you know my Jake's something of a hero?" She gave free rein to her imagination. "In York a couple of months ago, he ran into a mugging. Two youths snatched and made off with a Chinese tourist's handbag containing all her holiday money and her iPhone – that alone was worth hundreds of pounds. So what did Jake do? Without a thought, he dived in a rugby tackle and took the one with the bag down. Of course, he had to fight both of them off to secure the hand-bag, and he got a black eye and a split lip for his trouble, but he drove them away and restored the bag to the girl. Not bad for a pacifist, wouldn't you say?"

"I don't know what the world's coming to. It never used to be like this when I was a girl. It must be all these horrible drugs. But thank goodness there are people like Jake to stick up for the defenceless."

"I just hope the truth comes out and that we can go ahead with our weddi–" Here, Heather deliberately choked the word and wept to the dismay of her hostess, who tried to comfort her, even crossing the room to hold her in a tight embrace. In truth, the person who needed comforting was Mrs Lucas, who was feeling self-disgust, and her honesty reduced to something like the smallest doll in a nest of Russian Matryoshka dolls.

Thanks to Heather's convincing performance, the widow was feeling shaken and ashamed when she said goodbye to her visitor, the latter burdened with Jake's rucksack and a carrier bag of his possessions. It was therefore the ideal time for Kate to rejoin the fray. She had been sitting, waiting in her car, parked a little farther down the road.

She rang the doorbell and noticed at once that the widow had been crying, by her red-rimmed eyes.

"Is everything all right, Mrs Lucas?"

Without a word, the woman shook her head and held the door open for Kate to enter.

"It's the matter of the boot, isn't it?" Kate launched straight in.

Again, no reply except for a nod of the head.

"That's why I came back. I felt something was amiss, and as a lawyer, I couldn't let you walk into trouble."

"Trouble?"

"Of course, Mrs Lucas. As things stand, you'll be called to testify in the High Court – and you're a religious person, I know – you'll have to swear to tell the truth on the Holy Bible. If you continue with this lie, you'll perjure yourself, you know. It's a very serious offence that carries a prison sentence."

"Oh, my goodness!" Her eyes filled with tears and she mumbled something incoherent.

"Come. Sit down and tell me all about it. We can work it out together. There's always a solution."

The landlady recounted her tale starting from the churchwarden's visit and underlining her well-meaning intentions as far as the parish was concerned but dissociating herself from any knowledge or approval of the violence used.

"You must tell all this to Inspector Shaw, Mrs Lucas. Don't worry, a clean confession means there'll be no consequences for you."

"But what about Mr Hibbitt? It'll get him into trouble, won't it?"

"I should hope so, Mrs Lucas. He's hurt four people and tried to send a good man to prison. We can't let him get away with that, can we?"

"No. Will you ring the police for me, miss?"

"Of course."

Kate had wanted to pass the landlady the phone, but the incredulous police officer told her to wait because he wanted to see the situation for himself.

"It's my duty to ensure that undue coercion hasn't been brought on the witness."

"Not by me, it hasn't."

"We should be there in half an hour, Ms Mack."

Detective Inspector Shaw drove away from The Elms with the woman's statement ringing in his ears and transcribed word for word in his notebook. He was seething, having read the forensic report on Conley's boots and bloodied T-shirt; the three things together corroborated the suspect's statement and pointed to his innocence. Also, he now had to drive to the churchwarden's house and interview the man who had supplanted Conley as suspect number one. Was it possible that his instinct about Conley had been wrong? He still believed he'd killed his fiancée, and it would take a good deal to shake that suspicion.

Next on Kate's agenda was a visit to the hospital to further strengthen her case for Jake's release. All three victims were sitting up in bed, and it was reassuring to learn that none had suffered serious consequences from the hefty blows they'd received. A doctor told her that it was standard precaution to keep them under observation for another day as concussion had, he said, a *vexing habit* of delaying its reaction.

She visited the exorcist first, out of curiosity, never having met one, whereas for her working with the police was routine. The elderly Jesuit, bespectacled and white-haired, seemed pleased to have company. He took her hand and recommended that she entrust herself to the Lord because he could sense the goodness in her.

"What about this man, Father?" She showed him the photo of Jake.

"Is it your boyfriend, miss?" The priest smiled and looked at Kate enquiringly.

"No, Father, he's my client. The police say he's the man who struck you."

"I shouldn't have thought so," said the cleric. "There's no wickedness in that face."

"I already have some proof, in fact, that it wasn't Jake."

"Jake Conley?"

"Yes, do you know him?"

"I don't, but Father Anthony in York told me all about him. He's the reason I came here and just as well. I had to cast out several demons from that cavern. It was a draining experience, believe me." The old priest made the sign of the Cross and took the same hand to his lips. He thought for a moment.

"You are his lawyer, then. I wish I'd seen who'd hit me, but in all honesty, it could have been anyone. I was coming out of the cave, and the light was blinding. So I'm afraid I can't help you, miss."

She left him and showed the photo to the policemen, but neither claimed to have seen Jake at Elfrid's Hole. This simple exclusion helped her case, but she blamed herself for forgetting to ask D.I. Shaw about Hibbitt's alibi. It was something she needed to discover.

TWENTY-EIGHT

EBBERSTON, NORTH YORKSHIRE

KATE MACK, SMARTING FROM THE SHORT SHRIFT GIVEN HER BY Detective Inspector Shaw, and she, being a young woman of strong character, decided to ignore his warnings and veiled threats to pursue her own inquiries. Her interpretation of his attitude was he was hiding behind formalities to delay her involvement in the case. With these words, the officious detective had treated her like a schoolgirl:

"I'm not obliged to reveal that information, Ms Mack. There are many types of police records we do not have to disclose. There are two main reasons why they aren't publicly available. First, divulging the information you seek could undermine our ongoing investigation. Second, it could jeopardize the witnesses' privacy and safety, not to mention your own." And here he had sneered. "We'll divulge certain information related to the report, such as to a reporter doing a story. However, you're a lawyer...in any case, we rarely release a full copy. So good day to you, Ms Mack."

The non-cooperation left her with no alternative; she'd drive over to Ebberston and find out for herself. In search of solidarity, she called Heather and explained the situation.

"I'm coming over to give you a hand just as soon as I clear it with Professor Whitehead."

No number of polite refusals and counterarguments would dissuade the archaeologist. Recognising a spirit as determined as her own, Kate desisted and admitted she'd be glad of the support. The logical thing to do was to drive to Driffield, pick up Heather, and make the trip to Ebberston together. They could hatch a plan in her car. The dark blue Mazda MX-5 was Kate's delight, especially because there weren't many of them around this area. It was just sober enough for a lawyer and ideal for a single professional woman. On a sunny day like this, she loved riding open-topped, feeling the caress of the wind in her hair. Thank goodness she'd opted for an extra-short pixie hairstyle months ago, which flattered her delicate facial features and big grey eyes. She'd taken that decision before buying a convertible, and just as well. She smiled at the thought of the tousled mess her long hair would have become. She thought she'd better warn Heather to tie hers back.

Heather sank back into the leather upholstery with a contented sigh and reflected on her career choice. Would she ever be able to afford such a comfortable and sporty motor? She smiled at her thoughts and ruefully admitted her passion for history would never change. Now she'd met Jake, with similar interests, she'd found another love. What a twist of fate had thrown them together and torn them apart to place her in a car with his lawyer.

"Where do we start, Kate?"

"Well, what have we got? Someone's trying to frame Jake, and that person also struck him and locked him in a shack. Or else, more likely, had an accomplice do it. I think we're looking for a number of people. Nobody could have managed it alone."

"Jake told me he'd been threatened by the churchwarden."

"I know. I suspect he's behind this whole business." Kate glanced in her rear-view mirror and pressed down on the brakes. "Bloody speed traps," she grumbled. "Take all the joy out of driving."

Heather glanced up at the yellow and black roadside box on its pole and grinned. "They discipline hot-headed drivers, so I'm all for them."

Kate rose to the bait.

"Spoken like a true non-driver."

"Getting back to the matter at hand, do we start with the churchwarden?"

Kate frowned and, irritated by a red traffic light for road works, pulled up, blew out her cheeks in frustration, and said, "I prefer driving in the country. These main roads are full of delays." Almost as if their mission were of secondary importance to the issue of driving, she said with an air of distraction, "I hardly think so. It would give him more opportunity to cover his tracks. No, I think we need to find out who his accomplices are most likely to be. We can start with his weak link," she said mysteriously.

"Do you mean Mrs Lucas?"

"Unless you have a better suggestion, Heather."

Heather's brow creased in concentration, broken by g-force jolting her back in her seat as Kate roared away from the green light.

"Don't you think Mrs Lucas will have told Inspector Shaw everything?"

"I know she'll have kept things back from him. He's obviously not making progress in the case, else he'd have released Jake, wouldn't he? We'll have to scare the truth out of her. This is what we'll do..."

Kate realised she would have to hold nothing back from the archaeologist, who might prove to be an invaluable ally. She outlined her intended approach as they neared the turn for Ebberston and had finished when she parked opposite The Elms.

The pleasant greeting the landlady afforded them could not veil the anxiety and shiftiness in her eyes. The two investigators were in no hurry to put her on the defensive, so they stuck to the plan.

"How are you, Mrs Lucas?" Kate smiled sweetly. "We were in the area and thought we'd call round to make sure you were in the best of spirits."

"Why shouldn't I be, young lady?"

"With two police officers and a priest in hospital, it's a serious business, and there are people with a great deal to gain by perverting the course of the investigation. I'll be honest with you, Mrs Lucas, I think you may be in danger, and our main concern is for your safety."

Heather gave the frightened woman her most reassuring smile.

"Oh, Mrs Lucas, we wouldn't want anything to happen to you. My fiancée is still locked up." She feigned an anguished expression. "Which means that the guilty party is scot-free and will want to keep things that way at all costs. We wanted to make sure nobody had threatened you; in that case, Kate can help you."

The furtive look in the landlady's eyes, although fleeting, when Heather had mentioned threats, escaped neither of the young women.

Kate pressed home their advantage.

"Don't be taken in by appearances, dear lady; the man who threatened you is dangerous and will stop at nothing to keep you quiet."

"I-I don't know what you're talking about."

"Don't upset yourself, Mrs Lucas. You can trust us," Heather said. "We want to keep you safe. Tell us what you didn't tell the inspector, and Kate will know what to do in your best interests."

The silent battle with uncertainty showed on the elderly woman's face.

"When this case comes to court, which it must in the end," Kate used her strongest argument, "the more you have cooperated in doing the right thing, the safer you are from prosecution."

"Oh, my goodness! What is the world coming to? Ebberston used to be such a peaceful place, and we were all friends, what a state of affairs!"

"Right! We obviously haven't got through to you," Kate said, "so we'll bid you good day."

This left Heather open-mouthed, and as Kate intended, the archaeologist hesitated to try and comfort the distressed woman, whose unconvincing excuses she ignored. It gave Kate, who'd noticed the parish newsletter lying by the phone in the hall, the precious seconds she needed to slip it into her shoulder bag.

"That was a complete waste of time," Heather complained.

"Not at all." Kate whipped out the newsletter with a flourish and a triumphant grin. "This is invaluable. It will have all the names of the people involved in the parish."

Heather pondered the significance of this. "You're thinking it might be a conspiracy, aren't you?"

"It has to be. Hibbitt can't have acted alone. Let's see what the newsletter has to offer." She flicked through the pages before thrusting a hand into her shoulder bag and repeating the earlier flourish, brandished a yellow highlighter under the archaeologist's nose with a broad grin. "The lawyer's best friend! Now, we're not interested in dog fouling or window locks, not even in worthy causes like the Yorkshire Air Ambulance charity. There are good people doing splendid work, but we have to remove a couple of bad apples from our basket."

Heather laughed and said, "Kate, I would never have thought of you as a light-fingered lawyer."

"All for a good cause, my dear." She highlighted names with frantic determination. "In any case, this newsletter by its very contents gives us an insight into the pride the parish council has in its village. It's there in every line, and while they display an excellent spirit of protecting local values and standards, as well as aiding the needy, it doesn't take much imagination to understand how easily those could be perverted by someone despicable for their own purposes."

"What are you going to do with all those names, Kate?"

"*We* are going to sort apples, my friend. The sooner we start, the quicker we'll track down our false witnesses."

"What then?"

"We squeeze them till the pips squeak!"

Heather sighed and bit her lower lip. Kate's flippancy gave her courage, but it didn't lull her into thinking it would be an easy task.

TWENTY-NINE

PICKERING, NORTH YORKSHIRE

Sick of the supercilious expression of Detective Inspector Shaw, Jake battled to restrain himself. The daily interrogations had reached a new low in his opinion, and this latest offensive suggestion made him lose his composure.

"I don't care what deals you want to strike or what you say." His voice reached a new shrillness. "I didn't kill Liv –" He didn't finish his denial, and a look of abject terror induced Shaw to follow his gaze.

The policeman's eyes widened, his eyebrows shot up, and his mouth fell open. Jake had smelt the same graveyard odour as before and seen the hideous skull-like face with remnants of grey-green decaying flesh and red eyes fixed on them from across the room. In the bony grasp of the creature from Hell glinted a battle-axe.

Seeing the tense white face of the detective, Jake was left in no doubt that he was sharing the same vision. Shaw's seat flew back as he leapt to escape from the nightmare. Jake's foot tangled in his own chair and he tripped, barely keeping his balance as he plunged forward to flee with the policeman, whose raised voice betrayed his panic.

"Quick, all of you! Tasers! Get him!"

Jake spun round at the sound of a great blow and splintering wood. Aghast, he saw the table of the interview room split into two parts to remain standing like a great letter M, each side supporting the other. What a formidable strike must have been delivered to create such devastation! However, he was relieved to see no sign of the demonic warrior.

There was no time to consider their situation, as four policemen were now bearing down upon him brandishing Tasers.

"Not him, you idiots, the Saxon; get the Saxon!"

"Sir?"

The policemen looked around them in puzzlement.

Shaw brushed past them and gazed at the wrecked table and overturned chairs. Apart from the foul stench in the room, there was no trace of the warrior. Alarmed, he had no desire to stay in the room after what he'd seen.

"*You*, come with me!"

Jake followed obediently.

In the safety of his office, Shaw turned on Jake.

"I think you have some explaining to do."

"What? Do you think I pulled some sort of trick on you in there?"

"I don't know how you did it, Conley, but it was impressive."

"Don't you understand that I didn't do anything? That creature is following me because I was involved with Elfrid's Hole. The monster has unfinished business; otherwise it has nothing to do with me. I certainly didn't summon it. I'm just as scared as you are, can't you see that? I've been saying so all along. Why won't you believe the evidence of your own eyes? I don't know what I have to do to make you believe me."

"Are...are you saying that...thing...is real?"

"I don't know what you mean by 'real,' inspector. I'm saying that it *exists* – and that I didn't invent it. I've been saying it all along."

The detective's face passed from incredulous through horrified to an approximation of professional comportment.

"Did you see the force it used to smash your table? That's solid wood, isn't it? Now do you believe me that the monster killed Livie? Oh, my God, it doesn't bear thinking about!" Jake shuddered.

"As of now, all charges against you are dropped, Mr Conley. It seems I owe you an apology. But," the inspector's voice took on a more confidential and friendly tone, "where do you think it...that thing's...gone now? And why did it come here?"

"My guess is it's gone back to Elfrid's Hole. If I were you, inspector, for the time being, I'd close off the area to the public and wouldn't let even your police go near it. I have a theory about how to put an end to its malign activities once and for all."

"Let's hear it, then. I still don't know how we can charge a ghost with murder!"

"You can't."

Jake took the proffered seat and outlined his detailed plan for ridding Ebberston of the ghost.

When he'd finished, the detective looked at him with something akin to admiration – a new experience for Jake.

"Are you saying that it doesn't want to harm you, but wants you to complete this scheme, and it appeared because we'd been talking about it and the cavern?"

"Exactly."

"What about the people in Ebberston who tried to frame you?"

"I don't particularly wish to press charges. But what about your officers, are they badly hurt?"

"They'll survive, but I'll get to the bottom of that, don't worry. At the moment, my main concern is how to tell my superintendent that I've solved Ms Greenwood's murder but can't arrest the culprit. He's not going to like it one bit. I'm sorry to trouble you further, but I'll need a written statement about what happened in the interview room to corroborate my account."

"Of course, no problem." Jake was seeing the inspector in a whole new light.

In less than an hour, task completed, he was on his mobile to Heather.

She answered at once. "I'm with Kate. Yes, Kate, your lawyer. Right!"

"Can you tell her I've been released, and all charges are dropped? Yeah, I know. I'll explain later. I'm in a café just up the road from the police station."

Just time to consume a cup of tea and a toasted teacake when through the café window he noticed a blue sports car pull up across the road. He'd not seen Kate's car before, so he was surprised when he saw her slip out of the driver's seat. Heather emerged from the passenger's side.

Settled across the table from Jake and their order of coffee and cheesecake taken, they exchanged news with the happily relaxed man.

"What do you mean you're not pressing charges, and without consulting me, your lawyer? Take a look at this. Someone placed it under one of my windscreen wipers."

Kate took a piece of paper from her shoulder bag and slid it across the table to Jake. In bold capital letters it read: LAST WARNING. STOP MEDDLING IN EBBERSTON AFFAIRS.

"Have you forgotten that these are the bully boys who beat you up? We're onto something, or they wouldn't have left this."

Jake stared hard at Kate. "We?"

"Yes, Heather and I are investigating, seeing that the police aren't making progress."

"Heather, is that wise?"

"They beat you up and then tried to frame you. I'm with Kate on this." The archaeologist turned her head to smile at her new friend.

"You realise you could be putting yourself in danger, don't you?" But even as he said it, he knew they would not let the matter drop. "I just want to bring this whole matter to an end, and the only way to do it is to do what the Saxons should have done in the eighth century – lay Aldfrith to rest where he wanted to be buried."

"Do you really suppose that will stop the ghost from continuing its violent activities?" Kate asked.

"I'm banking on it."

"Well, I don't know how soon you can carry out your plan, Jake," Heather said. "There's so much yet to be gleaned from the king's remains. I doubt Professor Whitehead will see your scheme as a matter of urgency. Then you'll have to get permission from the Church to inter the king in the chancel of St Mary's."

Jake sucked in his cheeks, stared hard at his girlfriend and pondered. "If the ghost visited James, he'd soon change his mind. It's that I have to communicate to him. There might be a way." He stood and smiled grimly. "See you two ladies later – this is on me." He dropped a banknote on the table, ignored their protests and questions, and walked back to the police station.

This visit was conducted in a completely different atmosphere from his previous ones. The inspector was now a willing and cooperative listener. He stared at the note from under the wiper that Jake had kept and stroked his chin.

"Leave that with me. I see what you mean and I'm in complete agreement that the sooner we can bring an end to *happenings* at Elfrid's Hole, the sooner certain people in Ebberston will return to normality. I'll back you on this. Fancy a ride over to Driffield?"

In the back of the police car, Jake smiled to himself. This was the first time in this situation that his stomach was not in a knot. He was even able to relate the finding of the tomb to the detective in a relaxed conversation and to describe the eccentric archaeologist to him; he felt it wiser to forewarn the policeman about the professor.

There had been considerable progress on the excavation since Jake had left the site under stranger circumstances with the same policeman. Professor Whitehead, wearing a classical tweed suit and his usual bowtie, this time dark green with white spots, greeted him like a long-lost son. He was only too keen to demonstrate the headway they'd made.

"It's essentially a Romano-Celtic site, dear boy, and as you can see, we've exposed the hexagonal shape of the base. These British temples were less grandiose than their classical counterparts. It's their form that gives them away. One of our gals turned up an exquisite figurine of Epona, protectress of horses, ponies and donkeys; she was also a fertility goddess, by the way – not the student, ha-ha! There's enough here to keep us busy right through the summer."

"The sarcophagus of Aldfrith must've been brought into the temple by those who considered it an alternative to a Christian church," Jake mused.

"Or, more likely, the pagan temple had been consecrated, as just such a church."

"I see. That sounds probable, professor. But why didn't the building survive?"

"Good question for historians. A better query might be by what miracle did Aldfrith's tomb remain intact? I'd hazard a guess that most of the temple finished as building material at some point. Might it be that the sarcophagus was deliberately buried to leave it here undisturbed? It's all speculation, of course."

"I'll be honest with you, professor, we're here about Aldfrith's tomb..."

He continued to relate all the events concerning Elfrid's Hole, his arrest, the various apparitions, and the exorcism.

"In the name of all that's holy! Are you telling me that you've both seen a Saxon warrior – a ghost?" the professor spluttered. "Now look here, Jake, I don't believe in ghosts – and I don't expect any sane man would, either."

"That's why I came along, professor." Detective Inspector Shaw assumed his most formidably serious police expression. "It's taken me months to change my opinion on the matter. But I couldn't ignore the evidence of my own eyes. The thing I saw was straight out of a horror film. I doubt I'll sleep tonight."

"Just a minute, inspector, are you telling me that you've *both* actually *seen* this ghost? I'd have expected something more sensible from a man in your position."

"I understand your reaction, sir. It would have been my own

yesterday. But apart from our own experiences, we also have the testimony to the existence of these – er – beings from a Jesuit priest."

"Oh, my goodness, and you say this ghost is dangerous?"

"Deadly. It murdered my fiancée, I told you. My fear is that it won't go away until Aldfrith's tomb is laid to rest in St. Mary's church in Little Driffield, where I believe the king had ordered his remains to be taken. I fear that anyone hindering this may be in mortal danger."

"We're still studying the king's remains and the grave goods interred with him. That will take time. You'll have to speak with the vicar of St. Mary's. These matters require all sorts of permissions and debates."

"I think there's no time to be lost, professor. I'll expect you to cooperate to the best of your ability."

"Why, of course, inspector. I'll get straight in touch with my colleagues in Bradford, though goodness knows how I'll explain to them there's a ghost on the rampage."

"No need, professor. It'll be quite sufficient if you tell them we're coming over to speak with them on a matter of the greatest urgency."

"Indeed, I'd prefer that. I'll ring right away."

After his call, they took their leave, but not before extracting directions to the archaeology laboratory at Bradford. They would have to follow the campus signs and take the charmingly named Tumbling Hill Street into the grounds where the tall building to the left of the workshop block housed the Archaeological and Forensic Sciences Department.

They parked and entered the gleaming new STEM research laboratory.

"STEM?" asked Shaw, perplexed.

"Science, Technology, Engineering and Mathematics, inter-disciplinary stuff, all the rage nowadays," Jake explained.

"Impressive place, very avant-garde and well-lit."

A man in a lab coat hurried towards them. He'd been expecting them, following James Whitehead's call. While Jake left the formalities to the inspector, his eyes roved around the huge room and settled on the sarcophagus in one corner next to workbenches staffed by white-coated individuals all wearing face masks.

He reconnected with what the archaeologist was telling the detective. "...some preservation techniques, such as those used on the sword blade, require time and optimum atmospheric conditions, but of course there's no reason why it should be returned to the sarcophagus. It might just as well finish up in a museum."

Don't let the ghost hear you say that, my friend.

Jake kept his thoughts private and his expression neutral. Anything that would expedite the release of the stone tomb suited him.

"So, as far as we're concerned, inspector, with a concerted effort, I think we can release the sarcophagus as early as the end of next month, with the proviso that some artefacts will remain here in the laboratory for reasons of conservation."

They left the laboratory with a feeling of mission accomplished and decided that the next appointment must be with the vicar of St. Mary's at Little Driffield. Jake looked at his watch. "I seem to remember from my visit that evening prayer is at 4 pm, so maybe we could catch him after the service." This agreed, they drove towards Driffield, and Mark Shaw launched into a conversation about life after death. As an agnostic, he'd been badly shaken by the apparition of a centuries-old warrior. Jake listened politely to the policeman thrashing about out of his depth before interrupting.

"If we start out firmly convinced that there's no God, no soul, no cosmic justice, then, okay, the idea of an afterlife is going to seem implausible. But what if we admit we may be wrong? I mean, look at our ghost. Well, what then?" Jake paused and reflected. "Could anyone tell us anything at all about the afterlife? If so, on what basis? Personally, I've never met anyone who's been there. But believing in an afterlife is not a matter of evidence. It's a matter faith – at least while we're still in the here and now."

"You know," the inspector replied, "what happened today has changed me in a way that's difficult to explain. I feel I've become less cynical but more vulnerable. I just hope it doesn't stop me from doing my job to the best of my ability."

"Don't be offended when I say this, inspector, but I believe you'll be a better policeman for having wider horizons."

Perhaps luckily, given how the conversation was shaping and the set jaw of the detective, they arrived at their destination and got out of the car. The vicar was at the church door chatting to three middle-aged women. They waited politely until the group had concluded their parish matters, and then the inspector introduced himself. The vicar was surprised by a visit from the Pickering police, but when the detective provided an explanation for the visit, he grew extremely interested. An intelligent man, the vicar at once saw the immense potential benefits to his church of housing the tomb of Aldfrith. At the same time, anxiety at the implications of church bureaucracy and the subsequent dealings with the press modified his enthusiasm. He did agree to contact his superiors and explained that all decisions in the end would have to be taken by the Archbishop of York.

THIRTY

EBBERSTON AND PICKERING, NORTH YORKSHIRE

Bewildered by Jake's behaviour at the café, the two women decided to proceed with their investigation. With this in mind, Kate drove over to Ebberston and pulled over to consult her notes and sat-nav, into which she typed a postcode and drove to the house of a certain Councillor Mrs Hodges. They had planned to catch her with her husband but were thwarted because he was still at work in York.

A stout woman with a florid complexion, Mrs Hodges allowed them into her house with an edginess that aroused suspicion from the start. After a brief explanation of the reason for their visit, Kate plunged straight into the accusations.

"We have reason to believe that there's a conspiracy among parish councillors to pervert the course of justice. My client has been wrongfully arrested, and we intend to get to the truth, councillor. If I were you, I'd think very carefully before continuing with this misplaced solidarity. Are you quite sure you can trust your fellow councillors to do likewise? I should warn you that the first cracks are appearing in your collective barricade."

With satisfaction, Kate saw that her words had unsettled the formidable hauteur of the woman. It showed in the shifty movement of her eyes and the increased ruddiness in her cheeks.

"You have no proof that there's anything of the kind, and you have nothing on me!"

"That's where you're wrong, Mrs Hodges, and—"

She stopped short and leapt from her armchair at the crashing sound that carried from the road into the room. Dashing to the bay window, she was just in time to see a hooded figure brandishing a baseball bat take another swing at her windscreen.

"Hey!" she shouted and banged ineffectively at the window. A flash of a white face in her direction and the hooded figure began to run away.

"What more proof do you need!" Kate hissed into the face of the startled householder. "I'll have the full weight of the law on you all for your crimes."

"Assaulting police officers and a priest is a serious matter." Heather thought she ought to participate. "And now wanton damage to a lawyer's car. I really think it's in your best interests to cooperate with us, madam."

"I'm going to ask you just once to leave my house, otherwise I'll call the police and report you both for intimidation."

"Yes, why don't you, councillor? Go ahead, make your situation worse, by all means. We were just leaving. I need to photograph the vandalism that's taken place, *by chance*, in front of your premises."

On the road, Heather gazed appalled at the damage.

"Oh, good Lord, Kate, they've shattered your windscreen, what now?"

"Don't worry, my windscreen is insured, and the policy provides for emergency call-out cover. I have the number; someone will come and replace it in no time, you'll see."

She made the necessary call, strode back down the garden path and hammered on the Hodges's door. Heather watched a heated exchange, but Kate triumphed and returned bearing a brush, dustpan and bin liner.

"Ah, the milk of human kindness, I don't think! She almost refused to lend me these, you know. Anyway, I'll clear the glass from our seats, the dash and the floor."

She set about the task with a vigorous determination, and Heather had to insist on relieving her. When they'd finished, they had a bin liner full of glass shards, and Heather had to dissuade Kate from flinging them all over the Hodges's neatly kept lawn.

"No point in losing the moral high ground, Kate. Your photo will be enough to persuade D.I. Shaw to take action in this village."

"I wouldn't bank on his professionalism," Kate said bitterly, for she couldn't know he was a changed man.

She fumbled in her shoulder bag and pulled out a slim pack of mini cheroots. She offered one to Heather, who shook her head and said, "I didn't know you smoked."

"I don't unless I'm stressed." She flicked a throwaway lighter and inhaled shakily, spluttered, and wiped the corner of an eye.

"I can see you're no expert," Heather said. "Even a non-smoker like me knows you shouldn't inhale cigar smoke. Just blow it out. Here, let me take these things back to our friend in there."

Kate, curious, watched Heather prolong a conversation at the front door. When the archaeologist returned, she couldn't resist asking.

"I explained that they're achieving the exact opposite of what they want by their behaviour. You know, I think I almost convinced her. I gave her your card and told her to ring you if she comes to her senses."

"Well done! Are you sure you don't want to join the police force? We could do with her confession."

At that exact moment, Kate's mobile rang with the gentle melody of The Cure's *Lullaby*. It wasn't a confession but the windscreen repair men seeking directions. Soon a blue van with the writing Auto Windscreens on its side appeared.

"I see you've cleaned away the mess; that makes our job easier," the cheerful driver said. "Now, let's just cover your baby – nice little motor." His assistant, also wearing blue overalls bearing the firm's logo, helped spread the protective sheeting over the bonnet and the roof. The younger man removed the wipers, and the other took a tool to remove the old inner trim around the aperture. They fitted a replacement trim and spread glue around it. Heather was astonished at the speed of the operation and even more surprised at the special suction handles they used to slot the new screen into place. The whole operation had lasted less than five minutes.

"Who said replacing windscreens wasn't easy?" The cheerful operative beamed and thrust paperwork at Kate to sign.

"Ready to go, now, miss." He winked at her and nodded at Heather before leaping into his van to depart with deliberate wheel-squeal.

"Some men!" Kate growled.

"It was relatively painless, and they're efficient," Heather observed.

"I don't think windscreens cost you your no-claims bonus," Kate murmured. "Let's go and see our none-too-friendly copper."

She got into her car and squirted the new windscreen rather pointlessly, just to check her wipers.

"Ok, we're off." Her wheels squealed, too.

"Some women!" Heather teased her and earned herself a sour look.

By the time they reached the Pickering police station, D.I. Shaw and Jake had returned. They found the detective receptive and attentive.

"Did you get a good look at him, Ms Mack?"

"I'm afraid not, inspector. Only a glimpse. Whoever he was, he was white-skinned and young, I'd say, but he was wearing a hood. He ran off as soon as I'd spotted him – but here's a picture of the damage."

"Hmm. All sorted now, is it?" He glanced out of his window at the parked car below, sunlight sparkling on the new windscreen.

"Yes, but I'd like to know how they knew I'd be parked near Councillor Hodges's house."

"They didn't. That's the price you pay for having such a recognisable vehicle, Ms Mack. Nice car, by the way."

"I suppose so, thanks."

"I'm pleased you came in about this. It's exactly what I need to return to the investigation on Ebberston. I have some chasing up to do there. Now, just a few more questions..."

Kate left the police station in a much better mood, amazed at the transformation in the detective.

She made the point to Heather who'd been joined by Jake.

"Perhaps he's seen a ghost!" Jake said, and Heather and he laughed at their in-joke while Kate stared at them in frustration. "Is there something I should know?"

Jake recounted the events of earlier in the day.

"So, you've persuaded him of your innocence. That's marvellous! I'll still be sending you my bill, though."

"Unless, as chief bridesmaid, you want to forgo it as a wedding present." Heather laughed.

"Hang on! I thought it was the bloke who's supposed to make the marriage proposal," Jake protested. "But, yes, I will marry you. But under one condition..." Heather looked at him anxiously, "...only when King Aldfrith is in place among the wedding guests."

"Condition accepted!"

"Congratulations then, come on, let's get a drink! Champagne's on you two!" Kate linked an arm under Heather's. "We need some serious talk about dresses, young lady!"

Jake groaned and wondered how a would-be novelist could support a wife.

———

Mrs Hodges gave way under pressure, but instead of ringing Kate's number, she rang Pickering police and confessed to her minor role in the plot hatched by Hibbitt, the churchwarden. It was she who put the detective on to Mrs Lucas, who when confronted by the inspector and a woman police officer and realising her friend, Maggie Hodges, had cooperated with the police, did the same. The two witnesses were quite sufficient for Mark Shaw to arrest the church-warden and four Ebberston youths. One of the youngsters came clean about smashing the lawyer's windscreen, largely to wriggle out of the more serious charges of assaulting Jake, police officers and a priest, which were ascribed to his three cronies. So, all in all, Shaw told himself, a satisfactory day's work. All that remained was for him to find the courage to close the Greenwood case, but as he told himself, there was no rush, and he would wait for the Archbishop of York's decision.

———

THE DIOCESE of York is one of the largest in the Church of England, spreading between the Rivers Humber and Tees and from the York-shire east coast to the foot of the Dales. It contains 602 churches in 469 parishes, so its head, the Archbishop of York, leaving aside his political agenda in London, is a very busy man. His typical day begins early and includes prayers and gym. By the time the 8.30 morning prayer at Bishopthorpe Palace comes around, he's well into his stride. The sort of clergyman who deals personally with indi-vidual problems and reserves the same treatment to the great number of letters arriving daily, he would not have passed over the request coming from the vicar of Little Driffield, even had he not been so intrigued. The vicar of St. Mary's, together with a Jesuit priest, a psychic, an archaeology professor and a police Inspector, was seeking an audience 'over a delicate matter.'

Making a considerable rearrangement to his overcrowded agenda, the archbishop graciously agreed to the meeting. The presence of a Jesuit caused the prelate some considerable perplexity. His ever-curious mind wrestled with the meaning underlying the strange composition of the delegation, and, at a complete loss, he decided to meet singly with the vicar of St. Mary's before welcoming the others. In this way, he hoped not to be caught unprepared for the 'delicate matter.'

The vicar expounded the situation as far as he understood it and trod very carefully around the matter of the ghost. Sensing his unease, the archbishop reassuringly told him, "My son, do not fret; I have authorised quite a number of exorcists in this diocese. The Church of England provides a training course which is run by priests and psychiatrists - they instruct on how to diagnose the symptoms of paranormal activity and to distinguish between it and a purely psychological disturbance. Most paranormal activity can be explained by science or psychiatry."

"Your Grace, that is why I have brought along Mr Conley, Father Sante, and Detective Inspector Shaw, who are all witnesses to this extraordinary phenomenon."

"I think it's time we met." The archbishop gestured to a secretary, who hurried to escort the small delegation into the room.

Jake, overawed more by the ecclesiastical robes than by the benevolent presence of the archbishop, relaxed and returned the greeting.

"Honoured to meet you, Archbishop." He hoped that was the correct form of address.

All the introductions completed, the archbishop questioned Father Sante about the *presences* at Elfrid's Hole and alluded to the possibility of psychological disturbances on the part of 'well-meaning but misguided or disturbed individuals.'

The Catholic priest was swift to describe his experience at the grotto and the response of the 'evil spirits' to the ritual he'd used, which he repeated before the astonished listeners.

"There seems little doubt, in light of what you've just told us, Father, that you were contending with otherworldly entities."

At this concession by the archbishop, Jake spoke. "If I may, Archbishop, I can describe my encounters one by one with one of these diabolical entities..." Fascinated, the prelate listened attentively, and when Jake had finished, looked around the taut faces scrutinising him for his reaction.

"Have you all seen this Saxon warrior that Mr Conley has so graphically described?" The archaeologist and the priest shook their heads. Professor Whitehead added, "Good heavens, your Grace, I don't believe in such hocus-pocus!"

At this, Mark Shaw spoke for the first time, rounding on the archaeologist. "I told you, Professor, neither did I, that is, until I saw the thing with my own eyes. I don't know if it's a ghost or...or... something worse. What I do know is that it possesses infernal strength and is a danger to anyone who has the misfortune to encounter it." If there ever was meaning to the phrase 'a haunted expression,' Inspector Shaw exemplified it at that moment.

The Archbishop looked at him with compassion, "A terrifying experience, I imagine, inspector."

"One I have no wish to repeat, I assure you, Archbishop. In fact, that's why we asked to meet with you." The detective looked to Jake. "Mr Conley, why don't you explain your theory to the Archbishop?"

Jake swallowed hard, feeling inadequate before such an eminent personage, and he questioned for the first time whether he was being foolish, but commenced, "It's like this, it started with a battle in 705 AD..."

When he had finished, his throat was dry and he felt belittled by the extravagance of his own theory, which he now saw was based only on intuition.

Relieved, he heard the prelate say, "I think it's a sound possibility. The Bible teaches that troubled souls may frequent the site of their torment after death, taking the form of a ghostly presence. The whole point of exorcism is," here he stared hard at the Jesuit, "to put an end to their torment and to provide peace to them."

"Indeed," the Catholic agreed. "But in this case, there may be more than a ghostly presence, your Grace. I fear we are dealing with the diabolical as underscored by the sad death of Ms Greenwood."

"Quite. So there is a likelihood, Mr Conley, that laying King Aldfrith to rest in St. Mary's church may not end the nefarious activities of this entity."

"Whether or not it does, archbishop, there is something essentially right about interment there, where the King surely intended, rather than leaving him in a museum or returning him to a pagan temple." Jake moved on to the ace up his sleeve. "Besides, the influx of visitors to Little Driffield after the publicity surrounding the re-burial of a great Anglo-Saxon King will only help the church. Anyway, I just want to say that after my road accident I've become a synesthete, and my cross-wired brain," here he gave a self-deprecating laugh, "tells me that the *entity* will vanish when the King is laid to rest in the chancel."

The archbishop considered this carefully and consulted Professor Whitehead about the briefest time needed to conclude investigative work on the sarcophagus. He also enquired as to the state and aesthetics of the stone coffin. For the first time, hope grew in Jake's bosom.

"I'm inclined," said the archbishop after hearing out the professor, "to grant permission for the sarcophagus to be placed in the chancel as a free-standing tomb to the memory of King Aldfrith. This operation, however, must be concluded before Advent. That should give your boffins sufficient time to finish their research, shouldn't it? Also, it means I will be able to free a day for the official ceremony of collocation of the tomb if it pleases you, vicar."

"We'd be honoured to have you in our church and parish, your Grace."

"My goodness, yes," said the professor, who'd waited patiently to reply. "May I say, archbishop, what a jolly splendid outcome to our meeting. My heartfelt thanks."

"Another time, I'd love to have a much deeper conversation about your work, professor, but if you will all excuse me, I have an impossibly crowded schedule today."

AT THE END OF NOVEMBER, Jake thrust the day's issue of *The Daily Press* into his fiancée's hands. "Here it is Heather, the fruits of the last two month's haggling and incessant phone calls." She read:

WORLD EXCLUSIVE
FROM YORKSHIRE MURDER SUSPECT TO HERO OF DRIFFIELD

THE FULL AND EXCLUSIVE STORY OF JAKE CONLEY IN TOMORROW'S EDITION OF YOUR *DAILY PRESS*.

"I just hope they're paying you well for all those hours of interviews, Jake Conley."

"No worries, Heather, let's say it's a six-figure sum."

"What! More than £100,000?"

"Yes, so we can start house hunting and leave this pokey flat with its bad memories behind. We can easily afford to put down a deposit now. Also, I'm going to write a novel about King Aldfrith, and *The Daily Press* had agreed to give it major coverage when it's published. There's even talk of printing it in a ten-part serial. To think I was worried about getting married and being able to support a wife."

"That's bloody old-fashioned nonsense, Jake Conley. I can support myself, thank you very much! Mind you, if you write a bestseller, it might become a film and we'd be rolling in cash. I wouldn't turn my nose up at that."

They attended the ceremony of reburial and appropriate blessing of Aldfrith's tomb, conducted by the Archbishop of York. The next day Father Sante checked on Elfrid's Hole and declared the cavern free of paranormal activity. The ceremony was not confined to being a local event but treated as something of national importance with the television and major newspapers sending journalists. Jake had to be particularly astute, because he was bound by contract to *The Daily Press* not to release interviews to their competitors. However, he did prime Heather to let slip that they would be marrying by special permission in St. Mary's Church, Little Driffield, on Christmas Day. It was once quite customary in England to marry on that day, she informed the eager journalists. Her fiancé glanced at the sarcophagus and silently blessed King Aldfrith who'd made his – Jake's – fortune thirteen centuries after his death.

Just one thing bothered him. He did not want one particular uninvited guest turning up at his nuptials complete with battle-axe.

THE END

Dear reader,

We hope you enjoyed reading *Elfrid's Hole*. Please take a moment to leave a review on Amazon, even if it's a short one. Your opinion is important to us.

Discover more books by John Broughton at https://www.nextchapter.pub/authors/john-broughton

Want to know when one of our books is free or discounted for Kindle? Join the newsletter at http://eepurl.com/bqqB3H

Best regards,

John Broughton and the Next Chapter Team

ABOUT THE AUTHOR

I was born in Cleethorpes Lincolnshire UK in 1948: just one of the post-war baby boom. After attending grammar school and studying to the sound of Bob Dylan I went to Nottingham University and studied Medieval and Modern History (Archaeology subsidiary). The subsidiary course led to one of my greatest academic achievements: tipping the soil content of a wheelbarrow from the summit of a spoil heap on an old lady hobbling past our dig. Well, I have actually done many different jobs while living in Radcliffe-on-Trent, Leamington, Glossop, the Scilly Isles, Puglia and Calabria. They include teaching English and History, managing a Day Care Centre, being a Director of a Trade Institute and teaching university students English. I even tried being a fisherman and a flower picker when I was on St. Agnes, Scilly. I have lived in Calabria since 1992 where I settled into a long-term job, for once, at the University of Calabria teaching English. No doubt my lovely Calabrian wife Maria stopped me being restless. My two kids are grown up now, but I wrote books for them when they were little. Hamish Hamilton and then Thomas Nelson published 6 of these in England in the 1980s. They are now out of print. I'm a granddad now and happily his parents wisely named my grandson

Dylan. I decided to take up writing again late in my career. You know when you are teaching and working as a translator you don't really have time for writing. As soon as I stopped the translation work, I resumed writing in 2014. The fruit of that decision is my first historical novel, *Die for a Dove*, an archaeological thriller, followed by *The Purple Thread* and *Wyrd of the Wolf*, published by Endeavour Press, London. Both are set in my favourite Anglo-Saxon period. Currently my third and fourth novels are available too, *Saints and Sinners* and its sequel *Mixed Blessings* set on the cusp of the eighth century in Mercia and Lindsey. A fifth *Sward and Sword* will be published in November 2019 About the great Earl Godwine. Creativia Publishing have released *Perfecta Saxonia* and *Ulf's Tale*. about King Aethelstan and King Cnut's empire respectively. In May 2019, they published two more, a time-travel tale, *Angenga,* and *In the Name of the Mother*, a sequel to *Wyrd of the Wolf*. *Elfrid's Hole* is the first novel in the Jake Conley series, look out for future publication of Books 2 and 3: *Red Horse Vale* and *Memory of a Falcon*. I am currently working on Book 4, as yet untitled.

You might also like

In the Name of the Mother by John Broughton

To read the first chapter for free go to:
https://www.nextchapter.pub/books/in-the-name-of-the-mother

Lightning Source UK Ltd.
Milton Keynes UK
UKHW012134120121
376933UK00006B/344/J